FOREST PARK

FOREST PARK

By Valerie Davisson

Copyright © 2019 Valerie Davisson

FOREST PARK is a work of fiction. Names, characters, places, and incidents are the product of the author's imagination or are used fictitiously. Any resemblance to actual events, locales, businesses, or persons, living or dead, is coincidental.

Published by Vaughn House Publishing, Depoe Bay, OR

Second Edition

Previously Published by Hauser Publishing in 2016

Print ISBN - 978-0-9838696-4-1

Ebook ISBN - 978-0-9838696-5-8

Cover and Interior Design by Kimberly Peticolas, www.kimpeticolas.com

Library of Congress Control Number: 2019912521

10 9 8 7 6 5 4 3 2 1

FOREST PARK

A Logan McKenna Novel

VALERIE DAVISSON

For Dad.

PROLOGUE

Major Nguyen Van Chinh ignored the bold, red-lettered signs above the shops: "Nguyen Van Dac," "Perlon Dental Cream," "Photo." He strode quickly past bright-green umbrellas blossoming over café tables and produce stands glowing with mango yellows and rich reds.

Slim young women, sheathed in traditional, white *áo dài*, floated around traffic on bikes, their faces protected from the hot sun by broad, conical straw hats. Busy mothers shopped for dinner or gossiped with friends while their children ran laughing around their feet. Toothless old men, shopkeepers, soldiers, and traffic clogged the street.

In three short months, this scene would not exist, but for now, the army was holding and everyone was looking forward to the upcoming New Year celebrations which would begin in a few short weeks.

You would not be so calm if you knew.

Knowing would not save them, anyway, Major Chinh thought grimly. *Not now.*

And where would they go . . . into the ocean? There is nowhere to run.

The term "boat people" had not yet been coined.

Chinh navigated deftly through the crowd, focused only on arriving on time. Even in this time of stress, and maybe because of it, the brim of his cap sat square above his brow, and he had taken particular care trimming his thin mustache this morning. His uniform was crisp. A solid, brace of medals filled the area above his left pocket. No one paid the thirty-six-year-old military officer any particular attention. Saigon was filled with military men, from both the ARVN and the US.

His purposeful stride and manner gave him a confident air, but today there was an additional undercurrent of urgency. Not panic, for Major Chinh knew outright panic to be a useless emotion. He elected instead to use the strong danger signals his brain was producing to keep his body sharply focused. Every step he took in the next few days and weeks had to be placed perfectly.

So much to do; no time to waste. Even though the Americans thought they could hold Saigon through the dry season, and even until the beginning of the next year, Chinh knew better. From the latest reports, they had very little time. He needed to arrange for the safe passage of his wife and Dinh before it was too late. Hence the appointment he was walking to now.

Rounding onto Vung Tau, his path was blocked by a large white Mercedes pulled half up on the sidewalk. Some American officer, no doubt, or someone they'd bribed. Irritated, he walked around the behemoth and continued on. Everything American was too large. Until recently, he thought that included their commitment. They hadn't had enough supplies or equipment for months. Empty promises. How did the American government expect them to win? His men had recently had to cannibalize some of the older planes they could have used, just for parts. His friends in the American Air Force felt the same way. It was always the governments far away that made a mess of things.

Crossing the street, dodging traffic, he arrived at his destination, La Vie Café, and went inside. An elegant crystal vase filled with Bach Ma orchids curved over a gleaming mahogany table. Ceiling fans spun lazily overhead. Thankfully, it felt at least twenty degrees cooler, even just inside the door. It took a moment for his eyes to adjust to the dark. When they did, he found his friend had arrived first and was waiting for him at a table in the back of the restaurant, sipping a coffee.

Chinh smiled. Cong looked much the same, only fatter. As a child, his friend had been frail and small. Born with a pronounced spinal curvature, the other boys in the village teased him mercilessly when Chinh was not around. Cong came from a household of women. He had no brothers, and his father died two months before he was born. In all likelihood, if Chinh had not fought Cong's battles for him, Cong would not have survived his childhood. No one knew why the tall boy had taken the damaged one under his wing, but from the boys' earliest years, they were inseparable. Chinh always felt a bit guilty for the praise showered on him for this. Chinh's father had died when he was only four, and Cong was the brother he would never have. The war separated them, but more than the war kept them apart now.

Cong, unable to join the military due to his birth defect, made his way south to Saigon with nothing more than the rice in his stomach. Once Chinh had left to join the South Vietnamese Air Force, there was nothing for him in the village. The exhilarating chaos of wartime Saigon suited Cong well.

He soon built a profitable black-market business, which had obviously continued to flourish, if his weight and choice of restaurant were any indication.

Their paths rarely crossed anymore, and when they met occasionally over the past couple of years, they spoke only briefly, and never about business. The less Chinh knew about Cong's black-market dealings, the better.

He knew if you needed something, you went to Cong. And Chinh needed something now. But so did Cong. Money couldn't buy everything. Once again, Chinh would save Cong, but this time, his friend could help him, too.

Chinh's heels clicked softly on the hardwood floor as he walked to the back of the restaurant, past a series of French doors that opened onto a lush garden with a fountain, to join his old friend.

✳✳✳✳✳

Cong placed his coffee down and watched his friend approach. *Straight and tall as ever.*

He did note a few more gray hairs when Chinh took off his hat and placed it neatly on the white tablecloth to his right. The war was aging them all.

"How are you, my friend?" Cong began. "I have already ordered for us. I hope you don't mind. I included some banh mi. I know," he replied to the surprised look on his friend's face. Banh mi was a popular street vendor sandwich, not something you would normally get in a restaurant. "Banh mi are my weakness. They make them for me here. And some wine. Here, they have the best. I would have ordered more, but you said this meeting must be short."

Cong nodded to the waiter across the room to let him know his guest had arrived. Chinh would have been happy with just a quick, simple bowl of noodles from one of the vendors outside but was glad to indulge his friend. And given the importance of their meeting, a more formal setting seemed appropriate.

"I am well," Chinh answered, "and you seem to be quite well."

Both smiled at the reference to his increased girth, of which Cong was proud. The surgeon said it was too late to do anything about his curved spine, so he pragmatically put up with the pain and decided to enjoy what was, indulging his many passions, which included good food, sex, math puzzles, and calculating his next business move.

"I enjoy my life here in Saigon," Cong said, waving his hand across the view. "It is my city. The French, at least, left us with some things of value. The Americans are just leaving, or so I've heard."

The sandwiches arrived first, and further conversation was put off while they ate.

Cong took a large bite of his banh mi, savoring the crackly crust of the airy baguette spread with pork pâté, layered with cool, spicy chilies, cilantro, and thinly sliced vegetables. It did not do to rush these things. His friend had arranged this meeting. Let him speak first. Besides, the sandwich was true perfection.

"It is our rice flour that improves on their bread," he said. Seeing his old friend made him want to be proud of being Vietnamese. "But their music," he added, closing his eyes as a middle-aged female violinist began to play a sonata in G minor near the piano. "The French also left us with their music. I do like Senallie. Do you know him?"

"No, I'm afraid I do not," replied Chinh. Deciding not to play the waiting game any longer with Cong, who could always beat him at it when they were boys, anyway, he spoke directly, but at a much lower volume, the one thing Cong wanted to hear, "I can get you out."

Neither spoke while the waiter cleared their plates and another waiter set large steaming bowls of *pho* in front of them, with fresh bean sprouts, cilantro, peppers, and quarters of fresh lime in small dishes between them.

Cong's body language remained the same, a short man with a full face, enjoying a leisurely lunch, but his eyes flicked instantly to his friend's. He would have tested anyone else, but he knew Chinh didn't lie, so he didn't waste time.

"When?"

He had heard the rumors the army could not hold much longer. He knew his money could bribe his way out, but to where? Smugglers and pirates couldn't be trusted. He did not want to wind up in Thailand in some refugee camp, living on a concrete, twelve-by-twelve rectangle, waiting for some country to take him. He wanted a straight flight to America in a US military plane. And only Chinh's American Air Force friends could supply that.

"Soon. I have to make final arrangements." Chinh paused. "And you can't bring anyone—just you."

"Who would I bring?" Cong said, shrugging his shoulders, lifting a thin piece of spiced beef to his lips. He had long ago accepted that no woman he valued would want him. But other women were always available. They would have those women in America also, he knew.

"Good."

"How much?"

He did not think Chinh would accept a bribe, but maybe some American doors higher up needed to be opened.

"No money will be necessary. People are expecting you."

Cong raised his eyebrows, but said nothing, waiting for his friend to elaborate.

Chinh set his jaw, unwilling to ask the favor, but knowing

for his family's sake he must. He leaned in. "There will be three seats. My wife and my son. He is eight. They must get to America safely."

If all Chinh wanted for the price of his ticket out was for him to babysit the wife and son on a flight to America, while Chinh and his men were flown out with the regular military, Cong was delighted.

"Of course! . . . I would be happy to . . ."

"That's not all. I have responsibilities here. You must promise that if I cannot meet you right away . . ." Here he hesitated, then went on. "They do not speak English. They will need your help."

Cong's English was very good. Americans were some of his best customers.

"I am not without resources," Chinh added. "I have prepared. They will have enough."

Oregon. That's where he wanted to go. Everyone thought LA or San Francisco was best, but they were too large. Too much competition. He was thinking he might try farther north. Yes, Oregon. Portland was about the right size for his needs.

Cong looked at his childhood friend as he ate his meal. They were so different. What would this man sitting across from him be doing if their country were not at war? Probably teaching at a university. A vision of the thick stand of bamboo surrounding and protecting their childhood village came to his mind. Chinh was like that, strong and straight. Always protecting. Always doing the right thing, while he, Tran Van Cong, was more like the river, running ceaselessly away.

He understood what Chinh was asking, and how unlikely it was for him to make it out of Saigon if he waited too long. He, too, had heard the rumors.

With a nod to his friend, he accepted both the gift of his own life and the responsibility of theirs.

*****

Chinh needed one more thing. Somewhere to change his cash into something more transportable. Something for Minh and the boy in case he didn't make it. Or something for all of them to build with if he did.

Chinh was not familiar with such things, so Cong told him what narrow street to go down and which old shopkeeper to find.

When he got to the shop, Chinh didn't ask what a poor man on a back street was doing with diamonds at all, let alone such a stone as the largest one in the bunch. Diamonds, gold, and other currency changed hands frequently in Saigon at that time. Everyone wanted whatever was worth the most, weighed the least, and could be smuggled through whatever customs inspections they may need to pass. Thieves worked overtime, too, and instead of risking a formal appraisal, sold their gleanings to anyone with a chunk of cash. Most people over- or underpaid. Few knew what they were getting. Major Nguyen got lucky. Cong saw to that.

When Chinh left the old man's shop, a small envelope of diamonds tucked securely inside the waistband of his uniform, his step was lighter. At least now he knew his family would be taken care of whether he made it out to join them or not.

1

Valentine's Day loomed.

It's not that she wasn't a romantic, but Logan hoped Ben hadn't planned anything. He'd been hinting, but she wasn't there yet. They weren't there yet. Were they? It had only been a few months. A great few months, but . . . she counted backward on her fingers . . . six months. Was that a long time? She had no idea what was considered long these days. Widowed for almost three years, with a twenty-three-year old daughter, Logan had been out of the dating pool a long time.

"It's time to seal the deal, girl," her best friend, Bonnie, said.

Ben was great, a solid guy. And she really liked him. They'd spent a lot of time together over the summer, and so far he passed all the tests: played well with others, a hard worker, and he cooked—a definite plus. In addition to all those virtues, he'd been patient in the sex department, a rare attribute among Orange County males.

How well should she know him before she "sealed the deal," as Bonnie so bluntly put it?

Things were so different now. With Jack, she'd waited for the ring. That's what you did. Now, she didn't need a ring. She could take care of herself. It wasn't that.

She wanted to be sure what was developing between them was real. At times, Ben seemed too good to be true. He'd given her no reason to doubt him, but subconsciously she kept looking for flaws.

After all, she thought Jack was great when they married, and he turned out to be not only unfaithful, but adept at lying about it. Sure, she was older and wiser, but what if Ben showed his true colors one day . . . she did not want to go through that pain again.

How had six months gone by so fast?

She'd been busy, that's how. In the first half of the summer, a young glassblower had been murdered at the Otter Festival, where Logan was helping her friend Thomas at his Native American arts booth. For reasons that later turned out to be false, Thomas was the primary suspect. Logan's incorrigible digging had helped flush out the real killer and clear Thomas's name. It all still felt unreal, like it happened to someone else.

Pushing back from her desk, she looked up from her computer and took in the full expanse of the view out of her new office windows. Ben had helped her convert the garage over the summer. Studio downstairs, office above.

The Pacific Ocean was showing off again. Shameless, really. Even in winter, the Southern California sun revealed more blues and greens than Logan could name.

"Ms. McKenna? Are you still here?" Brandon, one of her project leaders from the high school, shouted up the narrow stairs. "We just finished. Do you want us to lock up?"

"Thanks, Brandon. Just the studio door—I'll lock up when I leave," Logan called back down the stairs. "See you Monday— you guys have a good weekend."

The boys made scuffling noises and shut the door behind them. She watched the top of their heads as they bounced down the street to the bus stop, guitars strapped to their backs.

FOREST PARK

Brandon and Jeff were recording a couple of songs to include on a CD they were making to raise money. She needed to replace instruments once the grant funding for her program phased out. It was pretty good. She'd promised to lay down a track for them with Bella, her violin, after spring break.

She again rested her eyes on the ocean, allowing herself a few more minutes to savor the view. So many blessings.

Ben, of course. Without him she wouldn't be sitting here. They'd worked side by side all summer on the studio and office, shared life stories over long beach walks and stargazing sessions on the rooftop deck. What they'd both avoided, she realized, was any talk of the future.

Her daughter, Amy, was another blessing in her life—one she never took for granted. Amy loved her work in Africa, and her new botanist fiancé, Liam. He seemed like a good man. Of course, you never knew. She'd only met him once over Thanksgiving. She hoped he was worthy of Amy's trust.

Trust. A wonderful and dangerous thing.

Her first real home. That was a biggie. She bought it with the proceeds from the sale of the business and loved every inch of its 982 square feet, particularly the French doors in back and the rooftop deck she and Ben often enjoyed.

Luckily for her, due to the steep incline of Killer Hill, even with the addition of a second story on top of the studio, she hadn't lost the view of the ocean from her house. Lola, however, was not happy about the arrangement. Logan's sapphire blue '58 Corvette had lost her garage in the remodel. She had yet to forgive Logan for making her sleep outside.

The fact that Logan found a fixer-upper back in Jasper, where she was raised, was a big plus. It gave her more time to spend with her brother, Rick, who worked as a K-9 cop on the Jasper police force.

And her friends. She only had a few, but they were good ones. Which reminded her, she needed to give Glenda a call. Her old school nurse, she had been a friend of the family for years. They'd been playing telephone tag for days. She hadn't talked with her since before Thanksgiving when Amy brought Liam home to meet the family.

Liam had been nervous, but after Ben got him to talking plants, he relaxed. His eyes lit up and Logan could see what her daughter saw in him. He was passionate and had an endearing sense of goodness about him. She hoped he was as good as he seemed. If not, she would seriously have to get on a plane for Africa and hurt him.

*****

Putting in her wireless earbuds, she looked up the number Glenda had given her and tapped the screen. While she waited for Glenda to answer, she lifted the metal pole off its hook in the corner and used it to close the upper half of the long rectangular window above and behind her desk.

When she retired from the school district, Glenda had taken a job at an experimental, project-based school in Oregon. A skilled herbalist as well as a nurse, she wore several hats at the New School and seemed to be loving her new job. She'd been trying to get Logan to come visit.

"Hello." Glenda's brisk greeting was always cheerful, but to the point.

"Hi Glenda—it's Logan. Sorry it's taken me so long to call you. How is everything? Are you still enjoying Portland?"

"Dundee. We're about an hour outside of Portland."

"Right, Dundee. How's the school?"

"Good! Very good! You would love it here," she said. "How's the new program coming? *Fractals*, right? Such a great idea to integrate math and music."

FOREST PARK

Over the last year, Logan had been forming and directing an innovative program for the school district. It was based on all the latest brain research about how kids learned. The basic idea was to immerse students in both math and music—because the two together created a synergistic effect that helped learning across all subject areas. AND the lessons were designed to be fun. The research also proved that humans learn best when they are enjoying themselves vs. chained to their desks prepping for paper and pencil tests.

"Great! It's a work in progress, but it's going well," Logan said. "Admin doesn't love it, but the kids and teachers do."

For the next thirty-five minutes, the two women talked shop. An afternoon onshore breeze rattled the window before Logan realized how long she'd been on the phone. Her rescue cat, Dimebox, needed to be fed.

By the time they said their goodbyes, Logan made an executive decision. Because of the school district's alternate calendar and her new job, she had as much as three weeks off coming up soon. Two weeks for spring break—February 17 – 28—and up to another week for her to meet with some Portland University professors doing promising new research about how music influences memory.

Ever since Glenda took the job at the New School and moved up to Oregon, she'd been trying to get Logan to come up for a tour and meet Rita, the director, whose vision for education was similar to Logan's. Since she was going up to Portland anyway, she could combine some of her spring break time with that and zip over to visit Glenda.

If she left a few days early, she could even avoid having to decide what to do about Valentine's Day. She'd break it to Ben tonight.

2

Mrs. Nguyen paused at the entrance of a functional concrete building. She was exactly on time for a meeting with a man she despised.

Without her permission, her mind drifted back to 1975.

Thinking her husband was leaving with her and their son, she boarded the transport only to find Cong sitting in what should have been her husband's place. It was the one thing for which she would never forgive Chinh—putting his country before his family, staying when he could have gotten out with them.

It should have been you, Chinh, my love, not that deformed dwarf, sitting next to me on that plane.

Just before takeoff, noise and confusion swirling all around her, she thought she saw her husband's face. A thrill raced up her body. She thought he had changed his mind and was coming with them after all. But it was not his face, and she left their country alone. She did not consider Cong company, nor speak to him for the entire flight.

Wanting to get this over with as soon as possible, Mrs. Nguyen collected herself before pushing open the heavy steel door in the imposing wall. She was uncomfortable on this side of town. All warehouses near the river. But she would do what she must to help her son. She distrusted banks more than she disliked Cong.

The inside, she was surprised to discover, was not ugly. Polished concrete floors, sleek reception desk. Skylight and chandelier. You'd never know by the outside. One of Tran's thugs, ersatz doorman, noted her entrance without expression and pointed toward the elevator.

"Mr. Tran is expecting you," he instructed. "Seventh floor."

So you are Mr. Tran now.

The man had helped her and her son during their first difficult months in this country, but she disassociated herself and her son from him as soon as possible. How he could be Chinh's friend, even as a boy, she would never understand. Tran Van Cong had been a criminal back in Vietnam, and as soon as he stepped onto American soil, she was sure, he had become even more of one.

Whatever money you have, you owe it to my husband, who saved your life. We made our own way here. I will collect on that debt now.

Alone in the elevator, she pushed a gold filigree number seven. Top floor.

Of course.

She noted the gaudy finishes with some smugness, thinking of her son's tasteful restaurant downtown and the refined elegance with which she had decorated it. Over her son and his wife's objections, she had the ivory and black-veined marble for the foyer flown in from Carrara, Italy. It was perfect. Some things were worth it. As was this visit, if she could stomach it long enough.

Thanh was a good daughter-in-law, though. She could give credit where credit was due. She made a good match for her son. Such a hardworking, obedient girl would have been hard for her to find here in America. Luckily, she didn't have to. Thanh and her son met at chef's school, and all she'd had to do was put her stamp of approval on the union. Twenty-five years ago. Twenty-five? Had it been that long?

At least they had some good years together. More than Chinh and I.

When they opened the restaurant, her daughter-in-law was content to work in the kitchen with her son while she, Mrs. Nguyen, filled the role of gracious hostess, smoothly greeting customers with imperial grace.

Holding her Louis Vuitton clutch at her side with one hand, Mrs. Nguyen patted her already perfect French twist. As the elevator doors opened onto the seventh floor, she put her game face on.

A second man waiting there motioned for her to follow him down a short hallway. He knocked once on an oversized door, received the okay from a man's voice within, then ushered her in and closed the door quietly behind her.

Tran, having embraced all things American, had sent her and her son annual Christmas cards, even though they were Buddhist, even Tran, if he was anything. In each card he included his most recent contact information, with a brief note encouraging her to call if she ever needed anything. That's how she'd known how to reach him. He wasn't exactly in the book.

He looked much the same. Still deformed.

A young man slouched in a chair to Tran's right. She didn't know him.

"Mrs. Nguyen, please come in. How good to see you," he said, half rising from his chair to greet her, listing slightly to the left, before sitting down as she did. He really was very American.

She avoided staring at his body, which twisted grotesquely from between his shoulder blades to his pelvis.

Motioning to the young man, he says, "This is my nephew, Sonny. My sister's boy. Born here." The last two words were more of an apology than an introduction. "Sonny will be leaving us now."

Tran's nephew insolently unfolded himself from the chair and stood to his full height, which was almost six feet. Grabbing a jacket off the back of his chair, he swung it over his shoulder, glaring at Mrs. Nguyen as he sauntered out of the room.

He certainly was born here. My son would never behave in such a way.

She kept her thoughts to herself and got straight down to business.

"You know my son and I have a restaurant, yes? Vietnam Pearl, downtown. You have seen it, I am sure," she added proudly.

"Yes, it is a very fine restaurant. You and your daughter-in-law own it along with your son. It is doing very well. Open for nine years now, correct?" He let this sink in. "Much better times for all of us, now, than back in Vietnam."

If she was surprised Tran knew so much about their business, she didn't show it. Of course, he would know. He had his fingers in everyone's business, legitimate or not. And he had promised her husband. She had to give him that. He had honored his promise to Chinh. That's why she was here.

3

"**M**y son wants to expand. The economy is good, but we do not want to deal with an American bank."

And they would not loan you money, anyway, since you deal only in cash. None of you have established credit in this country. Living by the old ways has not helped you, woman.

And what, I wonder, did you do with your diamonds?

Let her keep them. He owed Chinh that much.

"Columbia Gear next door is clearing out when their lease is up, relocating to a larger property on Yamhill," he informed her, as if she didn't know already. "That location would provide adequate space, I think."

Surely Mrs. Nguyen knew all about Columbia's lease and had already redesigned the space in her plans to the square inch. It would double, maybe triple their profits.

"I know the owner of the building," he said, knowing the remodel would be expensive. "Would that be satisfactory?"

"Yes, that space sounds adequate," she said casually.

"Then it is done."

"Let us decide on terms now," she replied, attempting to reassert control of the conversation, so she didn't feel like she was asking a favor of this man. "Business is very good. We will repay the loan within one year."

You could pay me now, probably. I know Chinh sent you here with something, but you can keep whatever he gave you for hard times, which always come. I would. Maybe I'll borrow from you someday.

He allowed himself a smile at the thought.

"I will have one of my associates bring the paperwork by, and unless you have selected someone already, my architect will meet with you next week for the renovations," he said.

"Yes, that will be good." She would not thank this man.

Meeting over, she rose stiffly, indicating he need not get up, and let herself out. It wasn't until she exited the building and got into the waiting taxi that she allowed herself to take a deep breath. Her heart soared with happiness for her son. And his wife, Thanh. Maybe now they could hire another cook, and her daughter-in-law could begin fulfilling her most important role, providing her with grandchildren.

*****

Back in his office, although he had other business to attend to, Cong sat for a moment, looking out the window, considering Chinh's widow's visit.

With the economy as strong as it was, he knew she could easily repay the loan for the expansion. He was not worried about that. America had been good to him. He could afford to loan her the money. And even if something happened and she could not repay the loan, she had never asked a favor of him in all these years. He was happy to finally be able to repay a small part of his debt to his friend.

He thought back to those chaotic last days. Through Chinh's American friends, who respected him for being one of the few

South Vietnamese officers that could not be bribed, Chinh obtained seats on an American Air Force transport for Cong, his wife, and their eight-year-old son. He could see on his face how difficult it was to not go with his family, but there was no talking him out of staying behind to fulfill what he saw as his duty, even though he could see by the look on his wife's face, she also had tried.

Chinh did not make it out. Cong may not have had his friend's other positive character traits, but he was loyal. For his old friend's sake, he could put up with this woman's distaste for him and do what he could for her and Chinh's son.

As long as he was alive, Mrs. Nguyen would never want for anything.

Thinking of the call he needed to return, and his surly nephew, he sighed. Why did family come with all these obligations? He would have to find a way to keep Sonny busy, so he wouldn't keep pushing him to get involved with the Canadians. BC bud may make more money, he had tried to explain to him, but they involve people you cannot trust. He preferred the cleaner business he'd established for himself here in America: identity theft, counterfeiting, and banking fraud.

Very lucrative, and less violent. He needed to convince Sonny to complete high school so he could get a degree, any degree, but preferably one in law or finance. Then he would be ready to take over the business someday. They'd argued over this many times.

"Sitting through classes is boring! You made it without a college degree, why can't I? Why make money the hard way? We can make so much more if you would just open your eyes, old man!"

Their conversations usually ended with Sonny slamming a door on his way out, then getting drunk with his friends. Cong had had to bail him out of jail several times lately. He was getting worse, not better.

4

Clad in ripped jeans, long-sleeve thermal, and combat boots, Sonny burst out of the elevator and slammed open the front door, pulling on his jacket. His I-don't-give-a-shit look cost over a thousand dollars.

He threw himself into his G5, gunned the engine, and peeled away from the curb.

The guard watched impassively.

That kid is trouble.

*****

When he got to the restaurant, Teng had already grabbed a table.

"Hey, Sonny! How's it hangin'?"

He'd heard this line once in an American movie and never got tired of using it.

They'd both gone to school together in Beaverton. Boring Beaverton. Teng hadn't done very well in school. Sonny could have gotten really good grades, but never tried. Said the teachers were assholes. Besides, he had bigger plans. Went to work with his uncle. Partying helped. What else was there to do?

Sonny scraped out a chair and plopped down. Over steaming bowls of *pho,* he expressed his frustrations. Teng just listened. He'd heard all this before. Sonny's rants were not new. He just needed to spout off. Then maybe later they could go back to that new place. The girls were cute there.

"Can't see what's right there for him to grab. He's just so fucking ancient." He stuffed more noodles in his mouth. "He wants me to go back to school this fall. Says he'll cut off my allowance if I don't finish. Keeps *pushing me!*"

"Yeah," Teng agreed, "but didn't you say your uncle is turning the business over to you as soon as you're done?" Teng liked to look on the bright side. He laughed at his own joke. Sonny really needed to lighten up, or they wouldn't have any fun tonight.

Sonny stared into his almost empty bowl. "Yeah . . . Uncle's old all right . . ."

A couple of minutes went by, which Teng did not feel inclined to fill. He finished his *pho* and burped.

"You still know Michael?" Sonny asked Teng. "Is he still around? I heard he was back."

"Yeah, keeps to himself pretty much, but we hang out now and then. He lives over in Gresham with an aunt. Not happy about it, either. Why?"

"Is he working?"

"Part-time security—he was some kind of sharpshooter over there," Teng said.

"Bring him tonight, okay? Tell him I might have some work for him. Make sure he knows I can pay him a lot more than whatever he's making doing security."

That night Sonny was all smiles. Michael, a Vietnamese man whose body language and buzz cut screamed ex-military, had indeed shown up. Without hesitation he took the job. Even said he could do it that night.

"Don't you have to, like, follow him around—learn his schedule and all that shit?" Sonny asked.

"He lives alone, right? Works in his office until late, which is right by the docks? Why wait?" Michael said. "Follow your normal routine. Go out—make sure you're seen by people."

The guy was scary. But Teng knew him. Said he could be trusted. A former sniper in the Army, Michael didn't party and he knew how to follow orders. He also had a less-than-honorable discharge from the Army. Seemed he enjoyed his job a little too much. But for this employer, that little piece of information was a plus.

Sonny and Teng had no problem following Michael's instructions. They went to the club where people knew them, picked up some cute girls. *E* all around ensured they all stayed happy for the rest of the night.

✶✶✶✶✶

8:00 A.M.

Sonny swung his legs out of bed, grabbing the phone off the hotel nightstand.

"That you?" Even though it was a burner, Michael had insisted they not use names.

"Done."

Silent fist pump.

Yes!

They disconnected. Arrangements for payment had already been made. Cash. That's one thing his uncle had taught him. Never leave a trail.

He looked back at the bed. The girl still had on her purple wig. The rest of her clubbing outfit, which wouldn't have fit in the shot glass on the nightstand, was scattered on the floor. Leaning over, he shook her.

"Hey—get up."

She groaned and rolled over, burrowing into the pillow to escape the light streaming in the window. Her wig didn't make the complete trip, exposing mousy brown hair underneath.

Skank.

A second later, Sonny's foot made contact with her nineteen-year-old behind. She hit the floor with a satisfying thud, sat up, and glared at him. He jerked a thumb toward the door before flopping back on the bed.

At least her friend knew the score. She was already gone.

"Whadja do that for?"

When no money, not even an offer to call a cab, was forthcoming, she got dressed and left.

"Cheap bastards," she mumbled on her way out.

Normally, he would have taught her a lesson for that remark, but he was in too good a mood. Ignored her exit completely, even though it was punctuated with the slamming of the door. He ordered room service, then lay back on the bed, rubbed his face, pushed razor-cut bangs out of his eyes. With great pleasure, he contemplated the first day of the rest of his life, sans Uncle Cong. This Michael could prove useful.

He'd call Vancouver today.

5

Alaska Flight 421, nonstop, departing SNA at 8:34 a.m., arriving Portland at 10:49 a.m. . . . no bags . . . aisle seat . . ."

Logan scanned the boarding pass she'd just printed, making sure everything was correct. It was, so she detached the advertisements, threw them away, and folded the pass into a flat cross-body bag that held all her essentials within ready reach for tomorrow's flight. Scooping up her computer, she took a last look around her office before heading down the narrow stairs.

After letting herself out and locking the studio door, Logan walked the twenty steps home, following the curving flagstone walkway that meandered around her little hobbit hole to the front door. The asymmetrical path had been a must for her. She'd always wanted one. French thyme was filling in the spaces between the stones nicely, and coastal sage and tall lavender brushed her ankles and arms as she walked to her front door. Several different types of ornamental grasses and herbs grew at varying levels, softening the edges of the boxy, 1940s house. She loved breathing in the sharp, pungent aroma of the herbs and the distinctive, sweet fragrance of lemon blossoms from

Ben's tree when it was in bloom. The low wooden fence she left to the morning glories.

Inside, Dimebox rubbed against her ankles as if she'd been gone for days, not hours. Logan placed her computer bag on the bench by the door and reached down to pick him up, kicking her shoes off and pushing them more or less beneath the bench as she did. This was easier said than done, seeing as he weighed almost twenty-seven pounds.

After rinsing out and refilling his water and food dishes with fresh fare, Logan opened the French doors and let in a good cross breeze. Ben was coming over to barbecue, but the 55 was a parking lot this time of day, so she had some time before he got there. She always made the easy sides. Ben was the real cook. Putting some potatoes in to bake, she made a quick tossed salad and popped in the little domed fridge.

As much as she loved her new office space, she loved her home more. Satisfied her part of dinner was taking care of itself, she walked back into her living room and surveyed her domain with satisfaction. A lifelong renter, she was still enamored of her first actual home. She loved every bit of it!

Gleaming hardwood floors she'd discovered under dull, shag carpet and refinished. A saddle-brown leather couch with a queen-size sleeper for extra sitting support and overnight guests sitting comfortably across from a working rock fireplace. Across the coffee table sat the handmade rocking chair she'd splurged on last year at the festival. Not the most expensive one in Soren's booth, but more than Logan had ever paid for a single piece of furniture in her life. It was beautiful, and the bottom curve fit the small of her back.

Lifting her violin, Bella, down from the wall next to the built-in bookshelves, Logan dug her naked toes into the thick Persian rug before sitting on the coffee table. As much as she loved the chair and the couch, she couldn't sit up straight enough in them to play. She usually played standing up or perched on the edge of a kitchen chair.

It was almost 4:00 p.m., and neighborhood sounds of children walking up the hill from the bus stop drifted in the open doors. Putting bow to string, Logan took a deep breath and got lost in the music.

Created by a young, Italian violin maker in love with Logan's Appalachian great-grandmother, Bella was not only a glowing work of art, but it also produced rich, resonant tones. Knowing only that her father had inherited the violin from his grandmother, Logan often wondered how a poor mountain woman could afford such an exquisite instrument.

After *Tchaikovsky's Violin Concerto*, Logan moved on to the soaring notes of *O Mio Babbino Caro*. For years, Bella had been pushed to the back of Logan's closet while she and Jack built up the computer business. Another blessing in her life, this rediscovery of her music.

Playing was very zen for Logan—along with swimming and walking, her other two favorite forms of moving meditation. It freed her mind from every day, frontal-lobe thoughts of planning errands, tackling her taxes, or reworking student schedules. It was only after a full-on workout or playing Bella for a while that long-buried wisdom, insights, or new creative thoughts floated up to her conscious brain.

Today the voice of her old physics instructor, Professor Goldstein, came to mind.

"All forces in the universe are composed of tiny, vibrating strings," he told them. "Each unique vibration creates different kinds of matter. String theory can't be called a true scientific theory," he added wistfully. "It will remain a philosophy until we have instruments small enough to test it."

Even though her double majors had been music and math, not science, she'd stumbled into his class and wound up taking several more from him, as her schedule would allow. Often, when Logan played, she felt Bella's vibrating strings in every cell of her body and wondered what her music was creating.

As she played today, her mind continued to flow. Her new job made her increasingly aware of how all knowledge overlapped, not fitting into neat academic departments. As one of the neuroscientists at UC Irvine had told her over lunch one day, there were no real boundaries between academic fields, or shouldn't be—each informed and inspired the other.

The world was a messy place, but Logan didn't mind messy. She liked a bit of mystery mixed with her science. She had long ago abandoned formal religion as a source of absolute answers, but didn't think of herself as an atheist, either. She'd become more comfortable not knowing. In fact, she'd taken to liking the questions. Who knew? Maybe God played the universe into existence on a celestial fiddle like Bella.

Smiling at the thought, she looked at her cell phone and wondered where Ben was.

6

Logan checked on the baked potatoes. Perfect. The fork went in smoothly, so with two thick oven mitts, she removed them from the oven and their skewers and wrapped them in foil.

No pain, she realized as she straightened up. Good. The sciatica that used to shoot down her left leg was occuring less often. She used to only be able to sit for a few minutes at a time after the accident. Tava'e credited the Pacific.

"The ocean is our mother," she'd informed her.

Tava'e and her husband, Jean, owned the coffee shop at the bottom of Killer Hill. A good friend of Logan and Ben's and a mother to all, the Samoan woman was also Jasper's reigning chess queen. Tava'e was right about most everything else, why not a powerful, female ocean? Another place science and spiritual beliefs intersected. We evolved out of the oceans, didn't we?

Ben rapped a knuckle on the wooden frame of one of the open French doors, "Hello! Anybody home?" he called. She loved that he smiled with his eyes as well as his mouth.

When everything was ready, they carried their plates, the tray, and wine glasses up to the roof, along with a roll of paper towels. Dimebox trotted up after them, hoping for leftovers. Dimebox was no longer the emaciated tortoiseshell kitten he'd been when she found him at the pound. He was a proper cat now and dominated his kingdom and all living things within it accordingly. Even Ben's Greater Swiss Mountain dog, Purgatory.

"Where is Purgatory?" Logan asked.

"Vet," Ben replied, cutting into his steak, tearing off some bread to sop up some of the juice. "Ate something that didn't agree with him."

Purgatory's gastronomical issues were legend, coming to their full expression on the inhalation of Polish sausages, the dog's favorite. She'd learned not to invite the dog into the house until at least an hour after he ate one of those. She was glad to hear it was nothing serious this time, just some habanero sauce he'd gotten into.

"Hammond said he'd be fine in a few days," Ben said. "Tyler's going to keep him when I come up next weekend. He's taking on Dimebox duty, too. He loves cats."

Charlie, Rick's K-9 partner, would be disappointed her buddy was indisposed for a few days. At 145 pounds, most of it muscle, the striking female German shepherd intimidated most other dogs, but not Purgatory. He also didn't seem to realize they'd both been fixed at some point in their childhoods. It certainly hadn't lessened his ardor. Purgatory was in love with Charlie.

"What time is your flight tomorrow?" Ben asked.

"Not until eight-thirty," Logan replied, taking a green wool blanket from the small teak nightstand that served as a side table and storage unit. Ben lit the fire pit and pulled her chair over to his, then reached over and took her hand into his large, calloused one. She felt his love as much as his physical warmth. Simple.

Logan helped spread the blanket and pull it up to their necks. Then they snuggled down to do some serious stargazing. Coastal clouds prevented only the largest stars and planets from poking through, but they spotted Sirius, the Dog Star, and could make out Orion and what had to be Jupiter. The moon was a sliver hanging above the ocean.

Rick and Charlie were coming over in the morning to take Logan to the airport. Ben had to leave early to beat traffic for an inland job he needed to finish before he flew up to Portland for their romantic weekend. He'd been burning the candle at both ends in order to get it done. Tonight he'd driven three hours from Riverside in what her students would call "gnarly" traffic just to enjoy a last evening together before she left.

Now that Valentine's Day was going to be successfully avoided, she found herself looking forward to Ben's visit and the probable end of the platonic phase of their relationship.

✲✲✲✲✲

Ben had been a champ about Valentine's Day. He hadn't even mentioned it, just got excited with her about her trip to see Glenda and check out the New School. His intuitive understanding had created such a rush of warm feeling toward him she'd impulsively invited him to join her at the end of the first week. Something in her decided it was time. And now she was excited.

Everything was falling into place. Rick's new girlfriend, Paula, a dispatcher recently transferred from Oregon, had offered her a place to stay in her loft apartment back in Portland. Logan would be bunking with Paula's old roommate, Rheanna.

"Won't I be infringing on her territory?" Logan asked.

"Hell no! I still have six months left on that lease. Rheanna's paying half rent for a whole apartment all to herself. She's in no position to complain. Besides, she's not like that. You'll love her. Rheanna loves company," Paula said. "And she's hardly ever there. She really only uses the apartment as a place to sleep. When she's not working, she sings around town—she's really into her music. Good, too. She's been dispatching long enough she gets days or swing, can request a schedule, so it works out for her."

Rheanna said she'd pick her up at the airport and show her how to use the MAX. She'd stay in Portland until Sunday when Glenda would drive her out to Dundee. She'd check out the school, interview some teachers, look at the new computer lab, then back to Portland for her romantic weekend with Ben. After Ben left, she'd wrap up her stay with some interviews at Portland University and head home. Everything was working out great time-wise.

When she asked Paula for hotel recommendations downtown for when Ben came, ones with some history, not slick, generic chain hotels, she quickly listed several, including the Benson and the Governor. When she and Ben did some research online, the pictures of the historic Governor won, hands down. It was right downtown and steeped in Portland's history, and its Lewis and Clark mural alone was worth the stay. It was pricey, but they decided to book a three-night stay.

7

Sure you got everything?" Rick asked, leaning out the window of his patrol car after dropping Logan off at John Wayne, the Orange County airport.

"Yep." Logan patted her travel wallet containing her boarding pass and ID. Hoisting her computer bag onto her shoulder, she adjusted her grip on the handle of her roll-on luggage. "Thank Paula again for me for setting me up with Rheanna for a place to stay. I probably couldn't have gone otherwise."

"Okay, I'll tell her. Call us when you get in." Rick pulled smoothly away from the white curb. People tended to get out of the way when a cop car wanted to merge in front of them.

Rick and Paula's relationship had progressed a lot faster than her and Ben's. Paula had moved in a month ago. Luckily, she loved dogs.

Even though she could have justified taking it out of program funds, Logan decided to pay for the trip herself. Half of it was going to be personal time, and the work she was planning on doing felt more like play, anyway. From what she'd learned so far, it sounded like Rita Wolfe was accomplishing at the New School what she was trying to do in her program—integrate learning so it was joyful and meaningful and stuck with kids. Even with what they'd been able to accomplish so far, she knew it was only baby steps. She wasn't sure how much more leeway the school board would give her. Some members still couldn't see beyond test scores. She had to prove Fractals was working or her program would get cut and she'd be out of a job . . . again.

*****

After an uneventful but packed flight, she landed in Portland just a couple of minutes late. Rheanna, who was on time, was even tinier than Paula had described her. Hard to believe the woman ordered police and firefighters around. She looked about fifteen. A deep-purple crocheted dress hung loosely over a black T-shirt and leggings, ending in beat-up, half-laced combat boots. With a huge canvas bag slung over one shoulder, she waved Logan down.

"Hello! Welcome to Portland!"

After a huge hug, which she had to deliver on tiptoe, Rheanna guided her charge down the escalators to the ticket kiosks.

Buying a MAX ticket was easier than expected. Since she only had a twenty-dollar bill, Logan was delighted to receive her change in one-dollar Sacagawea coins, which, for lack of a better place to put them, she stuffed into a zippered side pocket of her computer bag. She pulled out her wool wrap. The air outside was definitely colder than what she'd left in California.

Rheanna's short hair shone blue-black in the winter sun. Logan wouldn't have been surprised if the tops of her ears were pointed. Her elfin guide bounced up into the train as soon as it stopped and the automatic doors slid open. Logan followed and they found some seats.

FOREST PARK

The surrounding scenery they rolled through was more rural than urban, although Rheanna said they were in Portland. Train passengers were a mix of students in Columbia jackets and beanies; a Hispanic mother with her children doing their grocery shopping; and a finely suited businessman—African by his accent—with a watch that cost more than Logan's first car, and possibly her first house. Which reminded her, she hoped she'd remembered to leave a key to Lola for Ben. Lola usually didn't like anyone but Logan driving her, but she positively purred when Ben got behind the wheel.

Traitor.

*****

Fifteen minutes and a few stops later, they crossed a river.

"Say hello to the Willamette!" Rheanna chirped, "We're crossing on North Steel Bridge. South of here is the Burnside. Hope you're hungry. I'm going to take you to the Saturday Market—most of the vendors only open on Saturday, but some good ones set up on Friday, too. You're going to love it! My friends'll watch your stuff while we walk around, get some lunch, then head back to my place."

When the melodic computerized voice announced Skidmore Fountain, Rheanna stood up. When they got off, Rheanna insisting on taking Logan's rolling suitcase. After they did some exploring, Logan asked if the Governor was nearby. She wanted to see if it looked as good in person as it did online.

They almost missed it. It didn't show up on her phone's navigation because it was in the middle of a name change. The Governor was going to be called the Sentinel. Rheanna had promised lunch, and Logan was starved. Starting at Tenth and Alder were several blocks of food trucks.

"Welcome to Portland's very own United Nations of rice

and noodles," Rheanna said, leading them to a small blue-and-white place facing Eleventh called Thanh's Pho.

"Best *pho* in town," she declared.

Orange County had a large population of Vietnamese immigrants, so Logan was already a fan of the Vietnamese comfort food, a large bowl of rice noodles and thinly sliced beef swimming in clear, spiced broth, topped with fresh bean sprouts, sprigs of cilantro, and a slice of lime. Logan liked hers with lots of hot sauce, which an older woman at the order window efficiently added to Logan's order when she asked.

A younger woman, somewhere in her forties, Logan guessed, worked in the back, stirring something in a huge steaming stockpot almost bigger than herself. Slim in a double-breasted white chef's coat, she checked the gas flame under the pot, then adjusted the wide blue bandana on her head with the back of her hand. Just skimming her eyebrows, the bandana tied up and around, securing a short ponytail at the nape of her neck. Kept the sweat out of even mahogany eyes set in a small, delicate face.

Satisfied, she wiped her hands on her apron and gripped a cleaver to finish thinly slicing a hunk of frozen meat on a cutting board atop the stainless steel counter in front of the stove.

Several large stainless steel bowls filled with vegetables consumed what was left of the space. Above the counter, shelves were stacked with various spices and bottles.

Handing a steaming bowl of broth up to the front, she smiled. Steam swirled around her face, revealing light but long laugh lines around her eyes and mouth. Yes, forties, probably.

Admiring her efficiency, Logan wondered how they could cook enough food to fill the orders in such a minuscule kitchen.

FOREST PARK

The truck next door, Damascus Dining, wasn't much bigger. Providing the only place to sit and eat, the enterprising owner had squeezed in a couple of white plastic café tables and chairs between the front of his converted silver travel trailer and the narrow, buckling sidewalk.

Holding the steaming bowl of *pho* in her hands, Logan wasn't sure what the seating protocol was. A handsome middle-aged man, dark hair curling at his collar, shirt sleeves rolled up to his elbows, nodded his permission for them to sit there. She gratefully did so, city sidewalks being much less forgiving on her feet than the soft, sandy beach she usually walked on.

Lunch rush over, the man finished wiping the counter in front of his order window, then began refilling condiment bottles. He also continued to surreptitiously sneak glances at the younger of the two Vietnamese women next door, who had come around the front on the same mission. The older one frowned her disapproval.

Nosy by nature, Logan wondered what their stories were. The crowded lot filled with customers and vendors from all over the world. She'd heard German, French, and Japanese just in the ten minutes they'd been sitting there.

If they all worked as hard as these guys, Logan thought, slurping the last of her soup, she hoped all their stories had happy endings.

***

Later that night, after a long, hot shower, Logan got ready for bed. She rummaged through her travel bag for a brush and managed to get out most of the snarls the Portland wind had created. She hadn't thought to bring warm slippers because she didn't need them at home. Rheanna found an extra pair, and Logan gratefully pulled them on before padding out to the couch in the living room to enjoy the spectacular view out the loft's floor-to-ceiling windows. It wasn't the ocean, but nature was still evident. Clouds scudded across a crescent moon, which rose above the buildings. The cityscape had its own beauty.

"Ready for your Valentine's Day treat?" Rheanna called from the kitchen.

She'd forgotten it was Valentine's Day. Before Logan could answer, Rheanna appeared with two oversized bowls of ice cream with spoons sticking out of them.

"Cool Moon's own chocolate cherry, 'a decadent combination of Oregon bing cherries and dark chocolate,'" she said delivering the dessert with a flourish and a bow.

Accepting it with a royal nod, Logan took a bite. "OMG! Is this even legal?"

"Well, if it's not, we're in trouble. The police know where I live!"

For the next hour, Rheanna regaled her with tales from her job as a police dispatcher, including the reason she was flying solo this Valentine's Day. Missed dates were part of the package when your boyfriend was a homicide detective.

Taking her big sister role seriously, Logan tried to learn as much about Paula as possible. Rheanna had nothing but good things to say about her, so Logan eventually ended her not-so-subtle inquisition. Rheanna saw right through her and joked it was more thorough than the formal background check she'd taken to get her job.

"Not that I object," she said as they carried their now-empty ice cream bowls into the kitchen. "I have a little sister, and believe me, I give every guy she dates the third degree. Twice." She grinned mischievously as she handed Logan a fresh pillow out of the closet before mounting the open stairs to her open loft bedroom, waggling her fingers good night.

8

Stupid junkies.

Too stupid to know the little bottle of pills they stole off him wouldn't get them high. The joke was on them. They were just to help him sleep. It's what the VA doctors gave him after detox. Detox . . . that was fun. They told him he had PTSD from Vietnam.

No shit.

Detox was short, painful, and didn't include hand holding once your body rid itself of whatever it was addicted to. As soon as he was clean, they dumped him back onto the street with this bottle of pills and a bus pass. He'd been out for two weeks now. He was supposed to take one pill a night. At first, it didn't make him feel any different, but after a while, he didn't wake up in a sweat. Fewer nightmares. The pills didn't get him high, but they helped him stay clean and sober.

Having his medicine stolen was a setback but doing without the pills for a week or so couldn't be any harder than doing without his old drug of choice, heroin. He'd just have to keep busy.

During the day wasn't so hard. He had his regular routine. Places he liked to go. Nights were tougher. He had to find something else to do, other than get high, so he'd started going to St. Stephen's. Their shelter closed by eleven, but until then, he could always scare up a game of chess with the Jesuit in charge. A guy in his unit taught him how to play. Kept his mind off things. After he left, by eleven thirty or twelve, he was back to his area around Tenth Avenue, took his pill, and was tired enough to find a good spot and go to sleep.

This morning, stiff from sleeping in the doorway of an old theater in the process of becoming a shoe store, Joe stretched his long legs, pulled his jacket close around his somewhat concave chest, and sat up, hunched against the morning cold. So this is what the world looked like sober. At least it hadn't rained.

He checked his pockets to see what else was missing. They'd taken his Snickers, damn punk kids.

That was the one bad thing about the pills. They knocked him out pretty good. Slept like a log. That's why they wanted him to take them at night, so he wouldn't be sleepy during the day. As if he had some important job he needed to be alert for. Ha!

He barked out a laugh, which caused a woman walking by to give him an even wider berth. Didn't miss a beat on her cell phone, though.

What are you looking at?

It had been an eventful month. That hot shot he got eight weeks ago almost killed him, but the doc pulled him through. Why, he didn't know. Somehow he'd managed to use for thirty-five years, off and on, without killing himself, but it was only a matter of time. He wasn't the only one who wound up in the hospital lately. Bill didn't make it, and a couple of other faces were missing from around here. Must be some bad shit out there.

He'd been lucky so far, but things catch up with you. Time to get off the streets.

In order to do that, he had to stay clean.

He had no illusions about trying to revive his former life, which came with a two-bedroom duplex in the valley, a wife, and a four-year-old daughter, born while he was in Nam. First time he saw her, she was already two and a half years old. Spun-gold curls, dimpled arms thrown around his neck. Her smile lit up his heart. He'd never seen anything so perfect. Too perfect for him. He would have just messed up her life if he'd stayed. He hadn't seen them in years, anyway, and they sure as hell wouldn't want to see him. He left a day before her fifth birthday.

That would have been, what . . . '72 . . . '73? How old would she be now?

He couldn't work it out. A sweet aroma of cinnamon rolls from a nearby bakery wafted toward him. He sure wished he had that Snickers bar. Time to find breakfast. He stood and stretched. He could have stayed at the shelter, but there were bad people there, too. Besides, he liked being outside. He knew his way around. Which included good places to pee. He went around the back of the building and did just that. He'd do the rest of his business at the shelter.

With a last shake, he zipped up his pants and contemplated his life. All he hoped for now was one without nightmares, enough money to get a little room somewhere. He was getting too old for this. Maybe before he became a righteous citizen he'd take care of those punks. Get a gun to keep the Road Warriors off him. And their pit bulls. He'd love to put a bullet between the eyes of that white-and-black mutt they called Monster. They sicced him on the older vets for entertainment. It wasn't the dog's fault—it was the creeps who trained him.

They sure wouldn't have messed with him in '68. No sir. He'd have had their ears, candy-ass punks.

Maybe if he went back to the VA, they'd give him another bottle of those pills. The pills were working. But the doc told him he only got one bottle a month. He finished one in rehab.

Come back with the empty bottle at the end of the month for a refill.

He'd just have to wait. Hopefully missing a couple of weeks wouldn't matter.

And keep busy. They told him to keep busy. Deal with today.

He pulled out the square of paper he'd folded neatly into his jacket pocket yesterday. The Road Warriors had standards. They didn't steal anything they couldn't eat, spend, or get high on.

Blanchet House
310 NW Glisan
10:00 a.m.
Ask for Rita Wolfe

All he had to do was show up. Mary had been adamant about that.

"They take a limited number of people, Joe," Mary, his VA counselor, said, "so don't let me down. Show up and show up clean. Okay? Blanchet House is a shelter, but you won't be staying there. You'll be in one of their new programs. They've got a new place out in Dundee. It's like a small farm or large garden. You ever work on a farm, Joe? Garden, maybe?"

"Grew up in Vallejo. Worked summers picking. Should be able to handle a few vegetables." Realizing she was waiting for more, he added, "Thank you for the opportunity."

"You're welcome, Joe," she said. "Now, let's fill out this paperwork. I'll help you."

9

GI Joe—that's what the cops called him. Kind of funny because his real name *was* Joe. Joseph Maynard Watts, formerly from Vallejo, California. Army grunt. Saw the worst of the worst. While Joe was filling out the rest of the paperwork, Mary glanced again at his file, which she'd gone through in detail when it had first landed on her desk.

He'd served in Vietnam between 1967 and 1970. Home for about a year. Classic PTSD, but never received services. Wife waited, but finally divorced him a couple of years after he took off. Who knows where he was for those years in between. Says he did migrant work for a while. Seems to have found his way to Portland a few years ago. Might have died, but one of the food cart vendors on Alder found him one morning. Said a homeless guy had OD'd under his trailer during the night. Hot shots were becoming more common in recent months. The food truck vendor called 911. Saved Joe's life.

Boy, what a change. The filthy, wild-haired scarecrow described in the intake report was a far cry from the clean, subdued, brown-eyed man who sat before her now.

The police report said Joe had gone nuts when he came to in the hospital. Absolutely crazy. That wasn't a very exact term, so she'd called one of the EMTs who'd taken him in and asked for more details. He returned her call, but what he had to say wasn't very sympathetic.

"Here this little Asian nurse was, trying to save his miserable life, and all he could do was scrabble like a crab back on the bed, trying to get away from her. Called her a Gookinese bitch, as I remember. I feel sorry for these military vets, but you can't fix these guys," he told her.

Mary begged to differ, but knew arguing with him was pointless, so she thanked him for returning her call and downplayed his statement in her notes. She understood the young man's frustration, but he just didn't get it.

If he could see Joe now. This particular military vet was not hopeless. Joe wore new shoes, stiff jeans, a donated sweatshirt, and spanking clean white socks. He just completed the first few weeks of a relatively new multiphase drug and alcohol rehabilitation program. Three weeks in-house, three heavily supervised. Then, if he was still clean and sober, the transition work program she was recommending him for.

The only original item of clothing Joe wore was an old military surplus jacket. It was the one he came in with. He'd begged to keep it, so they sent it along with him when he was transferred to the VA hospital, where a kind orderly took it home, washed it, and returned it to him before he left.

Hundreds of homeless addicts—former military—came through her tiny office every year. Last estimate there were at least four thousand men, women and children living on the street in Portland. At least 25 percent of them were vets. She knew the VA services she helped provide were only making a dent.

A homeless Vietnam vet with a long-standing addiction to heroin and whiskey, Joe had all three strikes against him. After thirty-five years on the streets, the man had almost zero chance of full recovery. She usually didn't spend much time on cases like his, but the rangy man sitting in the chair across from her had something—some life left in his eyes. Some hope. Maybe he'd make it.

That's why she did this job. There were a few who kicked their addictions, kept jobs, and reconnected with the world. Some even reconciled with family. She had a slim "success stories" folder in her filing cabinet to prove it. Whenever she had a particularly bad day, she pulled it out and reminded herself why she hadn't gotten into computers like her mother wanted. That whole corporate world had never appealed to her, although she often envied the trips to Maui her sister and her husband took every year. She could go for a week on the beach with a mai tai in her hand. Any place warm and sunny.

★★★★★

"Their main farm is full, Joe," Mary said. "But they've contracted with a new place, a school a little farther out, near Dundee and Newberg. They've got a big organic garden. You work in the garden first, then the kitchen. They put you up—feed you. Lucky you, I hear the chef has never heard of macaroni and cheese."

Damn.

Macaroni and cheese was one of his favorites. St. Stephen's served it every Thursday.

Mary continued, "Then you qualify for the next step, HUD housing, work here in town. The first week's a trial run." She sat back in her chair, examining his face. "It'd do you good to get away from here for a while. From Portland. Your old stomping grounds. Is this something you'd like to try? You interested?"

"Yes," Joe answered. "I like trees."

Reaching across her desk, she handed him a piece of paper where she'd neatly printed the Blanchet House address and his appointment time. As if practicing for an etiquette class, after slowly folding the paper and tucking it securely in his front jacket pocket and buttoning it, he stuck a large-knuckled, bony hand out to shake on it.

Startled at first, she took his hand and shook it. It was pleasantly rough and warm. He rose quietly from his chair, as if afraid to wake a sleeping baby, nodded in her direction, patted his front pocket, and turned to exit her office. He had to duck down to avoid hitting his head on the doorframe. Watching him leave, she felt a wave of doubt washing over her.

"Trees," she muttered to herself as she picked up her land-line to return a call. "We all like trees, Joe."

But you won't have time to be looking up at the trees. You'll be looking mostly down at dirt, working.

God, she hoped he made it.

Blanchet House

310 NW Glisan

10:00 a.m.

Ask for Rita Wolfe

Hoping his appointment was today, Joe pointed himself south, in the direction of Thirteenth Avenue, a hot breakfast, and, hopefully, to step two in his program: meeting a woman named Rita.

✱✱✱✱✱

The grub was even better than Mary had advertised. And he ate every bit of it. He'd only been at the New School a few days, but he'd already begun to fill out his new jeans. It even felt good to have sore muscles at night.

FOREST PARK

The work was easy, compared with the picking he did years ago. Foremen back then worked you—they didn't treat the blacks any better than the Mexicans. And after ten hours in the sun, bent over those damn strawberries, they'd all gotten a few shades darker.

Things were different here. After showing him where he would sleep, Rita took him to meet the people he'd be working for. Neil and Brittany. They were nice. He ran the kitchen, and she was in charge of the garden.

He didn't know what to do with his very own room. He hadn't had his own room in over thirty-five years. Quiet. Clean. No Road Warriors. No cops rousting him, telling him to move.

He was afraid to use the dresser or nightstand, so each morning he placed his small stack of belongings—the change of clothes they'd given him at the VA and his razor kit, under his bed. Every evening when he returned, he was surprised they were still there.

They were all so nice. When the office manager discovered the new garden and kitchen helper had a sweet tooth, he'd found a fresh homemade cookie on his pillow—chocolate macadamia.

And just as Mary had promised, there were trees. They had been cleared around the garden and animal pens, where he worked during the day, but just across the little creek out back, the sharp, clean scents of pine and cedar surrounded you. Tall, straight trees, not humid, sticky jungle. No standing chest deep in bloody rivers with body parts floating by. Except in his dreams sometimes still.

In six more days, Rita said he would help her load up the vegetable crates, then she'd drive him back into Portland, where he would help unload them at Blanchet House. Part of the program was trust. It was not mandatory for him to stay there. After unloading the crates, he'd be free to go where he wanted until the next morning.

He just had to meet her back at Blanchet at 10:00 a.m. sharp and, she'd added, his breath better be clean and his eyes clear.

10

"**W**hat do you mean, she won't pay?"

"Says she doesn't have it," Teng said, shrugging his shoulders.

"She has it," Sonny said. "These old Vietnamese always have something hidden away. If not cash, then gold, jewels. Something."

His lean body curved like a capital C in his chair. Swiveling away from his sleek new desk to look out the window, he steepled his long fingers.

"We're going to collect on all these debts Uncle let slide." He turned back toward Teng. "How many are still stalling?"

"Eight, but I don't think Mrs. Nguyen's going to budge. Swears they were wiped out after her son died. Only have the food cart and what it brings in, which barely keeps her and her daughter-in-law in that little apartment they share."

✶✶✶✶✶

Teng didn't see what the big deal was. Why did Sonny always want more? He got everything after his uncle died, which was plenty. He had a killer place, a nice car, more girls than they knew what to do with, and plenty of time to enjoy them. What more did Sonny want? What good was all this stuff if you never had time to relax and enjoy it? All they'd done since Sonny's uncle died was work. Something drove Sonny.

Whatever it was had bypassed Teng completely.

✳✳✳✳✳

"How come your uncle never collected on her before? She hasn't paid in at least a year, right, since they lost their restaurant?"

"Honor. My *honorable* uncle thought he owed her. The old woman's husband came from the same village. They grew up together. The late Mr. Nguyen was too stupid to leave when he should have. That's how he became late." He smiled at his own joke. "Seems he was one of those straight arrows. ARVN officer. Felt duty-bound to stay. But he got Uncle a seat out, made him promise to take care of his wife and kid. The guy had some kind of connections with the American Air Force. But I don't owe that old woman anything. This is business."

"I want as much cash as possible by next week," he said. "If you don't do big enough deals with these BC guys, they don't take you seriously."

"Yeah, but why mess with them? Don't we have it good now?" Teng didn't want to admit the thought of dealing with these guys scared him shitless.

"They may have scared Uncle," Sonny answered, reading his mind, "but they don't scare me. You have to risk in order to make it big, and I'm going to make it big. As long as we keep up our end of the deal, everything will be fine. We're going to be rich, but we need cash or something we can quickly convert into cash. Go visit these losers again, including our stubborn

Mrs. Nguyen. One of them has to have a chunk hidden away somewhere. Find it. I want to make this happen. Soon.

"Oh, and take Michael. Scare her. We'll get something out of her, one way or the other."

11

Since Rheanna had to work, Logan spent Saturday catching up on Fractals paperwork and getting in a workout and a swim at an indoor gym down the street. Rheanna brought Thai food home and they shared pad thai, crab fried rice, and salad rolls. Logan offered to do the dishes, which involved throwing out the takeout containers and wiping the table. As they were polishing off the rest of the cherry ice cream, Rheanna got a call to sit in for someone at a blues place downtown later that night. Logan readily accepted the invitation to come along. She never said no to live music.

A few hours later, they entered the narrow club and grabbed a small table just as another party was leaving. Rheanna went up to talk with the band she'd be singing with. Taking a sip of an excellent, ice-cold martini, Logan put one foot up on the chair Rheanna had recently vacated and settled in. They started at about ten, and she enjoyed getting lost in the music. She started to fade around twelve thirty and lasted until one before saying her goodbyes. Another set was about to start. Rheanna was just warming up. Ah, to be young.

The next morning, Logan knew without a doubt her late nights were behind her. She couldn't remember ordering it, but she must have had at least one more martini. Her head was pounding, and her tongue felt like it had doubled in size.

"I am so not cut out for this anymore," she complained to Ben on the phone, not wanting to get out of bed. She could hear traffic noise in the background. He must be driving to work.

"Serves you right for starting the party without me," he laughed.

"Man, you're tough."

"Yep, tough love, that's me—don't want to enable the Irish in you."

"*Okay, then, I can see it's not any sympathy I'll be findin' here, so it's a shower I'll be takin' then—then off I go to find a cup o' joe,*" she intoned in her best Irish brogue, then added. "I'll call you when I'm feeling semi-human."

"Drink a lot of water, hon. You'll feel better. I'll have my cell. You can call me anytime."

"Okay, talk to you later," Logan said.

After a long, hot shower with a cold finish, she felt at least marginally better.

She wasn't averse to making her own coffee but had no idea how to work the complicated-looking espresso machine on the marble counter in the kitchen. She found Sisters Coffee Company, a few blocks over. One giant cup of Black Butte Gold, a strong, dark blend, and an airy brioche later, she hopped on the MAX and pointed herself downtown.

Her only time constraint was meeting Glenda at 11:30 a.m. in front of the Governor.

For the next few hours, Logan meandered happily, losing herself in the sights and sounds of a new city. Anonymity was a luxury she always enjoyed.

Her last stop was Nordstrom. She rarely stepped inside

a department store, assiduously avoiding malls whenever possible, but realized she hadn't brought anything nicer to wear to bed than her usual T-shirt and cotton bikini underwear when Ben came. She definitely wanted something more appropriate for the occasion.

She sighed. Relationships required so much maintenance.

She checked the sign by the escalator. Lingerie, third floor. A quick glance at the frilly offerings proved most of the inventory too little girl cutesy or French brothel for her, but with a little digging and the help of an understanding salesclerk, she found a simple Calvin Klein silk slip—black with double spaghetti straps—that skimmed her curves nicely.

First-night-sex attire purchased, she went down the escalator and back out onto the sidewalk, pulling out the map of downtown she'd picked up yesterday. Directionally challenged on a good day, she studied the streets and found Tenth and Alder. She wanted some more *pho*. It must be the air—all she wanted to do in this town was eat. It looked like it was only a few blocks away. Laid out on a grid, Portland was an easy town to navigate, even for her. She refolded the map, stuffed it and her hands into her pockets, and waited for the light at the intersection. The sidewalks were already filling with other hungry people running errands or grabbing a bite to eat on their lunch hour.

When the light changed, she got about halfway across the street when a tall, greasy-haired young man blocked her path. Rheanna had warned her about the panhandlers downtown. Thrusting his hand out, he blocked her path, stuck his hand out, and accosted her in a loud, cheery voice. "Well, hello there! Looks like you've got a friendly handshake hiding in that pocket. Got any change in there to spare?"

Something about his aggressive stance made Logan keep on walking. When he realized she wasn't going to give him any money, he didn't waste a millisecond. Instead, he turned pragmatically to the next person walking toward him, greeting them with the same shtick, "Well, hello there!"

She wondered how much money he made in a day and what would drive a young, seemingly healthy man to beg instead of work. Was there no work to be had? Rheanna had snorted when she asked that question last night.

"Oh, there's plenty of work for those who want to and can hold down a job," she'd said in a huff. "I work two jobs," she'd added proudly. "But why work when you can get three hot meals and a warm bed for free? The city makes it too easy for them—they can walk up to any policeman and ask for meal vouchers. That gives them three hot meals a day—no questions asked. Why work when you can eat for free and hang out with your friends all day?"

"Where do they sleep? Isn't it cold at night?" Logan asked.

"Portland has over a dozen shelters—they have a warm bed if they're willing to listen to a few prayers and want one. In fact, they don't even have to listen to prayers anymore. Against their rights. Some don't want to sleep inside." She shrugged and made a face, as if comprehending the thoughts of the homeless were beyond her. She continued, "They know how to work the system. A lot of them go down to California in the winter, then come back up here for the summer."

Logan wanted to say that some of the homeless who were without jobs or a place to live might have *legitimate* reasons, like mental illness or long-term health issues. But she could tell it was a hot button issue with Rheanna, so she let it go. Besides, Rheanna made some good points. It was a complicated problem.

After some successful shopping along the way, she arrived at Tenth and Alder, and joined the line in front of Thanh's Pho. As usual, she was starved, but the delicious aromas of garlic, soy sauce, and spices rising from all the food trucks would have sharpened anyone's appetite.

Logan studied the short menu nailed to the left of the order window on the side of the truck. Thanh's served mostly *pho,* which she was getting again, but also made spring rolls, which she decided to add to her order. Maybe some hot tea if they had it. She stomped her feet on the pavement and kept her hands deep in her pockets to stay warm, her shopping bags looped onto her arm. Unfortunately, there was a long line.

12

While she waited, Logan had nothing better to do than watch the women work. The same two Vietnamese women were there today, plus a man helping in the back. He was stirring the pots, and the older woman was keeping small bags filled with containers of hot sauce, hoisin sauce, lime wedges, fresh herbs, and bean sprouts ready to add to each order. How they all maneuvered in the small interior space was a mystery. A well-orchestrated dance of stirring, chopping, lifting, wrapping, and calling orders back and forth in short bursts of Vietnamese. The older woman placed each bowl of soup carefully in a plastic bag, adding individually wrapped small plastic bags of condiments to be added immediately before eating. Plastic forks and spoons or chopsticks were available, depending on preference.

Logan waited semi-patiently, the delicious aromas floating out the order window, making her ferociously hungry.

Finally, only two people were ahead of her in line, a tall, thin Vietnamese man and a short, stocky one. The tall one was younger, wore baggy jeans and had a shock of black hair, hung long in front across his eyes, with a thick gold chain too big for his neck. The stocky one wore army boots and sported short hair shaved close in back and on the sides.

The well-dressed older Vietnamese woman shooed the younger one to the back. Must have been her turn to man the order window.

The tall man leaned in, presumably to give his order. Logan didn't hear what he said to the woman, but her lips clamped into a thin line. After glaring at them, the woman pushed two large bags toward the men, not touching their hands, scowling deeply. Far from being deterred by her attitude, the young man replied with one or two words. She nodded curtly. Lingering at the window a half beat more than necessary, giving the woman a final stare, the two men then sauntered to their car.

Maybe they were relatives. They hadn't paid for their meal. Whoever they were, they'd gotten on the woman's bad side somehow. She definitely didn't seem pleased to see them. She said nothing about the incident to the young woman in the back but motioned for her to come back up front. When she had and taken her place at the window, the older woman huffed around in the back of the food truck, chopping things and vigorously wiping down the counter.

The younger woman pushed an escaped strand of hair out of her eyes, smiled at Logan, unfazed by the growing line, and asked for her order. "What would you like?"

"I'll have the beef *pho* again—it was so good yesterday. And can I get an order of spring rolls with that?"

While the woman rang up her order, Logan asked, "Are you Thanh?" pointing to the sign.

"Yes, I am Thanh." She smiled. "This is our truck," she added, gesturing back toward the older woman with her shoulder as she gathered the condiments and filled a bag, waiting for the bowl of broth to be handed to her from the man in the back.

"Your food is really good," Logan said, including the woman in back.

"Thank you. My mother-in-law makes the spring rolls. Are you visiting Portland, or do you live here?" Thanh asked. Straight hair pulled back into a plain ponytail at the base of her head. Smooth oval face—free of makeup, shiny with sweat. A delicate cross lay across her collarbones, hung from a thin gold chain. Her only other jewelry a pair of small gold studs.

"No, just visiting . . . from Southern California," she admitted.

While she talked with Logan, Thanh's hands never stopped—every movement efficient as she prepared and rang up her order.

"How long are you staying?"

"About two weeks."

"Well, you will have to come again," Thanh said, placing the steaming Styrofoam container carefully into the plastic bag, deftly tying the ends into a neat carrying handle with double loops.

Handing Logan her food, she added, "I put in some extra hot sauce and hoisin—try both. Different tastes on the tongue."

"Thanks, I will," Logan replied, taking the bag.

A couple of men in business suits vacated one of the tables where she and Rheanna sat yesterday, and Logan grabbed a seat. Feeling slightly guilty for undoing the woman's handiwork, she tore into the neatly tied bags and doctored her *pho* per Thanh's instructions. Both plum and hot sauce were delicious with the beef, so she piled on both. For the next ten minutes, between bites, she indulged in another of her favorite pastimes—people watching.

Hard hats, beanies, backpacks, strollers, cameras, sweatshirts, and suits denoted a diverse crowd. And of course, the ever-present panhandlers. One enterprising redhead in his fifties took the indirect approach, recommending food selections to people in line, worming his way into their good graces before hitting them up for money or a meal.

The lunch rush was slowing, but a steady stream of customers kept the food vendors busy until one o'clock. The Thai truck proudly displayed a couple of articles where they were featured in the local press, receiving glowing reviews. They had the longest line.

Checking under the table to make sure she had all her shopping bags—the small one from Nordstrom's, another with a cobalt-blue-and-gold Russian teacup she found for Bonnie, and one with a book on xeriscaping from Powell's Books for Ben. She was hoping Glenda drove her car in so she wouldn't have to lug them around—the landscaping book was beautiful, but heavy.

Placing her trash in an almost full can, she crossed in front of Thanh's Pho to get to the light, smiled, and gave a thumbs up for the delicious food. She was waiting for the light at the intersection when a loud noise, followed by a loud argument, erupted from the crowded space between the Korean food truck and the back of Thanh's.

From what she could see, the man who had been helping the two women out today was leaning out of the back door, trying to calm down Thanh's mother-in-law, who was screaming at a Korean man in what sounded like Vietnamese. And he was yelling right back, but in Korean.

Logan couldn't tell what they were yelling about, but it was clear the man's teenage son, who was sulking against the side of the truck, was involved. Thanh's mother-in-law kept jabbing her spoon toward his chest, then back at an upturned bucket and spilled garbage just outside the back of their truck.

FOREST PARK

Not wanting to stare, Logan walked across the street, hoping they worked everything out. It must be tough to land in a new country and try to make a go of it. Lots of stress.

13

Lola was fast, but Glenda's Tesla was faster. Newer and lighter, it made short work of the forty miles out to Dundee. Her small herbal business had gone so well she'd written a book, *The Herb Bible*, which was flying off Amazon's virtual shelves and onto thousands of baby boomers' e-readers and into young parents' diaper bags.

"And it's even Northwest-certified, granola green." She laughed as she took a corner at least forty miles over the recommended speed limit, showing her car-loving, California self.

Logan loved the idea of an electric car but wondered if relying on electricity was any greener than fossil fuel. Didn't hydroelectric plants decimate fish populations or something? Besides, if she ever bought an electric car, she'd have to get rid of Lola, and she couldn't imagine parting with her. She could convert her, maybe, but Lola didn't like change. She still hadn't forgiven her for commandeering her garage.

A couple of traffic snarls later, they were through Beaverton and Aloha, out of the city, and onto a two-lane highway. Someone had spray-painted everything green. Trees, grass, bushes . . . Amazing. How did they get it so green? Logan's neck and shoulder muscles let go. She didn't even realize they were tight.

✶✶✶✶✶

"So. How have you been?" Glenda asked, easily passing a slow-moving Toyota. "I mean, really."

With her herb booth not far from Thomas and Lisa's at the Otter Festival in Jasper, Glenda knew all about Logan's brush with death last summer. Few people went through being attacked with a knife by a crazed young woman without suffering some residual anxiety.

"If you're having any trouble sleeping, I'll mix you up some chamomile and valerian tea, and I think I've got some 5-HTP somewhere," she offered.

"HT what?"

"5-Hydroxytryptophan. Put simply, 5-HTP helps your body make melatonin, which signals your body to sleep," she explained.

"Thanks, Glenda. I'm okay. I've been so busy with the new program, I haven't thought about it much. It all happened so fast. Leah was arrested, she confessed, she's in jail—or a hospital jail, anyway."

"Where is she?"

"She's up at Patton in Atascadero," Logan said.

"What's her diagnosis?" Glenda's professional curiosity as an herbalist and a nurse often trumped her tact.

"Not sure what her diagnosis is, but it's enough to keep her locked up," Logan said. "Lisa would say it's an imbalance—she got out of balance with the natural world, the truth, and other human beings."

They both thought about that for a minute.

"Do you think it's possible for people like Leah, people that far off, to be brought back—cured?"

"Don't know," Glenda replied honestly. "I'm just glad that young woman is very far away from you, for a very long time."

They enjoyed the rest of the short drive in quiet companionship. Logan cracked her window a few inches to breathe in the moist, earthy air as Glenda took the next exit onto a narrow one-lane road that curved up and back, disappearing among tall pines hung with what looked like moss. Highway noise disappeared. The quiet hum of the Tesla's tires underscored the dense quiet.

Logan could hear, and occasionally see, a rock-strewn stream a small sign said was Whisper Creek and smell the oxygen-rich air. Like a mysterious woman, Whisper Creek kept the road company, occasionally dipping from view as they climbed up and back into a fairyland of pine forest.

Occasionally, Glenda pointed to a tree or plant, foreign to Logan, and explained its use, "Black willow . . . Pacific willow—it likes these wet places near streams and rivers."

Logan listened for the next ten minutes as the Tesla took the curves smoothly and climbed about a thousand feet in elevation, finally delivering them to their destination, the entry to the New School, spelled out in a distinctive, wrought iron arch. Spitting gravel as she turned left onto the wide unpaved drive, Glenda slowed her speed, so as to avoid damaging her new car.

The low, wide rock wall supporting the arch looked like something Robert Frost would have written about—rounded boulders softened by lichen and moss, placed one atop another with relaxed care. Formerly a wealthy lumber baron's estate, the generous proportions spoke to gracious country living and freedom from the worries of the less privileged. In reality, the former owner enjoyed only a few years of this insulated existence, losing everything in the stock market crash of 1929. Most of the estate was sold off to pay debts, going to those whose holdings were more diversified.

The private home and surrounding twenty acres, deemed the smallest area with which anyone could make do, was then purchased by a German duke. When the duchess passed on, he sold it quickly and returned to Bavaria. A US senator snapped it up next for him and his mistress to enjoy whenever his wife was in Europe. His children were already away at boarding school back east. In later reincarnations it served as a church camp and a writer's retreat. During the recession, it stood empty and had fallen into disrepair.

"Rita is a wonder at fundraising and grant writing. You should have seen this place when she got it. They'd already done a lot of work before I got here, and it was a mess then," Glenda said. "She picked it up for a song."

14

Logan checked her watch as Glenda pulled up to what must have originally been the lumber baron's private home. Although large, it wasn't boxy. The architect had avoided the temptation to show off and somehow managed to keep it human-sized and unimposing. Several large cedars grew near enough to caress the roof with its drooping branches and soften the corners. Long, low steps led to a wide wrap-around porch, complete with a couple of rocking chairs and side tables, one with a checkerboard painted on it.

The air was cool, and Logan was glad she'd worn jeans. Her boots made a satisfying sound on the solid wooden steps. To the left of the open double doors, a thickly glazed, misshapen pottery mug with a crooked handle, probably made by a child, sat near the foot of the nearest rocker.

"Rita?" Glenda called into the open door as she stepped inside.

Logan followed, rubbernecking at the rest of the property to the left and right of the porch as she went.

A warm but commanding voice boomed, "Come on back, Glenda. On the phone. Be off in a minute."

Glenda led Logan past a warm reception area, formerly the lumber baron's parlor, lit by retrofitted oil lamp sconces on pine paneling wainscoting. On the left, behind a simple reception desk were mounted open wooden cubes serving as mailboxes for faculty and office staff. A grandfather clock read 2:45 p.m. She'd been enjoying the scenery so much it had taken a little longer to get there than she realized.

"Rita keeps the original feel of the place, but don't let appearances fool you. Everything in here is state-of-the-art. She has some healthy donors. Wait till you see Huey's computer lab."

Glenda checked her box and grabbed a couple pieces of mail, tucking them into her purse as she walked around the unmanned receptionist's desk, leading Logan back toward a shaft of light slicing across the old hardwood floors and a faded, narrow runner.

They entered a large, light space. To their right, an energetic, wiry woman of average height stood behind the desk, phone to her ear. An athletic build and commanding stance: Amelia Earhart with white hair. She could be fifty or seventy. Hard to tell. The woman must have eaten all her vegetables and drank all her milk as a child, because her teeth were straight, white, and obviously all her own.

Acknowledging Glenda's mouthed hello, she directed them to sit at a small oval conference table across from her desk while she wrapped up her conversation.

"Yes, that will work just fine, Tim," Rita said, nodding as if he could see her. "Thanks for pitching in. See you Thursday . . . six is fine, just pull up to the side of the dining hall . . . Yes . . . You'll see it. It's kind of a wide driveway next to the back porch—that's our loading dock." She laughed warmly at her own joke, pushing long commas into her cheeks and deep crow's-feet around her eyes. "Okay, then, Tim. See you Thursday. Best to Ronnie."

Rita walked around her desk, extending her hand and looking Logan in the eye as she joined them, "Welcome to the New School, Logan. It's so good to meet you in person. How was your flight?"

"It was great, thanks. And thanks for letting me camp out here with Glenda while I'm visiting."

"Glad you made it. I was afraid that job of yours would keep you too busy to make it up here," Rita said.

"Well, the timing was right—it's spring break. We get two weeks."

"How is your music program going?"

"Well, I've been very lucky to find good people to head up the two schools I'm working with, and some very talented friends of mine are volunteering. I hope to bring them on full-time with next year's grant—if we get it. The kids are great, too. They practically run the program . . . but there is so much more I want to do . . ."

As they talked, Logan found herself really enjoying their conversation, hearing about the New School and all Rita had done and was planning to do. They were integrating so much more than music, and so much of the curriculum was project based.

She'd never gotten this excited about signing up a new client for the computer software training business.

Glenda looking pleased with herself for bringing the two women together. Satisfying herself with the role of geisha, making more tea whenever one of their mugs got low, she mostly sat back and listened.

"Do you think you'll be able to keep Fractals funded?" Rita asked bluntly.

"I hope so," Logan said. "Right now we're pretty dependent on one wealthy donor, but I'm always looking for more grants to write."

Rita nodded. "How are you measuring its success?"

"That's one of the challenges. Because Fractals is funded privately, we operate under the good graces of the school district. The only thing they understand is standardized test scores. It's hard to directly link student success with those. How do you measure joy in learning, or the foundation laid over several years in elementary school that will bear fruit in high school or college? That's one of the missing pieces I'm trying to fill by sharing the latest brain research they're doing at Portland U and UC Irvine. I'm going to be interviewing a couple of professors out there next week. Hopefully, they'll have something I can take back to convince a couple of the more stubborn board members of the benefits of an integrated music/math program. If I don't show progress somehow in a couple of years, I doubt they'll reapprove the program."

Logan and Rita continued to share stories of students as well as the challenges of creating and administering grant programs until the room began to darken. You could still see the buildings beyond the quad out Rita's back window, but just barely.

"Nick will have a fit if we don't get over to the dining hall by five thirty," Rita said, consulting a plain but obviously high-end thin watch on her wrist. Logan pushed her chair back, picked up her small travel bag, and stretched as she stood up. Rita closed her laptop and met them at the door, not bothering to lock it on their way out.

15

"**N**ick loves new guests. He gets to flex his culinary muscles," Rita said.

Dinner was as good as promised, and beautifully prepared. A large platter of an assortment of grilled meats sat alongside a bowl of shredded brussels sprouts topped with crisp-fried shallots. On each plate was a salad of freshly tossed butter lettuce with thinly sliced red cabbage for color and crunch.

And from what Glenda said, the meals he prepared for the kids were just as good.

"No hot dogs, tater tots or little cups of tasteless raw broccoli," Glenda said. "And ketchup is not considered a vegetable here."

All meals at the New School were made fresh and mainly from local ingredients or those produced at the school. Nick and another staff member, Brittany, started an organic learning garden. It was well maintained by a student agricultural team, who also cared for the animals, which included some chickens and goats. A certified nutritionist, Brittany also ran the woodshop. Multi-talented girl.

Breakfast, lunch, and an afternoon snack were served each day, and students went home before dinner. Rita said she'd considered a boarding school but really wanted to create a model for something public schools could emulate, should the state or federal government ever become so enlightened.

Nearby families tucked into quiet pockets of wealth in Carlton and other prime locations up in the pricey real estate off the 99 had quickly enrolled their children in Rita's school as soon as it opened. Their generous financial contributions helped support the attendance of students whose families ranged from the middle class to the working poor.

The only prerequisite was the willingness to work. The office manager, Carla, was a good example. A hardworking powerhouse, she quickly recovered from the humility of briefly living on the street after losing her job last year. She now claimed the reception desk and surrounding area as her domain. Tardy students both feared her wrath for being late and cherished the conspiratorial wink and contraband sugar-laden homemade cookie that often followed as she hustled them out the back door, down the porch steps, and toward their teachers. Both of her children attended the school.

Nick and Brittany joined them at one of the dining hall tables. Except for the fact that he had black hair and hers was honey blond, they could have been brother and sister.

After accepting everyone's compliments on the sophisticated spread he'd prepared, Nick poured everyone a crisp Marlborough sauvignon blanc to go with the roast chicken and venison, indicating a Two Vines cabernet if they preferred red.

"Speaking of chickens," Brittany said, "the one you're eating is Millie, one of our new Cornish crosses. We keep the Rhode Island Reds for laying, but nothing beats a Cornish for Sunday dinner."

Even talk of recently slaughtered poultry did not diminish Logan's appetite. She devoured an entire slab of venison, a slice of Millie, all her vegetables, plus a generous helping of the delicious wild huckleberry pie Nick served for dessert. With vanilla bean ice cream melting on top.

Feeling full and satisfied, Logan was feeling a warm glow. Glow was good—as opposed to the fire in her head she felt after her martini party with Rheanna the night before. A couple of glasses of wine were more her speed.

Logan could see why Glenda raved about the place. Good people. The party broke up about ten. Nick and crew were almost done cleaning up the kitchen when Logan started to feel sleepy. It had been a long day.

"Time for bed?"

"Absolutely," Glenda agreed. "I'm ready when you are. Anybody else ready?"

"I am." Brittany joined them.

Almost transparent, a silvery white crescent moon hung high in the pines. Glenda, with the help of a flashlight, led the way out the door and down a couple of wooden steps. Twenty yards over relatively smooth, open ground, they began to hear Whisper Creek's clattering, clean voice.

"Not far now," Glenda said.

They soon reached the new footbridge. Framed by trees, it was flooded by moonbeams breaking out into the open, the excess dancing along the flowing stream.

Thicker on the other side of the creek, the trees hid the cottages beyond the bridge from view. Sticking close to the others in the weak flashlight beam, Brittany shared the path until it split off to the left around a large yellow pine, leading to a cottage she shared with one of the science teachers, a biologist named Nan Parker. Nan was already there and had a light on.

"See you tomorrow, Logan. Glad you had a good first day," Brittany said.

Glenda and Logan continued until they reached Glenda's cottage. It looked a little more rustic than Brittany's.

"I took one of the older cottages so I have the place to myself. At least until Rita does more hiring, it's mine."

They went inside. "I could have had one of the updated ones, but I like this one. It's out of the way—quiet. But don't worry. The mattresses are good on the beds. I brought my own up, along with some quilts, so your back will be happy in the morning—they're extra firm. What time do you want up? Breakfast is at seven thirty."

"Seven works—if it's okay, I'll take a quick shower before we walk over," Logan said.

After Glenda showed her where everything was, she went into her room. Fading fast, she changed into a long T-shirt to sleep in, saving her Portland purchase for next weekend with Ben. Once Glenda was out of the bathroom, she went in and ran a washrag under hot water, squeezed it out, and pressed it to her face. The air in the cottage was cold, and the warm water felt wonderful against her skin. If she wasn't so tired, she'd take a full-on hot bath. Yawning, she brushed her teeth and turned out the light before returning to her room.

Lights out, she cracked the small window open for fresh air, then jumped into bed like a kid, shivering, burrowing under several layers of heavy quilts. It's true what they said about a change being as good as a rest. This may be a working vacation, but it was still fun. Snug and sleepy, she looked forward to meeting the rest of the faculty at breakfast in the morning and getting a tour of the school with Rita. Also, she'd have to find out where good cell reception was and give Ben a call.

16

The scrub jays were well into their day, carrying on loud, scratchy conversations back and forth as they hopped and flew among the branches and undergrowth along the path back to Whisper Creek. Glenda and Logan made it across the footbridge and to the dining hall a few minutes before it opened to students. A wonderful aroma of hot coffee and bacon made her realize how hungry she was.

"Over here!" a short woman half stood out of her chair, motioning them over to one of the big round tables scattered across the large dining hall. "Saved you some seats!"

After making their breakfast selections from the buffet, Logan and Glenda made their way to the table.

Glenda made the introductions, starting with the art teacher who'd called them over, ending with a conservatively dressed Vietnamese man—somewhere in his forties Logan thought.

"Mr. Le here is in charge of our computer lab and is making them do more than they were ever originally intended to. Nick's worried he'll be out of a job because Huey's just about got those computers in there making breakfast."

"Hello, Logan. Nice to meet you. Don't listen to Glenda—I'm

just a computer tech, not a computer genius," Huey Le said, reaching across the table to shake Logan's hand.

"Don't listen to him, Logan," Rita said as she placed her plate, neatly filled with a vegetable omelet and three strips of thick bacon, on the table. "Huey is a genius and he's taking you on your first tour of the day."

"I'll be happy to, but first, please eat your breakfast while it's hot, Logan," he said, "Nick's French toast is legend."

Next to join them at the table was Carla, the office manager. Before taking the first bite of her eggs, she said, "Nice to meet you, Logan. You're from Southern California, right? A music teacher?"

"Yes—sort of," Logan answered. "I play violin—but I'm only a new teacher. I run a program for the district. Just up here to learn as much as I can about how you guys do things."

"Do you get summers off?" Carla asked bluntly.

She hadn't shared this idea with her husband, but secretly, Carla was investigating going back to school to become a teacher. She loved the kids. Even more, she loved a steady paycheck and health insurance for her kids, something their dad had never been able to provide.

Glenda laughed. "Theoretically, yes, teachers get summers off, but most teachers spend a good portion of that time getting lessons and their classrooms ready for the next year. This one," she said, jerking her thumb at Logan, "had a particularly busy summer last year . . ."

Logan's mouth was full of French toast, so she couldn't object out loud, only shake her head.

". . . She not only got handpicked by a senior member of the school board to create and run a new music-math program, she found time to catch a killer."

"What?"

"You're kidding!"

"I don't think you mentioned that in our phone call, Logan," Rita chimed in. "Do tell!"

"The police caught her, not me," Logan said, downplaying her involvement. "I was just there, working with some friends at the Otter Arts Festival in Jasper, the town I grew up in."

"She put two and two together and rattled the girl's chains until she came after her," Glenda told her audience. "Almost got herself killed. The woman was criminally insane—murdered one of the young glassblowers just because she thought she was stealing her man. Had some very disturbed ideas. Claimed her actions were all sanctioned by God."

Glenda finished the meal by filling in the gaps of the story enough to satisfy the group's curiosity.

"All I know is, if I ever get in trouble, I'm calling Logan," Glenda said.

"Here, here," Carla agreed, toasting Logan with her mug of coffee.

Nick sounded a small gong by the serving window, signaling last call for seconds. Ten minutes later, a second gong signaled students to finish eating and begin bussing their tables. Logan marveled at the efficiency with which the students scraped, stacked, and cleared dishes. All vegetables and fruits went to the compost pile out back. A student team of helpers, which rotated weekly, she was informed, whipped through the dining room, gathering, wiping down, and storing the condiments and napkin holders before leaving for class.

"On Fridays we do community announcements in the quad," Rita said, "but Monday through Thursday, they go straight to class. I cleared Huey's class schedule. I'll leave you in his capable hands for the morning. See you at lunch, Logan."

For some reason, it felt like she'd met Huey someplace

before, but didn't see how. She'd been up to Portland once to do a computer training for one of their clients, but that was years ago.

"I'll be in the garden or the health office if you need me, Logan," Glenda said, pointing to a small building just past some classrooms.

Logan followed Huey out the front doors, turning right to walk across the quad to his computer lab.

Dressed comfortably but neatly in a pale-blue shirt tucked into charcoal-gray pants, Huey led the way. With inexpensive, but softly shined shoes, it was obvious Huey did not work in the garden. His thin, receding hair was parted on the side, combed neatly back, and trimmed close around his ears.

"I've never heard the name Huey. Is it a Vietnamese name?" Logan asked.

"My Vietnamese name is Le Hai Hieu, H-i-e-u. We put our family names first in Vietnam. To answer your question, I got the nickname Huey in college. It was easier for my professors and roommates to pronounce and spell, so I just left it at that."

The classroom they approached was portable, one of several connected end to end, bordering the south side of the quad. They were similar to some she'd seen on some of the older campuses in Tilcott, where enrollment had grown but they lacked the funding to build new classrooms.

Huey climbed the short stairs up to the door, holding it open for her.

"Welcome!"

17

Huey led Logan over to the first row of student computers and fired it up. "Are you ready to meet MuMu?"

MuMu, it turned out, was an animated dolphin that guided students through a series of visual math puzzles, building their skills conceptually. No written or oral directions were provided—either by the teacher or on-screen—so it was not only a good brain-building design, but also perfect for second-language students. The kids were given as many tries as they needed to figure out how to advance MuMu through the levels, which, according to Huey, most of them could do. For the seriously gifted child, there were a couple of levels even Huey admitted he had trouble completing.

"This is so awesome!" Logan said, her Southern California surfer girl emerging.

Huey grinned with pride.

What Huey was doing here at the New School would fit right in with Fractals. She'd have to talk about this with Rita. In the meantime, she offered to send Huey a music module to pilot.

Later that morning, Huey asked, "When do you have to go back to Portland?"

"Not until Friday," she said. "I have a friend flying in, and we're going to stay at the Governor. Sort of a mini vacation. Just a couple of days."

Huey's face lit up.

"You'll have to stop by my sister's place. She has one of the food trucks, Thanh's Pho, across from Jake's Grill, on the other side of the hotel. Do you know *pho*? Do you like Vietnamese food?"

"You're kidding—that's your sister's place? I just went there—I love *pho*," Logan said.

Neurons firing, she realized where she'd seen Huey before. He was the man she had seen in the back of the food truck on Sunday. Of course—he wouldn't have been there Friday when she first went if he worked here during the week.

"Oh my God! Was that you in the back of the truck on Sunday?"

"Yes," Huey said. "I go in most weekends. It's just the two of them. They work really long hours. I can't do much, but when I can I go in, it gives them some time off. They save me the heavy lifting."

"That's a pretty full schedule—working here Monday through Friday, then driving to Portland. How do you do it?" Logan asked.

"Well, I've only been doing it for a short while. For many years, Thanh, my sister, and her husband and mother-in-law, Mrs. Nguyen, owned a restaurant downtown. Very nice, called the Vietnam Pearl. My sister and her husband are—he was—both very talented chefs. Then one day he became ill. Meningitis. He was gone very quick."

Not wanting to dwell on sad family events, but feeling he needed to explain the story he'd started, Huey tried to wrap it up.

"When the economy got bad, they kept their restaurant for a while, but eventually lost it and then their home. Don't know how things were in California, but in Portland it was more like a depression than a recession. No one was eating out. A lot of restaurants went under. It didn't take long. Some simplified their menus and reinvented their restaurants as food trucks. Much less expensive to run. That parking lot across from your hotel filled up pretty quick."

Logan didn't want to be rude and start looking around for Glenda, whom she'd promised to meet, so she kept her attention on Huey. By unspoken consent, they had slowed to a stop near the gardens to finish this part of their conversation before going inside.

She could certainly empathize with his sister. Logan knew what it was like to lose a husband and have your life change overnight. She had some idea of what Thanh must have gone through, must still be going through, left to cope on her own. She knew what it was like to have to start over. At least Logan hadn't lost her home.

She and Jack had poured everything into the business and into raising Amy, so they had always been renters. After the accident, while she recuperated, Bonnie took her in. She lived with Bonnie and Mike for over a year in their wonderful, noisy, kid-filled house in one of the spare bedrooms.

Bonnie had been there for her every step of the way while she went through the painful process of grieving Jack's death and healing as much as anyone can from the psychic and physical wounds of the car accident that took her husband's life. She couldn't imagine going through that without someone like Bonnie. And from what she could tell, the scowling Mrs. Nguyen was no Bonnie. She hadn't looked all that close to her daughter-in-law the other day. Not the warm and fuzzy type.

Logan knew she shouldn't, but she felt guilty for having

some resources to help her get back on her feet after Jack's death. She sold her and Jack's computer business for enough to buy her small fixer-upper in Jasper. Her home represented the first stability she'd felt in a long time. She spent the last of her savings for the remodel and moved in last June. After hearing what Thanh went through, she was even more grateful for her little home.

"I am so sorry. That must have been very hard on your sister, to lose her husband and then the restaurant. She must be a very strong woman."

"Yes, she is, and so is her mother-in-law, Mrs. Nguyen," Huey replied.

She was surprised he had opened up to her and shared such personal information, but Logan had that effect on people—they often opened up and shared things they hadn't intended.

"And she has you," Logan said. "Brothers are indispensable. I have a good one, too. His name is Rick. He's a police officer back in Jasper—a K-9 cop. His partner's a beautiful German shepherd named Charlie."

Huey smiled and resumed walking toward the cafeteria. "You'll have to tell me about him at lunch."

18

As Logan and Huey walked toward the dining hall, they passed Brittany and crew coming in from the garden. Holding a variety of shovels and rakes, the students rushed ahead. They looked muddy, but happy.

A tall man in new jeans and a military jacket relieved the students of their burdens at the back door of the kitchen. As he carefully hung each tool in a neatly designed storage area attached to the back wall, the kids washed up at a large outdoor farm sink. Then Huey, Logan, and Brittany waited while the students followed the man inside.

"Who's the new guy?" Huey asked Brittany.

"He's part of a program with Blanchet House in Portland. Rita's trying him out. So far this new guy's good. Quiet. Keeps to himself. Does whatever Nick asks him to do and then some. He's going to help Nick get the vegetable boxes ready and go with Rita to deliver them Friday. You going into Portland this weekend, Huey?"

"Yes, but not until Saturday morning," he said.

Once inside, Logan didn't see Rita, but she spotted Glenda, who waved her over to a table. She had also just arrived.

"Follow me. You do not want to be late," Glenda advised.

They chose a couple of seats, turned over their water glasses to indicate they were coming back, then walked to the salad bar. Logan saw the students starting to line up on the front deck outside the main entrance. She wondered why adults got to eat first.

"Don't feel guilty about eating before the kids," said a deep voice drawn out in a Southern drawl, reading her mind. "You'll want to get to the salad bar before it's destroyed."

The deep voice belonged to a tall, handsome English teacher. When lunch was over and she and Glenda got ready to leave, it was also clear his Southern gentleman-ness was more than accent deep.

"Nice to meet you, Logan," he said, holding his tie back, rising out of his seat to shake her hand. "Hope to see you at supper." Warm. Direct gaze. Nice smile.

Hmmmm.

She didn't *not* like it.

Glenda gave her a look.

"What?" Logan asked with wide-eyed innocence.

✳✳✳✳✳

For the rest of the afternoon, she was under Glenda's wing, who gave her a walking tour of the back of the property, where the animals were kept, past her herb garden, and around the main garden, where they were met by Heidi, whose real name, Logan finally remembered, was Brittany.

She really does look more like a Heidi with those long legs and rosy cheeks. You expect to see a string of mountain goats loyally following her past an Alpine cabin to the barn.

After Brittany showed her around the Student Learning

Garden, Logan was impressed. This was a serious garden, bordering on a small farm.

"Do you guys use all the food you grow here?" she asked.

"No, we plant more than we need. Rita works with a couple of groups in Portland who provide temporary shelter, including meals, for families in transition. They get free meals during their stay in the emergency shelter while they complete the program, but we also deliver weekly bushels of fresh vegetables to them for three months after they get jobs and permanent housing. Nick goes out near the end of their stay at the main shelter and gives them lessons on how to prepare fresh foods. It's a great program."

"What a great idea," Logan said. "Who delivers the food? Do you take it out every day?"

"No, just once a week. Rita goes into Portland a couple of times a week anyway, errands and supplies. We pack up the bushels Friday mornings and volunteers deliver them that afternoon. Joe's going to help with that starting this week."

Brittany had to go help Nick get dinner ready, so they said their goodbyes before heading back to Glenda's cabin .

"Thanks again, Brittany," Logan said. "I really appreciate the time you took showing me around. I have a black thumb, but I know someone who would love to see all the great things you're doing here. If I give you my email address, could you send me some pictures so I can show him what I'm talking about when I get home?"

"Sure, remind me tonight," Brittany said, "Your friend can call if he has any questions, too. See you at dinner!"

Logan looked at Glenda, "Where's the best cell reception? I want to call Ben later."

19

After they enjoyed another of Nick's delicious meals, Logan walked back over to the computer lab area, where Glenda said she'd get the best reception, put in her Bluetooth headset, and pressed Big Ben's name on autodial. It was almost 7:00 p.m. Even with traffic, he should be home by now.

"Hey there, beautiful," Ben's warm voice answered, picking up on the first ring.

She heard highway noise again in the background, but could hear him clearly—as well as picture his solid face and cornflower-blue eyes. Bonnie called him Logan's Viking.

Logan loved the sound of Ben's voice.

"Hey there, yourself. You must have worked late—you still on the fifty-five? How's traffic?" Logan asked. She absolutely hated traffic, but Ben seemed to be more tolerant. In fact, Ben was what people call grounded. He had calmly seen her through the garage conversion and addition, which at times made her want to tear her hair out.

"Just passed Edinger. Not too bad. Should be home in about twenty minutes."

"Why'd you work so late?"

"Decided to finish up today. No sense making the drive again tomorrow when a few more hours got the job done. How was your day? You're out at the school now, right?"

"Yes. You would love it here, Ben," she enthused. "Listen . . . ," she said, holding her cell at arm's length for a few seconds, then back in. "Can you hear that?"

"Hear what?"

"*Exactly!* Just pine trees and stars," Logan said, soaking in the quiet, and then she launched into telling him all about the New School and what she'd learned so far.

✶✶✶✶✶

Ben loved to hear the excitement in Logan's voice when she talked about her work, Amy, or anything else she was passionate about. She made the next eight miles bearable by telling him all about Huey's lab and Brittany's garden.

He hadn't known he'd missed having someone to talk to at the end of the day.

At forty-two he was comfortable with his bachelor routine, traveling the familiar points of his self-sufficient world. During the week it was work sites, home, and on the weekends, the occasional jaunt to his sister's house to visit with his nephews or go see his parents. He had friends, but most were work related. He didn't date clients and had long since learned that satisfying his libido with casual sex didn't satisfy anything at all. Been there, done that, had the T-shirt.

His last serious relationship had been his first and only one.

When Julie the high school sweetheart wanted to become Julie the lawyer, Ben didn't hesitate to support her dreams. After all, they were a team, he thought. When she got accepted to UCSF, he moved to San Francisco to put her through law school doing landscaping jobs in and around the city.

FOREST PARK

As soon as she graduated, she left him for Alan, her new boss. The move to San Francisco was supposed to be only temporary. She promised Ben they'd move back home to Jasper when she passed the bar. But small-town life couldn't compare with Alan's steel and stone, very modern penthouse apartment, right downtown, near all the action. She wanted that life, not life back in Jasper, with Boring Ben, as she and Alan nicknamed him behind his back.

Ben's father, an attorney back home in Jasper, blamed him.

"You let the best thing that ever happened to you get way," he'd growled. "If you'd gone into the law, lived up to your potential, you could have kept her. I don't blame her for trading up."

This last stung but didn't surprise him. He already knew what his father thought of his taking over his grandfather's landscaping business.

Maybe it was where he lived. Most Orange County women were more into getting their nails done and going out to nice restaurants than backyard barbecues. He remembered his last disastrous date. He met her in line at the grocery store. Dark-brown hair pulled up in a ponytail. Friendly, nice smile. He'd taken a chance.

Keeping it casual, he suggested Juan's, a favorite of locals for great Mexican food. She said she'd meet him there.

He almost didn't recognize her when she showed up looking like a CEO, which it turned out, she aspired to be. Currently, she was VP of a wealth management group, aiming for the corner office. Stick-straight hair, carefully applied makeup, serious heels, Chanel suit, chunky gold necklace. Not exactly the outdoorsy type he'd met buying milk and eggs at Ralph's.

Her first question was about what he did for a living. Felt like a job interview. A second date was already in the Arctic range of possibilities.

"Landscaper," he said, ordering a chimichanga. He wondered how soon he could escape gracefully.

"So. You're a . . . gardener?"

Definitely a judgment, not a question.

The next hour was excruciating.

She ordered a cup of tortilla soup, no chips, small salad, no dressing. Within the first ten minutes, the date had died a painful, but natural death. In spite of her obvious disdain for his occupation, and the fact they had nothing in common, the woman pushed for a second date.

Right.

Ben didn't like dating. He was more of a one-woman man. And if there wasn't someone special, he was okay with being alone. He'd long ago become comfortable with his own company.

Logan had been an unexpected, and very pleasant, surprise.

*****

"So, that's about it for what's happening up here," Logan said, wrapping up her monologue. "You home yet?"

"Almost, just passed Tava'e's," Ben said.

She visualized him in his truck, pulling up Killer Hill from Pacific Coast Highway, past their favorite coffee shop on the corner, named after its owner, the monolithic Samoan chess queen, Tava'e. Everyone's touchstone, Tava'e's was where people went for an uninterrupted game of chess or huge maternal hugs that came with unsolicited but always spot-on advice. Oh, and they also came for her great coffee and Jean's incredibly delicious pastries.

She pictured Ben's T-shirt stretched over broad shoulders framed in the rear window of his truck. Her heart gave a lurch, and she suddenly wished she were there, sitting next to him in that truck, going home. Fixing dinner together, enjoying it up on the roof, looking out over the ocean, hearing the seals bark.

She wondered why she had even momentarily been distracted by that guy's attention at lunch. Was she really that shallow? Ben was great and all she wanted. He was nothing like Jack. She would just have to stop worrying that he would turn out to be unfaithful and hurt her.

Suddenly, she wanted him to get here sooner, rather than later. She was having a purely physical reaction to his voice.

Ben was visualizing Logan, too, and had gone way past her shoulders.

He pulled into his driveway and turned off the engine.

"I'll check on flights—see if I can wrap this job up early. What time's good for me to call tomorrow?" he said.

"Cell reception is spotty up here. If I don't hear the phone, just leave a message and I'll call you back."

"Can't wait to see you," she added, her voice automatically lowering to a softer, more sensual zone.

Anticipation is a lovely thing.

20

"It's about time you got here. Look what he did to me!" the tall one in the middle shouted, one hand pressing some takeout napkins against his bottom lip. "You oughta lock that guy up!"

With his other hand, he was barely hanging on to an excited white pit bull straining at the end of a short length of a skinny, yellow rope he had wrapped around his wrist.

Looked like he was going to be the spokesperson of this little group. The other two, a caramel-colored boy with dreadlocks, about the same age, and a stringy-haired blonde girl sat on their heels, backs pressed against the wall. Both looked amped up.

Officer Raitt, seventeen-year veteran of the Portland Police Department, nine of those years patrolling downtown, double-parked, lights but no sound, got out of his vehicle. His partner exited the other side. The coffee shop on the corner had called in the disturbance.

One glance told him who it was, and he was not surprised. Five-ten, shaved head, black eyes, ribbed sweater, baggy pants, wool beanie, couple of long scarves wrapped around his neck.

Gold cross earring. Surprisingly, no tats. At least none were visible.

Tommy.

He and his bunch showed up about two years ago and, like a lot of these kids, decided Portland was a pretty good place to be homeless. He was surprised to see them in the winter, though. They usually headed south for the winter, but here they were, like the flu.

Except for the cut lip he was nursing, with a hot bath and some clean clothes, Tommy could have passed for one of the boys on his son's football team. They'd all shaved their heads in solidarity last week before the big game against St. Mary's.

Not for the first time, he wondered how these kids got here. And how did they take care of a dog when they couldn't even take care of themselves? Not his problem. It was late, and he just wanted to get home. Better get this over with.

"What guy, Tommy?"

Whoever hit you must have been pretty quick to get past Monster. If we find him, we'll have to buy him a drink.

He did not say this out loud.

"Yeah, it's always us you're hassling. You need to do something about *him*!" Tommy said.

"Him who?" Officer Raitt repeated patiently.

"GI Joe, that's who!" Tommy said, pressing his jacket sleeve against his lip to stop the bleeding.

"GI Joe? He wouldn't hurt a fly. He doesn't hang here. Not his area. What happened?" his partner asked, not taking his eyes of the two in the back.

"Why are you wasting time talking to me? You should be going after him. He just took off!" Tommy said, pointing north down Tenth toward Washington. "That way, toward the bridge."

Monster, as if to emphasize his master's point, lunged in that direction, ready to give chase.

Caramel Boy joined in, coming up from behind. "Yeah, man, Tommy was just messing with him and he exploded! Wasn't no reason for that."

The girl tried to struggle up to add her two cents, enjoying the chance to be the accuser and not the accused, but swayed slightly on her feet and wisely decided to sit back down.

"Okay, let's all just calm down," Officer Raitt said, directing Tommy to sit down on the curb, feet straight out in front of him, well away from the others. He pulled out a notepad and pencil.

"Now, tell me what happened."

Tommy, when he realized the cops were not going to go after Joe, visibly deflated.

This wasn't fun anymore.

"Never mind. He's gone now," Tommy said, starting to get up off the curb, suddenly wanting to be as far away from the police as possible.

"No problem, Tommy. We're here anyway. We can give you a ride downtown and take your formal statements—all three of you," Officer Raitt said. "Right, Jay?" He looked at his partner.

Jay kept a straight face. "Absolutely. We can even arrange for you to stay overnight in a nice, clean, safe place. Want me to call and see if they have a vacancy?"

They let him up off the curb.

"We can do that," Raitt said, jerking a thumb back at the patrol car. "Shouldn't take more than two, three hours at the most. And we can get that dog of yours registered, too. He's had all his shots, right?"

Tommy narrowed his eyes, licking blood off his lip, then

turned and walked off with his crew, Monster still straining the other way. He jerked on the rope until the dog gave up and walked more or less beside him.

Fuck you, man . . .

Raitt snorted as they walked back to their vehicle.

"Hope he breaks the kid's nose next time."

"Yeah, what do you think got into him? I mean Joe. He never causes trouble."

"Don't know, don't care. I'm off in ten. It's taco night," Raitt said as they drove back toward the station.

Tommy turned back and watched them drive away.

21

Logan fished her phone out of her purse. Holding her it straight in front of her like a forked willow branch, she channeled a water witcher. She finally found good cell reception by the computer lab. Smiling that Ben's number came up under favorites, she tapped his name on the screen. She needed to find a ride into Portland, but first, she wanted to check on his arrival time in the morning, tell him how to catch the MAX, and hear his voice. The week had gone quickly, but now she was anxious to start the weekend with Ben. He picked up on the first ring.

"Hi. I was just going to call you," he said.

That didn't sound good.

She listened as he told her about a busted water pipe, a critical component of a major project he had just completed.

"No, of course I understand," Logan said. "You need to take care of that . . . okay . . . Let me know . . . We have reservations through Monday, and I'm sure I can switch things around if I need to with Rita . . . It shouldn't matter which day you get there. It's okay, really . . . We'll figure it out. Just do what you need to do there—stay as long as you need to . . . Yep, I want you to be able to relax and enjoy yourself when you get here."

She smiled at the thought of what enjoying themselves might include and was pleased when he vocalized similar thoughts. Sunday could not come soon enough.

"Okay . . . call you when I get in," Logan said. "I'll see if Rita can drop me at the hotel, or at least nearby."

✳✳✳✳✳

Ben apologized again for having to delay the start of their romantic weekend, then got off the phone, shoved the gearshift a little too harshly into first, and pointed his truck toward the disaster.

A water pipe that supplied the fountain at the entrance of the Otter Festival with reclaimed water had burst, taking out part of the new performance stage he and his crew were building for the owner of the festival, Solange Sauvage.

When he got there, he saw one of the sea otters on the dramatic sculpture in the center of the fountain was completely knocked off its moorings, bobbing in the water, facedown. It looked like it was paddling blindly out to catch a wave instead of floating on the surface of the ocean in its original position, happily cracking an abalone shell on its stomach.

Taylor, his usual go-to guy, picked up some studio work in LA earlier in the week, so wasn't available. This was Solange's fountain they were talking about—not a job he could easily pass off to anyone else to fix. An internationally respected sculptor, the famous artist decided to leave Paris and settle in Jasper. No one knew why, but everyone was grateful for all she did for the local arts community. Solange would not be satisfied with anyone else handling the job. She'd insist it be done to Ben's standards.

"But, Ben, dear," Solange implored when he spoke with her on the phone, "only you have the heart of this otter in your heart, and the heart of this festival and this land, in your soul."

Working for yourself was great most of the time, but not today. Normally, a wrench like this in his schedule didn't matter much. Other than his sister and nephews, and an occasional visit with his folks, he normally had no personal life to speak of.

But Ben finally had someplace he really wanted to be. And it wasn't at work.

Fighting rush hour traffic, it took him well over an hour to get to the festival grounds. The sight that greeted him was not encouraging. The city had stopped the flooding, but he needed at least three guys to clean up the mess, find the cause, and fix the problem. Kicking the low rock wall surrounding the base of the sculpture, he got back on his phone, called in some favors, and pulled together a temporary work crew that could meet him there in the morning.

Come hell or high water, he was going to be on that flight Sunday.

22

Impatient to get to Portland, Logan went looking for Rita. She found her in the back of the kitchen getting a van loaded with crates of vegetables.

"Sure," Rita responded when Logan asked for a ride into the city.

"Leaving in ten, fifteen minutes, though. I need to get these into Portland by six. We don't have refrigeration, just ice packs in the bottom of the crates."

"No problem. I'll get my bag from the office. You want me to meet you back here?"

She wasn't sure which way Rita would drive off the property, but assumed they had to go out the way she and Glenda had come in last Sunday, past the main building up front.

Rita continued directing the loading of the van. Several boys and GI Joe were rearranging the rows so more would fit.

"No, we'll meet you up front—just wait on the porch. I'll honk when we get there. Be there in ten, fifteen minutes."

Logan crunched across the gravel to the main building, where she found Glenda and Carla talking cookie recipes. She'd already said her goodbyes to Huey, thanking him again for taking up so much of his time and promising to stop by his sister's food truck again.

"Coconut's sweet," Glenda agreed with Carla. "You could use ground coconut, and maybe some dates, instead of sugar. Or applesauce."

"That could work. I tried stevia once—yuck!" Carla said.

"Couldn't agree more. Stevia tastes like shit," said Glenda.

Retrieving her bag from behind the counter, where she'd stashed it earlier that morning, not wanting to hike back to the cabin for it later, Logan hoisted it onto her shoulder and waited while Glenda finished writing down the address of a good place in Portland to buy the ingredients.

"Logan, give this to Rita and ask her if she can pick some of this up while she's there. Only if she has time. I can get it next time I go, too."

Logan took the list and put it in her pocket. Carla got up and came around the front counter to give her a mom hug and a huge, lumpy cookie. Smelled heavenly and must have weighed a pound. Glenda handed her some herbal tea bags she'd placed in a tin.

"My own blend. Better than Sleepytime. Just in case you have one of those nights. Always good to have on hand. Of course, with Ben coming in, I doubt you'll need—"

"Or *get,*" Carla chimed in.

". . . much sleep," Glenda finished. Both women looked up at her with wide-eyed innocence.

"Thanks, guys," she said, ignoring their not-so-subtle innuendos.

Glenda had obviously filled Carla in on who Ben was and what this weekend entailed.

Diverting their attention, Logan pointed past the two grinning women through the open back door toward the cafeteria.

"Here they come!"

Out for the day, students were beginning to stream across the quad, backpacks full. Cars were idling out front, waiting for their kids to sign out.

"No rest for the wicked," Carla said cheerfully, going back behind the counter, straightening the sign-out sheets, which were actually iPads, making sure each had a stylus, waiting for the onslaught of students to file by.

Rita honked, and Logan waved goodbye and went out to the van. She started to get in back, but GI Joe left the front seat for her, so she got to ride shotgun all the way into Portland.

*****

Rita dropped her off at the Governor. On the drive in, she ate half her cookie, sharing the other half with GI Joe, but was still starving. Her plan was to check in, call Ben, find some-place to eat, and make it an early night. If all went well, Ben would be there Sunday.

There was no rush to check in, so she got a tall Verona at the Starbucks and sat down to people watch. Caffeine-revived, she decided to go to the Portland Art Museum, then prowled through Powell's Books again. The place took up a couple of city blocks. It would take a week to just figure out how to find the bathrooms, let alone digest their inventory.

With a book on eighteenth century early American herbals for Glenda and an African tree book for Amy's fiancé, Liam, tucked under her arm, Logan didn't get back to the hotel until almost 6:45 p.m. She hoped they hadn't given her room away.

They hadn't. In fact, because it was winter and not a holiday weekend, she got upgraded to a corner room overlooking Southwest Tenth and Alder on the fourth floor, located in the hotel's west wing. She only had a small rolling bag and carry-on, so she declined the offer of help with her luggage to her room. It's not that she was cheap, but tipping always felt uncomfortable, and so did the helpless heiress role women seemed to put on the minute they stepped into a nice hotel. As long as she had both legs, she'd schlep her own bags.

She went directly to the elevator, and after a short ride, it pinged softly and opened onto the fourth floor. Padding down a thickly carpeted hallway, she admired the art nouveau sconces and oversized black-and-white portraits of Secretariat crossing the finish line and Muhammad Ali in his prime. Curious about why the sports theme, and with no one to ask, she found room 423 and inserted the key card into the lock.

Heavier than she expected, the door opened onto a well-appointed room, continuing the old-money theme from the lobby. Evergreen walls framed by plenty of freshly painted, thick white wood gave the room a wrapped-in-comfort feel.

More or less a square, with an additional, smaller rectangle for the entryway, bathroom, and closet to her left, the four-hundred-square-foot room accommodated a king-size bed, a generous round table with two leather chairs in the corner, and plenty of room in between for her morning salutations to the sun without stubbing a toe. A good-size gas fireplace topped by a large mirror over the mantle faced the bed on a short diagonal wall to her left, followed by a small minibar and refrigerator tucked into an alcove, topped by a coffee maker. But what caught and held her attention were the two walls of floor-to-ceiling drapes flanking the round table that promised a light-filled room in the morning. Crossing the room, she pulled one drape back with her left hand to reveal an inviting downtown view of maple-lined streets, pedestrians, and an eclectic mix of steel and stone commercial buildings.

Wanting a hot shower before bed, she went back to the bathroom. The old-fashioned black-and-white beehive tile floor reminded her of her great-aunt and great-uncle's Illinois farm kitchen floor, although she was pretty sure theirs was linoleum. Tile didn't curl up in the corners. And there were no mice. To be fair, mice didn't last long on the farm, either. Aunt Ethel's tuxedo cat saw to that.

Lifting her small suitcase up onto the bench at the end of the bed, Logan unpacked a few essentials and brushed her teeth before noticing the blinking red light on the hotel phone.

23

The hotel message was from Huey, wanting to know if Logan would like to join him and his sister for a drink at Jake's to welcome her to Portland. They also had food if she was hungry.

"We'll be there around seven," he said.

The clock next to the bed said six forty-five. Glad for the company, since Ben's arrival was delayed, Logan slipped her room key in her pocket and took the elevator downstairs. Jake's was recommended by Sarah at the front desk as not only the most convenient place to eat but serving the best steaks in Portland hands down.

When she got there, the restaurant looked a little upscale for the jeans, henley, and boots she wore in from the New School this morning, but her attire didn't faze the hostess, who took her back to one of the copper-topped tables in the bar where Huey and Thanh were waiting for her.

"Logan!" Huey said as she approached. "Glad you got my message."

Seated, Logan was surprised that Huey's sister was almost eye level with her. Freed from the bandana, Thanh's hair fell neatly into a smooth, shoulder-skimming blunt cut.

Huey made the introductions.

Smiling, Thanh reached across the table to shake Logan's hand.

"Hi, nice to meet you."

They ordered half-pound Tillamook cheeseburgers all around and fries. Upon Thanh's recommendation, Logan added a local Chainbreaker White to her order at the last minute.

"Nice." The waiter approved.

Huey ordered the same, Thanh a mineral water and lime.

When the tangy, gold ale arrived, Logan took a long pull. It definitely hit the spot. She nodded a thanks to Thanh for the recommendation. "Good call."

After eating, they made some students from the nearby College of Optometry very happy by trading their noisy table up front for a quieter one in the back. Logan got the next round, answered Thanh's questions, giving them the basic outline of her program and what she hoped to accomplish, and praised Huey to his sister, who glowed with pride.

Huey looked thoughtful, the warmth of the room, the beer, and the company relaxing him.

"Whatever I have accomplished, I owe to Thanh. I wouldn't be here if it wasn't for her."

Thanh immediately shook her head, downplaying her contribution. Searching Logan's eyes, briefly assessing her, she leaned back and explained.

"We were supposed to come together."

Logan settled in for the story.

✶✶✶✶✶

"I was thirteen. Huey was five."

FOREST PARK

Logan took another sip of her beer and waited for Thanh to continue. The noise of the bar blurred into the background.

"Our father was Hoa, ethnic Chinese. Our mother, Vietnamese French. Cultured. Educated. An unusual union. Her family was not for the marriage. Father was not from the same background. He owned a shop in Saigon. Things got worse for them after the Vietcong took over. By 1979, most of his relatives had escaped and persecution increased daily. He knew they needed to get us out.

"The smugglers had a price. One gold bar for each child got us on one of the large boats. Not the ones you see in the pictures—little rowboats filled with ragged poor people from the country. My father's family managed to scrape enough together for us, and the deal was made. We didn't know what night they would come for us, so we were ready every night. Every day I went to school, played with my friends, but could tell none of them, not even my closest friend, Hua, that I was leaving. Not coming back. I wanted to tell my teacher. I felt she could be trusted, but my father said you never knew. So I remained silent. And waited.

"Hieu knew nothing, of course. He was only a child.

"On the night they came, the smugglers informed my parents the price had gone up. Two. It was now two gold bars for one child. There wasn't much choice. Normally, the boy would go, but since Hieu was only five years old, it was decided that I would be the one to go. They hoped I would make it out and get a job—send money back for my brother."

Hieu excused himself to use the bathroom.

"You must have been so scared." Logan had a thousand questions, but didn't want to interrupt.

Thanh took a deep breath and continued.

"I must have been. What I remember is that the boat was much smaller and older than my father expected. He insisted on coming that far with me. He was very angry with the men, but there was nothing he could do. I got on the boat.

"There were pirates, but most of the time it was just boring. Nothing but ocean and sky. I was sick most of the time."

"Did you have enough food? Water?" She couldn't help herself.

"Yes. We were luckier than most."

"I can't even imagine what that must have been like."

"I don't think we thought much beyond surviving. I didn't understand why the adults on the boat were so worried. The worst part was over, I thought. We had escaped. I was too young to know that the main problem wasn't getting out, it was finding a place that would let us in."

"How long were you on the boat?"

"I don't know—about three weeks. Long enough I had my period. Something so easy to handle at home was not easy to deal with in such close quarters. Also, we couldn't waste the drinking water to wash out our underwear, so we had to use saltwater. You have no idea how bad menstrual blood mixed with saltwater smells. We were so embarrassed!"

Logan grimaced in sisterhood, but had no idea what to say, so wisely said nothing.

"The captain kept trying—we went to island after island. No one would take us. They wouldn't even let us land to get drinking water. Finally, the captain got us to the Philippines. There was a reef that prevented the boat from getting very close, so we had to walk in. I remember everyone's feet getting cut up on the coral. No one had thick-soled boots or anything. But we didn't care. We were off that boat."

24

"How did it work? Were there doctors? Did people take you into their homes?"

"A refugee camp was set up. They had basic first aid. You got a rectangle large enough to lay down in marked out on the concrete. There was a chain-link fence all around."

"Did you have enough food?"

"You got one gallon of water per day, canned meat, and rice. If you wanted fresh fruit or vegetables . . . medicine . . . that was more difficult."

"How long were you there?"

Just then Huey returned and rejoined them at the table.

Looking down, rubbing condensation off her water glass with her thumb, Thanh softly replied, "I don't remember much about that time."

Huey squeezed her arm. Lifting her head, she smiled.

"One of my mother's nieces was accepted by Canada the year before. A few years older than me. She made it to Portland, so I had somewhere to go when my application was granted. I arrived in 1981."

There was so much more Logan wanted to know. What was daily life like in the camp? How did she keep from going crazy? How did the process work for applying to get into one of the countries accepting refugees? Did everyone find a place? But she sensed Thanh had revealed all she wanted to share about that experience.

Huey took up the story.

"Thanh was amazing. She worked hard. Went to high school, learned English."

"I was lucky, a Vietnamese couple who lived next door to my relatives owned a doughnut shop. I worked every day from 3:00 a.m. until 7:00 a.m. Babysat on the weekends.

"But don't believe the perfect Asian student stereotype, Logan. The first two years I barely passed with Cs and Ds. Contrary to popular belief, not all Asians get straight As. Hieu did, though."

"What happened to your parents?" Logan asked.

"Our mother survived and took care of Hieu. Father was sent to reeducation camp. After that, we don't know," Thanh said.

"Many Chinese disappeared in those years," Huey said.

With the money Thanh sent, Huey said their mother was eventually able to clear all the bureaucratic hurdles, including substantial bribes, to get him out of the country.

"August 14, 1989. Thanh picked me up at the airport."

"And you've been nothing but trouble ever since!" Thanh said.

Sixteen when he arrived, Hieu didn't adjust as smoothly as Thanh. Lost in the large high school, he mostly skipped class and drank too much. Sophomore year he got Mr. James for chemistry. Great teacher. Chemistry wasn't Hieu's first love, but Mr. James also ran the computer lab. Hieu was hooked.

The others, boys who'd befriended him when he first arrived, Xuan, Teng, and Albert, drifted out of his life and into more serious trouble.

"That's when Hieu started to get all those As. Once I knew he was going to be okay, I started chef school. Met my husband that year. Hieu and I both became citizens."

"America has been very good to us," Huey said.

"Our parents and grandparents had it much tougher than we did, though," Thanh said. "They had a lot more to give up than we did."

"How did your mother-in-law, Mrs. Nguyen, adjust to having to leave her home and settle in a new country?" Logan asked. "Do you think she's happy here? Does she have friends? Are there many other Vietnamese people her age in the neighborhood?"

Thanh paused, then said, "Mrs. Nguyen is a strong woman, although I don't know if she has ever been truly happy—except when she was around her son, of course. Maybe when she was younger. I didn't know her then. She lost her husband in the war and when she got here, poured all her love into her son. She gave us the money to expand our restaurant. I owe her so much."

"And to answer your other question, yes, there are quite a few older Vietnamese people of her generation here. Mrs. Nguyen visits another widow who owns a café nearby."

"It must be nice for her to have friends who share her experience of growing up and living in Vietnam for many years," Logan said.

"Yes," Huey said, "but don't think all Vietnamese are as hardworking and nice as Mrs. Nguyen and her friend. People don't like to admit it, but in all the confusion during the fall of Saigon and the large number of refugees in the first wave, some criminals escaped detection and came over with the rest . . . we don't like to talk about them."

Thanh looked uncomfortable, so Logan steering the conversation back to more pleasant topics, asking about what it was like to be a chef and what other Vietnamese dishes she should try.

The bar, far from quieting down, had raised a few decibels in the last hour. Huey insisted on paying the bill. Logan thanked Thanh for sharing her story, knowing she'd skimmed over the more painful parts. She also noticed that Thanh looked unusually tired. Parting at the door, Logan promised to bring Ben by before they went back to California. Might even make it back out to the New School, depended on how her appointments went at the university.

Riding up in the elevator, Logan wondered how she would have dealt with the challenges both Huey and Thanh had faced and overcome.

I have nothing to complain about.

25

Back in her room, she finished unpacking, leaving one of the top drawers and a few hangers for Ben, like she always did for Jack when they traveled. She wondered if Ben was a folder or a hanger and how much he packed.

Logan pushed open the curtain again, sliding the sheers back, too, then turned on the gas fireplace. Tucking one leg under her, she settled into one of the leather chairs and took in the view. Even in the dark, the city had a likable, eclectic feel. Approachable. A mix of old stone buildings and polished sculptures gave it an artsy vibe, without being cute. From her vantage point on the fourth floor, she could see a block down Tenth, and halfway up Alder. The food trucks were shuttered for the night but visible behind a latticework of branches.

A couple exited a restaurant, strolling arm in arm down Tenth, dressed warmly against the cold. Very Parisian. Definitely a walking city.

Logan felt a stab of loss. It didn't happen often, but there it was—that feeling that she was a stranger in her own life. Things with Ben were good, but it was all happening so fast. In the last few years, a lot had happened. Why did everything have to change—and without her permission? Watching the couple made her really wish her father was alive. She wanted him to meet Ben—maybe he could give her some advice. She wanted to share with him all she had learned. Her dad had always liked Jack, but she knew he would really like Ben.

Thinking of Ben first, and not Jack, she realized was a good sign. Her mind continued to drift in that direction.

Of course, Jack couldn't meet Ben . . . I mean, there wouldn't be a Ben if Jack were still alive . . .

"God, you're losing it, Logan!" she said, smacking herself on the head.

The sky was clear—no rain until later in the week, the front desk said. She had been planning on taking Ben to the Saturday Market tomorrow, but that would have to wait for another day. The only thing missing was the ability to open the window—it only went up a few inches—and look out over the rooftops like she did in Paris from . . .

What was the name of that little place? Oh yeah . . . Hotel Saint Michelle.

All the foreign students and expats knew about it. Reasonably priced, and the woman who ran it liked Americans. At least she did then. Logan wondered how she felt now, after the Iraq invasion, and our other military adventures.

The French probably liked Obama better. Most Europeans preferred his urbane manner to the Bush's good-old-boy persona, but who knew if he was doing a better job? Logan still believed in the system and encouraged her students to vote, but she knew that until they got big corporations out of the campaign-funding business, nothing much would change.

Pulling her mind back to more pleasant thoughts, she remembered luxuriating in the deep, claw-foot tub in the tiny bathroom at the Saint Michelle, glass of wine in hand. Her first weekend in Paris, she'd taken the last room at the top of the narrow stairs no one else wanted to climb. The bed wasn't much more than a sunken cot, but the economy accommodations were worth the postcard-perfect view of scattered, moonlit rooftops.

Maybe that was where she began to really enjoy her alone time. It was a luxury she cherished more and more each year, but unless she made a conscious effort to schedule some white space into her weekly calendar, she rarely got it.

She tried again to raise the windows an additional couple of inches to allow in a little more fresh air, but there was no way.

Damn American safety features . . . takes all the fun out of being on the fourth floor.

Giving up, she went in the bathroom to brush her teeth and get ready for bed. One hot shower and a steamy phone call with Ben later, she snuggled under the comforter, reached up, and pulled the chain on the lamp next to the bed.

Ben had called the hotel already and extended their stay, insisting on putting it on his card. Used to handling everything herself, Logan was surprised, but pleased. It was so old-fashioned and male—like something her father would do. Knowing she was financially self-supported, his male "I'll pick up the check" gesture caused no tremors in the force. She liked knowing he wasn't cheap. It brought back memories of her dad's advice about what to look for in a man.

"Money's not everything, but a man's relationship to money is," her dad had said.

Maybe it was because her mother surprised as much as hurt them both when she took off. Her dad was always intent on making sure his daughter got it right when it came to choosing someone to marry. One night he was working on the sink, while she did her homework at the kitchen table, mapping out the military campaign course of Alexander the Great for ancient civ.

He suddenly looked at her all serious, wrench in hand, and said, as if picking up the thread of some previous conversation, "Gambling is a deal breaker. Drugs and alcohol? Definitely deal breakers. Can't hold down a job? Deal breaker."

He paused and pointed the wrench at Logan for emphasis. "It's okay if he doesn't make a lot, but look for a man who does honest work, pays his bills, stays out of debt, saves some, and is generous and has fun with what he has."

Not waiting for a response, he went back under the sink to finish the repair job.

Used to her father's occasional out-of-the-blue utterances, Logan nodded her head and went back to her map of ancient Greece.

Good advice.

From what she knew about Ben so far, he would pass all her dad's tests.

Shivering a little even in her flannel pj's, burrowing deeper under the duvet, Logan listened to Portland's night sounds drifting in the window nearest the bed.

No sexy slip tonight, but if this evening's conversation was any indication, she would definitely be wearing it Sunday . . . however briefly.

26

G. I. Joe sat on his heels, his back against the wall, rubbing the knuckles on his right hand. Why had he let them get to him like that? Punk kids! It was the dog. He could handle the boy and his posse. It was that pit bull, Monster, that scared him.

Normally, he knew, he could handle them. But he didn't feel good. He didn't want to go back to the shelter. Besides, it'd be closed by now. He would go back to the counselor in the morning. Mary. Where was her office again? He tried to clear his head, but all he could remember was what the front door looked like, not how to get there. But he'd find it, get himself there, and insist they give him some medicine to tide him over until the first of the month, which was only six days away. She would help. Mary would help.

He didn't want to lose the ground he'd gained. Sobriety was like a hill he'd taken and he didn't want to lose it. He liked Rita and Nick and the kids at the school. And the nice office manager always gave him those cookies. He wanted to go back. In order to do that, he had to meet Rita at ten o'clock tomorrow morning. If he could find Mary before that, earlier in the morning, he could make it. They filled their own prescriptions in the same building. He knew it wasn't far. He'd walked there before. Right now his brain was all jumbled. All he needed was some sleep. Then he'd remember how to get there.

Avoiding people he felt had more of a right to the sidewalk than he did, Joe went into automatic pilot, shuffled down the inside of the sidewalk, along the windows, as unobtrusively as possible, toward his old stomping grounds near the food trucks. Even when it was raining, you could find a dry spot under the trailers. The cops didn't bother you, and the vendors didn't mind, as long as you split before they started opening up in the morning.

A woman passing him on the street didn't make eye contact but stared at his left leg. He looked down and saw the rip in his jeans where Monster had clamped onto his shin until he kicked him clear. Blood, mostly dried, trickled down to his shoe. Not a big deal.

What he really wanted was a drink. The thought of that first, cleansing swallow, burning its way down his throat, warming his body. And he could disinfect his wound. No medic.

The VA office opened at 7:30 a.m. Hopefully Mary was working tomorrow. The pills they gave him kept the cravings at bay—helped him think—kept him calm. He just had to hold on until morning.

⁎⁎⁎⁎⁎

SATURDAY MORNING

FEB. 21

Rita paced in back of the van. "Ten o'clock, Joe," she muttered. "I said ten."

FOREST PARK

She'd already loaded the empty crates into the back. She heaved the door shut. Giving the handle a jerk to make sure it was locked, she stalked to the front and climbed into the driver's seat. Even though the dashboard thermometer read thirty-four degrees, she rolled down the window and stuck her elbow out.

"Five more minutes, Joe," she said.

Blanchet House's day manager came out and gingerly approached, hovering, anxious to appease Rita and not compromise future placements. They detoxed these guys and did their best to place them in supportive work environments, but most businesses didn't want to hire addicts and alcoholics.

"Something must have happened to him," she said.

"I wish he had stayed here with us last night. It's better if they don't go back on the street—even for one night," said the day manager, who was relatively new at her job. "He might still get here," she continued, without much hope in her voice.

"Yeah, well," Rita said. "If he gets here in the next five minutes, I'll give him another chance. If he's a no-show, I can't have that at the school. I hope you understand."

The woman nodded.

Behind them, Blanchet House hummed with activity. Participants in various stages of the program came and went through the large front door, on their way to or from morning signups, Microsoft Office software training classes, and resume writing, which should have been called Creative Bullshit 101. The neighboring prenatal clinic and daycare already had a line out the door. A toddler's indignant shriek pierced the air.

Ten minutes later, motor running, Rita ran her hand through her short, thick hair and took one last look down the street.

Adjusting her mirrors, she started the engine.

The day manager conceded defeat, and the women said

their goodbyes. Rita promised not to give up on the program altogether, even though the first Blanchet House candidate had failed.

She jammed the van into gear and pulled into traffic back to the school. Paperwork would be piling up on her desk even though she'd only been gone less than twenty-four hours.

*****

VETERAN AFFAIRS OFFICE
9:53 A.M.

"I'm sorry, Mr. Watts, but Mary isn't here. She doesn't work on Saturdays. We only have part-time staff on the weekends. Mary is your caseworker. She has your files. No one here can renew your prescription without authorization, and you can't get an exception without your case file, which your caseworker has . . . and who we have already established is not here today. I really am sorry, but you will have to come back on Monday."

Seeing the somewhat panicky look on the veteran's face, the man behind the window added, "They are very strict about prescriptions. You'll have to wait. I'm sure Mary can help you on Monday. She has your file, and the pharmacy will be open."

The counselor closed the window. He felt bad for these guys. They just didn't know how to organize their time and come for their appointments when they were supposed to or keep track of their medications. Poor man probably lost the bottle somewhere or took all the pills already. How these people survived from day to day, he had no idea.

*****

Joe stood for a while longer, looking at the man through the window, as if by some miracle he would change his mind and produce his medication. This was the place. He'd finally found the right street. It was near that big building with the boxes stacked in the window display. The red ones. They were supposed to help him here.

Well, if they weren't going to, he'd just have to do without. He would go to where he was supposed to meet Rita. He could do that. He could take care of himself. He would go back to the trees, to the nice people, to where he got to work with his hands.

If I can just get back to the school—if I can just stay busy, I'll be okay. Maybe they'll let me use the phone and I can call Mary on Monday.

He knew he was supposed to take the medicine regularly. The pharmacist had warned him about the side effects of stopping suddenly. When you did stop taking them, you were supposed to gradually reduce your dose—wean off them slowly.

Giving up on the guy behind the window, he went outside and turned right—toward Blanchet House, where he knew Rita was waiting for him. Like the counselor said, do what you can do. Keep your promises. He'd promised to meet Ms. Wolfe this morning where she dropped him off. He didn't have a watch, but it was still morning. He hoped she'd still be there. Thrusting his hands deep inside the pockets of his army jacket, against the cold, he started walking.

27

Glenda's shopping list wasn't hard to fill. Sarah, who was working the front desk again this morning, directed Logan to the farmers' market in Pioneer Square. The herb lady had an amazing variety of dried herbs, including lavender and comfrey, the two Glenda wanted.

Thanh's was open by eleven, so Logan stopped by for an early lunch. Huey was working, but it was busy, so they didn't have much time to talk.

Later, back in her room, Logan e-mailed Amy and called Bonnie. She tried a couple of times but wasn't able to get through to Ben. Probably left his cell in the truck or didn't hear it if it was noisy on the job site. Hopefully he was able to pull a crew together and fix that broken pipe. He finally texted saying he'd let her know for sure in the morning. Why he couldn't tell her now seemed odd, but she let it go.

She gave Rheanna a call to see if she was singing anywhere nearby tonight. Rheanna answered on the second ring. Happy to hear from her, she gave Logan directions to a small pub no more than five blocks away. Tonight she was singing some of her own songs, with a backup guitarist. The place hadn't filled up yet, but they were just about to start. Rheanna told Logan to grab a table when she got there, and she'd be able to talk during her first break.

After a quick rinse-off shower, Logan pulled on black jeans, a lightweight fisherman's sweater, and her favorite boots. She'd re-heeled them twice and they were due again. She checked her phone again, then put it in her jacket pocket, along with her hotel key, wallet, and some Burt's Bees lip gloss. Cranberry. Went with everything.

Not bothering with any other makeup, she took the elevator down, stopped at the desk for some general directions, then exited the hotel and walked a few blocks down and over toward the river.

Rheanna said to look for a wooden sign in the shape of a pipe, which she had no trouble finding. It's hard to miss a four-foot-tall, purple-and-lime-green-trimmed Sherlock Holmes pipe.

A young man standing under the sign opened the door for her, moving his cigarette away as he did, so the smoke didn't blow in her face. Nodding her thanks, she went in. A long bar ran along the right side of the room. De rigueur gold-veined mirror. Brass foot rail. Six or seven scarred tables of indeterminate material took up most of the uneven floor space. Half the bar stools and most of the mismatched tables were occupied.

Logan found a minuscule café table in the back corner, near a small stage, and sat down. The performance area barely held Rheanna, her guitarist, and the microphone she leaned into. A single spot spilled blue light onto the dispatcher's shiny cap of black hair, painting it sapphire.

Tonight, the petite chanteuse wore an ivory lace shift over a long satin tank and taupe leggings. Her black hair shone under the overhead spot. Her clear alto floated across the patrons' heads, commanding the attention of all but a few cellphone addicts, who wouldn't have looked up if Aretha Franklin belted out "Respect."

Logan ordered an IPA, gave Rheanna a wave to let her know she was there, and relaxed into the music. Forty-five minutes later, the first set over, Rheanna, after grabbing a Coke from the bartender, came over and sat down.

They talked music, and Rheanna caught her up on the highlights of her day job.

"Absolutely, stark naked—except for the garter belt," Rheanna said.

"Garter belt?" Logan asked.

"That's where he tucked the gun."

"And all of this happened in broad daylight? On the courthouse steps?"

"Yep," Rheanna replied, taking a sip of her Coke, "which was convenient, actually. When the call came in, they notified Keenan and his partner. They'd just finished testifying in a robbery homicide case. Brightened their day. They picked him up, escorted him to the car, and drove him straight to central." She took a long sip through the straw in her Coke. "Booked and processed before lunch. Kind of a nice break from blood and guts for the guys—all the stuff they usually deal with. It's only funny because the gun wasn't loaded. Speaking of Keenan, unless they catch a case, he'll be by later. He's supposed to have tomorrow off."

Elbows on the table, Rheanna, chin cupped in her left palm, absentmindedly pulled on a section of bangs over her right eye.

"It's a good thing the gun wasn't loaded. That whole thing could have gone a very different way."

Thinking of recent police shootings in the national news that had definitely not gone well, they avoided talking about them, not sure of each other's politics. Logan knew what a sensitive topic the shootings were with her brother, Rick. Not fair to judge all cops by a few bad apples, Rick said. But people did.

Instead, Rheanna asked about Logan's week at the New School. She shared her first impressions, which were all positive.

"I wish my high school had been like that," said Rheanna.

"Like what?" a male voice asked.

A tall man in dark slacks, jacket, and a blue dress shirt approached their table. Wool coat over his arm. Thick black hair waved off a high forehead. Pale skin. Blue eyes set close together. Long creases carved into his cheeks proved he must smile sometimes.

Striking. And a little intimidating.

He leaned down and kissed Rheanna as he pulled out a chair.

Rheanna returned the kiss very enthusiastically.

"I'm hoping you're Keenan." Logan laughed.

The intimidating face hinted at a smile. "Guilty as charged."

Folding his coat over the back of a chair, he loosened his tie and sat down. Immediately, Logan felt like a third wheel. He obviously would have preferred to have Rheanna all to himself.

<h1 style="text-align:center">28</h1>

She felt, rather than saw, his summary assessment, quick but complete. She doubted he missed much. Logan pegged him for about forty—maybe older—older than Rheanna.

"Logan," he said, holding her gaze as he leaned forward across the table to shake her hand, not giving away the results of his inspection.

Introductions made, Keenan sat back in his chair, taking easy ownership of the table. Not a direct action, just used to being in charge. Not one for small talk, either. Luckily, his girlfriend had no trouble carrying the conversation not only for their table, but the next three besides.

Soon, all the tables were taken and it was three deep at the bar. Around eleven, the guitar player, who had gone outside for a smoke, wound his way back through the crowd.

"Natives are getting restless, Rhe," he said, stopping briefly at her chair on his way back to the postage-stamp stage.

Rheanna checked her watch and stood up.

Turning to Keenan, she asked, "You going back out?"

"Not planning on it. Walters and Stillwater caught a

case—floater—Nelson and Taylor are on call tonight. I'm off till tomorrow morning," he said.

Rheanna's eyes twinkled.

Turning to Logan, she asked, "You staying? I'll be done by twelve thirty or one, depends on the crowd."

Knowing her boyfriend had other plans, Logan replied, "I'd love to, but I'm afraid that beer's making me sleepy. Time to tuck myself in."

Keenan didn't seem terribly disappointed she was leaving.

Logan couldn't blame him.

Given the sexual energy radiating off Rheanna, Logan knew she and Keenan would have no trouble filling the few hours Rheanna had between her last set and the start of her 4:00 a.m. shift. The woman apparently needed no sleep.

Keenan offered to call her a cab. Typical cop, bit overprotective like her brother. Must come with the territory. Rick was like that—always making sure she had pepper spray in her car.

She thanked him for the offer, but she preferred to walk. It was only a few blocks, and the sidewalks were well lit. After trying to pay her tab, which Keenan insisted on picking up, Logan let herself out onto the sidewalk. All in all, she liked him, although she wouldn't want to get on his bad side or be on the receiving end of those laser-blue eyes if she had anything to hide.

After being inside the stuffy bar, she welcomed the blast of cold air stinging her cheeks, making her eyes water. It cleared the sleepiness that crept up on her in the bar. She blinked a few times, brought the street into focus, and pulled her jacket tight. Being a Southern Californian, she didn't own gloves, so stuffed her hands into her pockets instead. Walking back to the hotel, she enjoyed the solid sound her boot heels made on the pavement.

A few blocks later, safely back at the Governor, she pushed against the tall glass doors and reentered the main lobby. What was it with heavy doors in this place? A single employee manned the desk, nodding at her as she made her way to the elevators. All quiet on the western front.

Upstairs in her room, she noticed the crisp turned-down sheets. Two sea-salt caramels placed exactly in the center of each pillow. Plucking the one closest to her, she unwrapped it and popped it into her mouth, falling back onto the bed, not bothering to remove her jacket first.

Oh . . . My . . . God! These things should be illegal. Perfect balance of salt to sweet.

Turning her head slightly to the left, she eyed the remaining piece on what would have been Ben's pillow. Housekeeping apparently hadn't gotten the memo he wouldn't be in until tomorrow.

Hmmmm . . . I could save it for him, or I could . . .

After making quick work of the second caramel, feeling only slightly guilty, Logan changed, turned out the light, and got into bed, proud that she had limited herself to two beers. She was in much better shape than the last time she went out with Rheanna.

The mattress was comfortable and the room dark, but two hours later, she was still awake. Staying up late threw her system off. The minute she lay down, her mind started its hamster wheel thing, thinking about what she'd gotten herself into.

What side of the bed would Ben want? Did he snore? Did she? How would sleeping together change their relationship? Maybe there was no busted pipe—maybe he was getting cold feet. What if they broke up later and still had to live next door to each other? What if . . .

No!

She would *not* spend what little of the night that remained second-guessing this. He wanted it. She wanted it. End of story.

Logan punched her pillow several times, rearranging it under her neck again. If she didn't get it just right, she'd feel it in the morning. Residual effects of the car accident. Most days it was fine, but sometimes, even after a hot shower, she could only move it a few inches left or right. She needed to get in to see the chiropractor when she got back.

No. Ben didn't sound hesitant on the phone earlier. He didn't sound unsure. And she didn't think he was the lying kind. Of course he really wanted to come.

Probably . . .

Eventually, Logan entered a fitful sleep and a series of murky ocean dreams—none of which she would remember in the morning. In them, she was some kind of small sea creature, darting in and around rocks and seaweed, urgently looking for something.

29

Checking to make sure the dead bolt was fully engaged on the front door, Mrs. Nguyen tugged at the bottom of her blouse and padded silently down the short hallway to her bedroom. The dead bolt ensured she'd have a minute's delay in case they came back early or forgot something, but she didn't expect them back for at least an hour.

She'd sent Thanh and Hieu to the market to pick up some more mint and fresh vegetables. Thanh usually went on Fridays but was too tired to go yesterday. She would have gone for her, but her daughter-in-law was very particular when it came to buying only the best ingredients. If Long's tried to push yesterday's bean sprouts on them, Thanh would make him go in the back to get this morning's delivery.

Now that her mind was made up, she moved confidently and quickly. The indecision and anxiety she'd lived with the last few weeks fell away, and she was her old self again. Minh of Saigon. Mrs. Nguyen. Not powerless.

Numb after her son's death, she'd gotten through the last couple of years in survival mode, doing her duty, taking no joy in the family she had left. And Thanh, she realized, was her family.

Yesterday, after they'd all put in a long day, she watched her daughter-in-law efficiently complete the last of the cleanup. She washed and dried the large stainless steel stock pot, hung it on the thick hook under the long wooden shelf that ran the length of the truck just over their heads, then deftly placed the clean knives on the magnetic strip above the counter. Backlit by the late afternoon sun streaming in the open back door, she had the vigor of youth, strong and clean. Her son chose well.

They would have had beautiful children.

And, she realized, *my daughter-in-law is still young. Too young to slave the rest of her life away in this cramped trailer.*

A wave of sorrow for all she'd lost overwhelmed her. Momentarily, the seventy-five-year-old Mrs. Nguyen could not breathe. A fierce, protective love for her daughter-in-law filled her heart. This surprised and amazed her. She thought she could only feel such love for her son.

The path now clear, for the first time since her son died, she slept soundly that night and woke refreshed.

If she was to finish before they got back, she needed to get started.

Thanh's room was across the short hallway next to the bathroom they shared. Hieu slept on the couch when he came.

Sliding open one of the doors, her eyes scanned the top shelf of her closet. Cheaply built, it was shallow, but held what she needed. Standing on tiptoe, she pushed bags and boxes over until her fingertips found the smooth surface of her old Samsonite suitcase. Steadying the loose shoe boxes stacked precariously on top with her left hand, she grabbed the plastic handle with her right, and pulled it down. Several leather purses came with it, tumbling to the closet floor, but she ignored them, turning instead to place the suitcase flat on her double bed. She didn't have all day.

FOREST PARK

Her graceful queen-size sleigh bed wouldn't fit in this room, so she got this smaller one, but refused to dignify the purchase with a headboard or good linens. It would be one of the first things to go, she decided.

She was glad her son did not have to see them living like this. He had died before the economic crisis, which Mrs. Nguyen did not understand, but certainly had been affected by. The restaurant went under. She and Thanh didn't even have time to grieve. To satisfy creditors, they sold everything, bought the food truck, and immediately had to go to work.

Bacterial meningitis. She still couldn't believe her strong, healthy son was dead. She didn't think people died of things like that here in America. But he had, and it had only taken three days.

"Just a headache, Mother. Nothing to worry about," he'd said. By the second day, he ran a temperature of 104 degrees. They got him to a doctor right away, but by then it was too late. One by one his organs had shut down.

Sighing for all she could not change, she dismissed these useless thoughts and clicked open the Samsonite's metal fasteners. With a narrow screwdriver she kept inside, Mrs. Nguyen removed the hollow handle and pried it open, shaking her daughter-in-law's future into her hands.

Twenty-four diamonds of varying sizes and cuts, worth about seven hundred thousand dollars, glittered in her palm. She knew this because, per her husband's instructions, she cautiously inquired of people with trustworthy families she knew back in Saigon and had been referred to a Vietnamese jeweler here in Portland who had appraised them for her. Her husband told her to sell the diamonds only in case of emergency. This may not have been the kind of emergency he had in mind, but Chinh was not here, and she was.

She could have used them to pay for the restaurant expansion, but that was not her way. Life was uncertain. One must always keep something back, have something set aside.

Expanding a restaurant is not an emergency. That was just good business. If the economy hadn't imploded, she could have paid Cong back easily. As it was, she took it as her due. He owed Chinh his very life. What was a few thousand dollars compared to the gift of a new life Chinh had given him? In reality, she owed him nothing. In fact, he owed her.

But now that Cong was dead, his nephew Sonny was demanding immediate repayment. Something had to be done. For herself, she was not concerned. With her son and husband gone, there was nothing they could do to her. But now those two thugs were threatening Thanh. This was not acceptable.

30

Her good daughter-in-law would not be safe until she paid off the loan. She would normally turn to the man of the family to handle Sonny, but Hieu was too soft, too gentle. Not tempered by war. He worked with computers and would not know how to handle these thugs.

She was mostly angry with herself for not having taken care of it before things got this far. The time had passed so quickly. She should have sold the diamonds long ago. What was she saving them for, anyway?

Those two men had come to the food truck again yesterday, insolent and disrespectful, wanting not just money, but free food, too. The tall one always did the talking. This time when she refused to pay, he just shrugged.

"I'm just delivering the message," he said. "Sonny's tired of waiting. You owed his uncle, which means you owe him. You've got to pay."

He had not very subtly implied with a glance to the back of the truck that harm would come to her family if she did not. Although the shorter man had not spoken, she felt he was the more dangerous of the two. He seemed to be in charge and emanated a coldness even Cong had not possessed. She told them she needed some time to get the money, shoving their food at them so they'd leave before Thanh noticed them. Her daughter-in-law, an innocent, must be protected. She had not had to deal with these types of people in her life, and if Mrs. Nguyen had anything to say about it, she would never have to.

Digging in her purse, she took out an Altoids container, opening and snapping shut the lid several times. Yes, it would do. It did not come undone easily.

She emptied the strong mints into the trash can by her bed, then poured in most of the diamonds. She funneled three back in the handle—the largest one and two smaller stones. One must always keep something back. Snapping the lid of the Altoids container shut, shaking it one last time to make sure it was secure, she put it in the zippered compartment of her purse. She would deal with Sonny tomorrow.

She'd have to find another place to hide the remaining three stones. If Cong's nephew didn't already know where she lived, he would soon. If he sent his thugs to come looking, she must make sure they would find nothing here. No, she would go to him first.

She shed no tears when Cong died, but then, she thought, our view of the dead often softens. At least he had the veneer of the old ways. Sonny was pure American, or the worst of this country, anyway. The sooner she could be rid of him, the better.

She smiled at the thought of walking down the street with half a million dollars of diamonds in her purse. Why hadn't she done this before? Her only excuse was that she had been in mourning for her son.

A stream polluted by grief takes time to run clear. She would never forget him, but she must begin living again.

She went through the plan for tomorrow in her head,

looking for any weak spots, any areas where things might go wrong.

Sundays, with Hieu's help, she and Thanh each took half days off. An early riser by nature, Mrs. Nguyen took the morning shift, opening up at nine o'clock for locals, giving Thanh a few extra hours of sleep. Thanh and Hieu got there at about eleven, when the food trucks officially opened. They worked the lunch rush, then ate something themselves. Hieu was not a cook but appreciated good food and was willing to help out in any way he could, like doing the heavy lifting. A good brother to Thanh. He also understood the old ways. He had always shown her respect and taken care of his sister.

Mrs. Nguyen usually left by two or three, leaving Thanh and Hieu to close. Hieu then drove the hour and a half back to his computer job at that school.

All she had to do was keep the diamonds safe until tomorrow afternoon, when she would go to Sonny's office in person. These would more than repay the loan in full, even with the exorbitant interest he'd tacked on. With the stones she left hidden in the handle of her suitcase back in the apartment, she could help Thanh open her own restaurant. A real one—worthy of her talents. Not as big as the Vietnam Pearl, of course, but one with a good location and kitchen.

In twenty-four hours, they'd be free.

31

Opening the door slowly, so as not to wake Hieu who was still asleep on the couch, Mrs. Nguyen let herself out of the apartment, closed the door, and listened. All was quiet. Good.

On the street, it was still dark, and the streets were empty of people. Small shiver. Almost giggled. She hadn't felt this alive since she was a young girl in Saigon, sneaking into an American movie with her friends.

Pressing her purse against her body, tucked securely under her arm, she walked briskly on the familiar Sunday morning route toward downtown. Her friend's shop wouldn't be open yet, but if she hurried, she would still have time for a visit later today, after completing her mission. She never missed a chance to sit and enjoy a pastry and steaming cup of cream-laden Vietnamese coffee with Mrs. Duong.

Thanh would be able to open a new restaurant worthy of her culinary skills. She couldn't wait to tell her!

Of course, she would officially give the diamonds to both Thanh and her brother, just as she had added Hieu to her life insurance policy recently. As capable as her daughter-in-law was, she felt it only proper she had a man to help her with finances. She would tell them both tonight.

Now that she made the decision, Mrs. Nguyen felt better than she had in weeks, since Sonny's thugs first started badgering her.

Recent years had been tough. Her son dying, so young. Gone in three days. She and Thanh had no time to grieve. The young couple had no life insurance. Her son had been young and healthy. Why would he need it? Why would they? Then suddenly he was gone. Their lives and the American economy collapsed together. No business. Lost their beautiful home.

But if her dear Chinh, her son's father, had not arranged for their escape, she knew her son's life would probably have been much worse, and most likely even shorter. She must accept the world as it was, not as she wished it to be.

Things would be okay. What was she saving the diamonds for, anyway? She may not have her son and she would never have grandchildren, but Thanh was her family now. Maybe Hieu would marry someday and she could be Auntie Nguyen to his children.

Thinking of Thanh, she thought of all the young woman had lost, leaving her parents behind when she was only thirteen years old. She had not had an easy life. She had no mother here to care for her, to do the things a mother did. Mrs. Nguyen felt ashamed that she had not done more, been more of a mother to her son's wife. She decided she would buy her a jade necklace. Something special, since her own mother was not here to take care of her. Why hadn't she done these things before? Why had she clung to the diamonds?

She could not change the past, but she could do better now.

Cooking made Thanh happy. Mrs. Nguyen had cooked because you had to cook to eat, and she wanted her son to eat well. She did not love cooking, but she loved her son. She made sure he had the best of everything she could provide as he was growing up. Thanh and her son, however, shared a great passion for creating delicious food. They could spend hours preparing and savoring a new dish for the restaurant or preparing a simple dinner at home, teasing out new flavors.

Another thought occurred to her. Once the debt to Sonny was paid and Thanh set up in a secure life, she, Mrs. Nguyen, could retire! Her duties complete, her debts paid, she would sit and visit with her friend every morning if she wanted to. Little Turtle still smoked, but they sat outside her shop to play cards, even in the rain, under the awning, so the smoke didn't bother her.

Everyone back in Saigon smoked. Or used to. She didn't know what they did now. It was probably outlawed, like the proper names *ladies* and *gentlemen* on the restroom doors. Friends who'd stayed or had not managed to get out when she did told her that one of the first things the North Vietnamese did when they took over the city was to change the names on the doors to rough, country names, designating basic biological differences only—*male* and *female*—trying to erase any and all remaining sophistication or culture they thought smacked of Western influence.

No better than animals.

Maybe she would take up smoking! Maybe not.

4:38 a.m.—she crossed the last street. Almost there.

Other than a homeless man curled up under Doughnut King's awning, which she skirted, Mrs. Nguyen saw and heard no one as she cut through the ring of closed and shuttered food trucks. Round propane tanks, like sleeping gnomes, hunched against the backs of the trailers, half hidden in shadow. Crossing on the diagonal, she quickly reached the back of their small silver trailer. Taking a ring of keys from her purse, she stepped up the three wooden stairs pushed up to the back door. Balancing at the top, she inserted her key into the single metal padlock, opened the door, and hung the keys on the hook above the counter.

Out of habit, she checked the small clipboard hanging on a string under the keys. Hieu's neat printing indicated the tanks had been filled yesterday. Reliable Hieu. He was such a help to them.

Pointing the flashlight beam on the floor in front of her, she located the small space heater inside the door and turned it on. No sense freezing while she was here. No lights, though. Probably no one was around to see her, but it was better to be safe. No sense advertising her presence.

32

She didn't need a great hiding place for the Altoid box. Just someplace temporary until tonight. Before the day was out, she would pay Cong's nephew Sonny the full amount owed to his deceased uncle.

Once Thanh and Hieu got there, she could leave for an hour or so without raising any suspicions. She knew she could tell them but didn't want them to know or worry.

She could easily use her hands as an excuse. Her wrists bothered her sometimes. Arthritis. More often than they knew. She didn't like to complain. It was the chopping. Even twisting those little ties on each bag made her hands ache so bad sometimes shooting pains kept her awake all night. Tiger Balm helped, but she couldn't use it when she was working with food.

She would use her arthritis as an excuse—tell them she was taking a small break to buy some Aleve. She would say she was walking to the pharmacy around the corner, then take a taxi, pay Sonny, and be back. She wouldn't be long.

Once she made up her mind, it was really all very simple. She would give Thanh the remaining diamonds tonight while

Hieu was still there, before he drove back to his school. Thanh was generous and would include him in the restaurant if he wanted to be a part of it. He had been kind to her. It would be proper to offer. They were all family now.

She looked around the trailer, looking for a good spot. Someplace that wouldn't be accidentally discovered by Thanh or Hieu as they worked in the truck today. Cups and pencils, takeout containers, plastic trash can, counter.

There!

That would do. That was a good place.

She went back to the drawer by the back door and found some duct tape, which all vendors kept on hand. It was amazing what it could fix or hold together until they could afford to repair whatever had broken that week. While she was there, she checked on the small space heater near the door. Yes, it was on. It used up some of the propane, but in the winter, it was essential to her old bones.

Back in the front of the truck, she laid the flashlight on its side so its beam weakly illuminated the counter in front of her.

Need to add batteries to the list.

She tucked a dishrag under it to keep it from rolling off. Next, she removed the Altoids tin carefully from her purse and placed it next to the flashlight, in the small pool of light it provided.

She looked over her shoulder. No, no one was there. The sound she heard was only a car driving by. Not stopping. No other vendors arrived this early.

Opening the tin, she checked the diamonds one more time. She knew they were inanimate objects, but in the dim light, they twinkled as if as excited as she was.

She was tempted to put one or two back in her purse but didn't. She needed every stone to pay off the loan in full. She didn't want there to be any question. She never wanted to see Sonny again or have anything to do with that world. And she definitely didn't want to give him any reason to send those thugs around here again to harass her or harm Thanh.

Snapping the lid shut, shaking it upside down first to make sure it was tightly closed, Mrs. Nguyen reached back and, with three wide strips of duct tape, secured the Altoids tin underneath the counter, in the far-left corner. Stepping back, she checked to make sure it could not be seen from any angle until she removed it.

Good.

There were no drawers, pipes, or wires there, no reason for anyone to look under the counter and discover the tin. And as busy as they were during the lunch rush, she would have no trouble retrieving it when it was time, but with the increasing crime in the city, how should she carry them out? What would be the safest way of transporting them to Sonny's?

She could simply put them back in her purse, in the zippered compartment on the side, but what if she was mugged along the way? More people would be out then. Not likely anyone would steal her purse, but she wasn't taking any chances. Absentmindedly, she patted her hair. She did that when she was nervous.

Of course!

Like many women of a certain age, Mrs. Nguyen's hair was thinning. As she had seen her mother and grandmother do before her, Mrs. Nguyen began collecting her own hair from her brush and pillow long before she needed it. In her youth, her hair had been a waterfall of black silk. Several years ago, when her French twist needed some help, she used this collected hair to create a French roll filler to create the illusion of her former, plentiful tresses. She could have purchased one, she didn't mind spending money on good clothes and skin care, but didn't need to.

The older, but still beautiful, Mrs. Nguyen, soon to be free of both grief and debt, scooped up the diamonds in her left hand while reaching to remove her hairpins with her right. Not even the savviest street thief would think of looking for valuables in her French twist!

She could see it now. When she got to Sonny's, she would simply excuse herself for a moment—an old woman who needed to use the restroom. Once inside, she would unwrap her bun, take out the French roll filler, shake out the diamonds she'd tucked inside, deftly put her hair back up, and walk back to his office. Like a James Bond movie she had once watched with her son, everything would go smoothly.

Her hair fell softly around her shoulders. How her husband had loved to stroke her hair.

She took a last look at the sparkling gems in her hand.

She couldn't wait to see the look on Sonny's face when she walked back into his office and let these diamonds fall carelessly from her fingers onto his uncle's desk!

4:58 a.m.

Good.

She still had plenty of time.

33

The beat-up green Subaru looked the same dull gray as everything else on Division Street this early in the morning. Sunrise wasn't for another three hours, but Michael didn't want to wait. What they were doing needed to be done in the dark.

"Take Morrison."

"What did you think I was gonna take?" Teng said.

A thin Vietnamese man in his late twenties, Teng continued to drive at the same leisurely pace. His hair stuck out at right angles from his head on one side, the result of another late night. Not a morning person. A straggly, wannabe mustache attempted to grow in the smooth real estate between his nose and upper lip. He was taller than Michael by at least five inches, his height giving him an air of irritating insouciance in the Vietnamese community.

"Just get me there," Michael said tersely, mad at Teng for being late. Teng needed to take work more seriously. He had a girlfriend but cheated on her all the time. He'd been out partying the night before, as usual. What a loser. He'd have never survived in the field. They drove across the bridge in silence.

Stocky, but gym-toned, Michael consciously lowered his tight shoulders, popping his neck left and right, easing the tension. He needed to relax. Teng was okay. Who cared about his personal life? He could drive anything on four wheels, even this old junker, wherever Sonny needed them to go. And lately, they'd been going quite a lot.

He didn't care about Sonny's ambitions or what this morning's errand was all about. Retribution or intimidation, it didn't matter to him either way. He liked the work. Like a shark, if he wasn't swimming, he'd die. Live for today. After Afghanistan, he knew tomorrow was never guaranteed.

Crossing over Morrison, Teng cruised smoothly into town up Washington. Traffic would be nonexistent this time of morning. The river—flat, black, and hard—kept its thoughts to itself.

Michael continued giving directions. "Left on Eleventh, left on Alder—go slow around the corner on Tenth."

He didn't care if he pissed off Teng. He wasn't about to get pulled over. He couldn't afford to. His Kalashnikov lay next to him on the backseat. Not exactly inconspicuous. The AK-47 was everyone's favorite assault rifle for a reason: it only weighed nine pounds and had six main parts. It was accurate, never jammed, broke, or overheated, and lasted forever. He'd used a 7.62 HEI incendiary round for today's job. Propane tanks didn't blow up by themselves. They needed a little help.

Almost there. Michael looked out the Subaru's rear window as they got closer to the target but didn't care about what he saw—he was focused on the job ahead.

Formless gray shapes huddled in doorways. Windows, deep set in old, gray stone, glowed softly, unseeing alien eyes. Above them, in luxury apartments, Portland's middle management workers still slept peacefully in five-hundred-thread-count

Egyptian cotton sheets. No one was around this early to pay any attention to the beat-up Forester.

He had Teng drive past the target and around the block again to check on the exact location. No room for error. Sonny wanted this job done quickly and cleanly. He wanted to get there two hours ago, before even the baristas were up, but Starbucks was on the opposite side of the Governor and down a block. They should be safe. Sunrise wasn't until 7:21 a.m.—he'd checked. Even if anyone looked their way, it was still dark. Food trucks didn't open until eleven on Sundays. Most vendors had kitchens off-site and didn't start arriving until around nine thirty or ten.

Lucky them. They'll miss all the fun.

He glanced again at his watch: 4:58 a.m. He picked up the rifle and placed it across his lap. Popped his jaw. The crowded rows of cheerful, multicolored food trucks filled him with disgust. Sleek office buildings and high-rise hotels were more his style. Vegas. Now there was a town.

This whole block should be razed.

Thai, Vietnamese, Syrians, Nigerians, Koreans . . . ignorant immigrants thinking hard work and long hours would get them the American Dream. Fat chance. His mother and sisters still worked six days a week for next to nothing in nail salons in Beaverton. Never a full weekend off. Ever. He'd joined the army just to get away.

Living up to the name his mother gave him, An Toam, Complete Peace, Michael got very calm. Wouldn't she be proud? The smile disappeared as soon as it started. He had done things in Afghanistan of which his mother would not be proud.

It was like this on patrol. You observed from outside your body. All focus. Everything came to a point, like the point on the horizon all lines aimed for in a drafting class he'd taken in high school. He liked that class. They used computers for most of the work, but his teacher was old-school, too. The feel of the steel ruler and mechanical drawing pencil, the precision of neatly printed letters. He liked that.

If you held the target in your mind, your eyes, brain, and body took over and did the work for you. No past, no future, just now. That's what Sonny paid him for, a lot more than he would ever make peddling *pho.*

Teng rounded Eleventh onto Alder, drove the short block, then smoothly turned left onto Tenth at the bulgogi truck on the corner. He slowed even more, without Michael having to ask, so he could get a good look down the narrow gap between the two trucks.

Propane tanks in the back. Empty parking lot beyond. Utility hookups located near the front of each parking spot, near the sidewalks. Michael ignored those. It was one of the tall unsecured propane tanks he was interested in. The one just outside the back door of the second truck in.

Teng slowed down even more. Not as nice as some of the newer ones, but clean, the blue-and-white truck rested low, more or less evenly on short stacks of cinderblock. A travel trailer in another life, it wasn't going anywhere now. Hand-lettered sign. Thanh's Pho. The flimsy order window facing the sidewalk was rolled down for the night, secured with a cheap padlock through a thin ring.

Some security. A child could snap that off.

Teng picked up a little speed now, but still kept it under twenty miles per hour, past Damascus Dining, no more than two feet from Thanh's. They had a large photo menu mounted along the side of a classic Airstream Silver Bullet.

The rest of the makeshift restaurants on the block were also parked end to end along the outer edge of the mostly empty parking lot behind them. Later in the day, the interior spaces would be filled with office and restaurant workers' cars, but this early, white buckets, hoses, and more propane tanks, some secured, some not, could be seen through the narrow spaces between the trucks. Trash skittered across the broken asphalt.

"Idiots. They almost deserve this," Michael muttered.

*****

On the third pass around the block, Michael was ready. When Teng looked back at him in the rearview mirror, he nodded. Teng stopped just around the corner by the Korean truck, allowing Michael to get a bead on the propane tank behind Thanh's Pho.

A solitary crow cawed overhead. Ignoring the distraction, Michael raised his weapon to his shoulder and took aim. If he did this right, he would only need one shot. Like playing pool, it was all about the angles.

The blue-tipped bullet was a beautiful thing. Flying swift and straight, trailing a two-foot tail flame, making a loud thump on impact, it neatly pierced the thirty-gallon propane tank, exploding out the other side. Knocked through the flimsy back door into the blue-and-white truck, the propane tank, safety features now breached, began rapidly venting.

Seconds later, as the Subaru sped away, a loud explosion sent a fireball into the air with a whoosh, followed by an angry, nonstop roar as the fire began its work.

"Sweet!" Teng said.

Satisfied, Michael dispassionately began dismantling his weapon as Teng drove away. The food court had no security, and no one was out this early, but it wouldn't matter if anyone saw anything, anyway. They'd be long gone before the police got there, driving another car. No need to worry about fingerprints or brass, either. Sonny still used his uncle's guys, and they were thorough. The Subaru would not only be completely clean, but a completely different color by tomorrow morning.

Thirty minutes later, they slipped across North Steel Bridge in a Honda Civic, baby-puke brown. Not exactly his style, but it got them out of town. As soon as he got enough, he was going to pay cash for a decent ride. Black and solid.

Grinning at Michael in the rearview mirror, Teng pulled into the fast lane.

"Sticky rice for breakfast? Long's makes good *xoi*. I'm starved!"

Michael nodded.

What they hadn't seen, couldn't have seen, but would have smelled if they had stayed to watch their handiwork, was a small, burned body—blown to the front of the truck by the explosion, jammed under a counter, clutching her dreams.

34

Chilled to the bone from her late-night walk back from the club, Logan kicked off her boots, stripped off her clothes, and jumped into a hot shower. She'd gotten caught in the rain two blocks from the hotel. Towel drying her hair, she decided to wait until morning to check her messages, and crawled into bed, pulling the covers up under her chin.

Damn it was cold!

While Jasper was on kissing terms with the Pacific, Portland was a good two hours inland, so lacked the moderate temperatures of the coast. Still, Logan liked fresh air, so left the window open a crack. The hum and rhythm of the city sounds floated in past the heavy curtains, lulling her to sleep just as effectively as ocean waves back home. She was out within seconds of her head hitting the pillow.

Logan's eyes flipped open.

What the . . . ?

Struggling to fully wake and get her bearings, she squinted at the alarm clock nestled under the watchful eyes of the stone owl on the small table by the bed.

4:59 A.M.

She rubbed her eyes, blinking to make them focus. She'd heard a noise but couldn't identify it.

She rubbed her eyes again, harder this time, and sat up, quickly surveying the still dark room.

A solitary flame reached for air in the gas fireplace.

Pilot light.

Had she been dreaming? She pushed off the covers and reached for the hotel robe she'd spread across the duvet last night for additional warmth.

A loud *whomp!* sent her scrambling out of bed.

Impatiently pushing her hand through the tangle of the robe's sleeve, Logan tripped on her boots as her bare feet tried to find purchase on the carpet.

"Jeez!"

She hopped over to the window, nursing a stubbed toe, and pushed back the curtains. The last of a giant fireball rose above one of the food trucks and lit up the parking lot across the street like it was day. Greedy fingers of flame reached wildly toward anything they could consume.

Logan grabbed the phone.

"911—What is your emergency?"

"Fire. I'm at the Governor, the fire is in the parking lot, diagonally across the street. There was an explosion—maybe two . . . Yes . . . Just a minute . . . It's at . . ."

Logan searched for a street sign.

"Tenth and something . . . Alder . . . Tenth and Alder."

She wanted to be brief so the emergency operator could do her job. Whatever information the woman needed to know she'd ask for.

FOREST PARK

Through the flames, Logan saw a man running away from the fire—low and in a zigzag pattern, open jacket flapping. He looked kind of crazy. No, he looked like the kitchen helper from the New School, GI Joe, or Gentle Joe as Glenda called him, but it was too far away to tell for sure.

"Do you need medical? Has anyone been injured?"

✲✲✲✲✲

Logan didn't think the man she saw running looked injured.

"No, I don't see anyone injured. I don't think any of the food trucks were open this early."

Cops were already showing up, positioning cars to block traffic and she heard a fire engine in the distance. It had been shift change when the blast hit and several cops had heard it on their way into the station or leaving it on their way home.

Even from her vantage point, Logan couldn't see much, her view obscured by thick smoke, but a few seconds later, she saw the man again, emerging onto the sidewalk on the far side of the lot. He seemed okay. Looking confused and unsure, he stopped, held both sides of his head between his palms, as if to shut out noise, then took off down Alder, away from her, out of view.

If it was GI Joe, why would he be on the street out in this neighborhood so early in the morning? She hadn't thought to ask where he was staying overnight. She'd assumed Blanchett House. He couldn't have had anything to do with the explosion. Was he hurt?

Probably a homeless guy who got a rude morning wake-up call.

No sense in involving someone whose only crime was to pick this parking lot to sleep in. Whoever it was, the man probably had enough problems without bringing the police into his life.

"No, I don't see anyone," Logan answered, not entirely comfortable with her lie.

Realizing she'd been shouting over the roar of the fire, and the commotion outside, Logan started pushing the windows closed. Once she reassured the emergency operator she was not in any danger herself, Logan provided her name and contact information and let the operator finish doing whatever it was she needed to do next.

She thought again about the man she'd seen running away from the fire, wondering if she should have told the 911 operator. It couldn't be him. Rita said they were going someplace on Glisan after they dropped her off to deliver the crates of vegetables to the shelter. Rita said she was going to visit friends and Joe, she presumed, to the shelter Friday night and that they'd return to the New School Saturday morning. Gentle Joe probably already left with Rita yesterday and was safe and sound back working in the garden. There must be dozens of men in army jackets and jeans on the streets. Could be anyone.

Another food truck in the row caught fire, refocusing Logan's attention on the scene below. Whatever those trailers were made of, combined with their interior contents, produced a roiling, acrid black smoke. She was glad she'd shut the windows.

She wished the firetrucks would hurry up and get here.

At the foot of one of the sugar maples Logan had admired the day before, lay part of a broken blue-and-white sign. She couldn't see the other half, but immediately recognized it.

Her heart fell.

Thanh's Pho.

35

Of course. How could she not have known? She knew right where Thanh's truck was . . . or had been. Amazing how the brain makes you focus on one thing at a time during an emergency, blotting everything else out. At least no one was hurt. It was way too early for any of the food trucks to be open yet.

She wanted to call Huey, let him know, but didn't have his number. Last week they had no reason to exchange numbers— thought she would see him back at the New School in a few days. Her original plan was to show Ben the school garden after their weekend and her other appointments at the university were complete. She wasn't scheduled to leave until Wednesday.

The hotel phone rang. Tearing herself away from the window, she walked over to the desk and grabbed the receiver.

A somewhat shaky young male voice, not able to hide his underlying excitement, read from a hastily prepared script. It sounded like a recording.

"Hello, this is the front desk. First, we would like to assure you that all guests are safe. A fire has occurred across the street. Although we are sure there is no cause for alarm, we are requesting that all guests close their windows against the smoke and stay in their rooms until the fire department arrives. We want to reassure you . . ."

Logan pushed the button for speakerphone. More sirens made it difficult to hear.

". . . that the Governor is not involved and is very safe. We are, however, asking guests to remain in their rooms for their safety until the fire department declares the surrounding area safe for road and pedestrian traffic."

The young man on the recording took a breath and continued, "Please accept our apologies for any inconvenience this may cause, but we place our guests' safety first. While we are awaiting the all-clear signal, for your comfort, we will be sending up coffee, juice, and some of Jake's delicious biscuits and marionberry jam. Again, we apologize for any delay this causes in your travel plans, but we will get you out and about as soon as possible. Thank you for your cooperation. We are sure this will be a very temporary inconvenience. We will notify you promptly with any updates and inform you immediately when we are cleared, so you can enjoy our beautiful city or get to the airport to continue your travel plans."

The recording ended and Logan pressed the button again, disconnecting the call. A fire truck had arrived and another police car parked across Tenth under her window.

The flashing lights and sirens brought back the night of the car accident that took Jack's life three years ago. She fought down a momentary stab of panic. This was different. She was safe in her hotel room, not lying face down on the asphalt, having been thrown from her car, unable to move, watching the EMTs load her husband's body into the back of the ambulance.

She shook the memory away.

More police came, parking their cars across Alder, and patrolmen secured the area. Customers from Starbucks, the only business open this early, stood a block away, behind the crime scene tape, cell phones out, recording, keeping Instagram and Facebook in business. Wouldn't want to miss the action.

In less than five minutes, four fire engines and two trucks arrived. Looking like something out of Sesame Street, the shiny red fire engines disgorged helmeted heroes in their familiar bright-yellow slickers. Like a well-orchestrated dance, even in their bulky gear, they quickly pulled hose and began battling the blaze.

Logan called Glenda on her cell to get Huey's number. He stayed with his sister and mother-in-law here in Portland on the weekends. She wasn't sure where they lived, but it couldn't be too far. She was sure they would all want to know as soon as possible about the fire, if nothing else, so they could contact their insurance company. She hoped they had one.

No answer. She tried again, but cell service wasn't getting through, or maybe Glenda's had her phone off. Logan looked at her watch. 5:15 a.m. It was still early. She left a message telling her briefly what happened and what she knew, which wasn't much, asking her to contact Huey and/or text her his cell number. She wasn't sure what she could do to help but wanted to offer anyway, as a gesture of moral support.

Next, she called Ben to fill him in and reassure him she was okay in case he saw it on the news. Probably not big enough news to make it all the way down to Southern California, but fires were always top viewing, sad to say. It reminded her of that old Henley song, "Dirty Laundry," skewering the media's ghoulish delight in disasters.

Ben answered on the second ring, in the middle of packing for his flight. Efficiently, of course, and fully prepared. Ben would have everything he needed, Logan needed, or any mother with fussy toddlers needed and still be under Alaska

Air's weight and size limit for carry-ons. The man was a treasure. Taylor was giving him a ride to John Wayne.

"Hey, what's up?" Ben said.

"Well . . . ," said Logan, proceeding to explain the morning's events as they'd unfolded so far, without alarming him.

Ben's first reaction was for her to catch the next plane home.

"Really, I'm fine, Ben. It's not even close to me. Fire and police are here getting everything under control. I just feel bad for Huey's sister. Probably some kind of fuel leak or something. It looks like Thanh's is where it started, but the fire traveled fast. The Middle Eastern place next door, and the Korean food truck—looks like they're both badly damaged, probably totaled. I feel so bad for Thanh and Mrs. Nguyen. They've been through so much already—losing everything. And now this."

Her attention was diverted by the action on the street below.

It felt nice to have someone worry about her. Jack hadn't been protective, leaving her to her own devices, just assuming she would handle everything from their business to raising Amy, which she had.

She was grateful Ben didn't take protectiveness too far, though. After his initial reaction, he didn't push her to cut her trip short. His flight was scheduled to leave John Wayne at 1:45 p.m., so he'd be there soon.

"Are they going to evacuate the hotel? Do you want me to call around, find you another place?"

"No, I really think they'll have everything under control by the time you get here."

"Do you want me to call Rick?" he offered.

She hadn't even though about that. Leave it to Ben to be the thoughtful one. Of course, Rick would be worried.

"Yes, thanks. Let him know I'm fine."

When they disconnected, she gave Glenda another try but she still couldn't get through.

Not wanting to miss anything, but also not knowing if the hotel guests were going to be asked to evacuate at any minute, in spite of what she'd told Ben, Logan decided to take a quick shower, brush her teeth, get dressed, and pack her things. Just in case.

36

Fifteen minutes later, showered and dressed in cargo pants and a long-sleeved T-shirt, she took up her station by the window. The firefighters had made a lot of progress.

Being practically on top of the intersection, only a helicopter would have given Logan a better view. In the summer, the overlapping branches of the maple trees lining Tenth Street shaded the food trucks with a leafy green canopy, but in February, they were bare. This morning, wet from the fire hoses, their slick branches formed a delicate black net she could see through to the smoking wreckage and a few remaining, desultory flames.

The only buildings on her side of the street were the third, fourth, and fifth floors of the hotel and Jake's Grill, directly below. The other side was all food trucks parked around the edges facing the sidewalks of two large parking areas across Tenth. She would later discover that the blast had taken out the bottom row of windows on the side of the galleria facing the trucks, but she couldn't see that from her angle. Jake's large picture windows had been spared, but she couldn't see them, either.

Although Rheanna hadn't been the one to take her 911 call,

Logan knew she must be on duty. She'd said last night that she was going straight in to work after she sang.

The dispatcher's smooth handling of the situation increased Logan's respect for Rheanna's job. Her artsy musician vibe probably misled most people to discount her strength and composure. It didn't show the pressure and responsibility of her day job. Logan would definitely have to give her more credit. And that went for Rheanna's former roommate, Paula.

She'd have to get to know Paula better—take her big sister duties more seriously. And soon. Last time she talked with Rick, her little brother sounded pretty serious about the girl.

A knock on her door told her emergency rations had arrived. When she opened the door, a small but determined woman pulling a large suitcase behind her barreled around the corner, almost colliding with the night porter's cart, which, if she'd been successful, would have landed him in Logan's arms. Luckily, he jumped out of the way in time.

"I am *not* going to stay in the room!" the woman hissed.

A tall man, presumably her husband, trailed behind her and mumbled something meant to calm, but the infuriated woman was having none of it.

"I will *not* be kept in my room like a child, and I *will* get a complete and full refund from this hotel."

Logan and the night porter couldn't help but stand and stare at her back as she stalked down the hall.

"I know you don't like it, Donald, but there's nothing wrong with asserting your rights. Imagine letting those people park those unsafe vehicles just anywhere in the city, across from a nice hotel like this one. No wonder one of them blew up. We paid good money to stay here! Don't they have city ordinances? I know it's not New York, but you'd think we'd landed in Podunk—"

FOREST PARK

★★★★★

The elevator doors mercifully cut her off. Logan pitied the desk clerk who had to deal with her checkout. Even if they could make her stay, she doubted anyone would want to.

Sharing an eye roll with the porter, she thanked him and carried her tray in to the table herself to save him the trip. He had a lot of deliveries to make. The wonderful aromas of hot coffee and fresh biscuits made her weak in the knees. She lifted the linen napkin off the basket. Real butter, marionberry jam, honey. Everything organic, local, and delicious—this was Portland, after all.

Now that the flames were out, only a few Starbucks lookie-loos remained. Even the media trucks were pulling away—they had their fire footage. They'd polish their stories with editing back at the office.

She ate a biscuit, loaded with jam, wiping the corner of her mouth with the cloth napkin. She washed it all down with the last of the hot coffee and went back to looking out the window. Logan was grateful she'd shut them and turned on the room fan, because even with the windows shut tight, smoke seeped in. Her throat and lungs still burned a little, but at least her eyes had stopped watering.

Several firefighters walked slowly, heads down, methodically working their way in from the farthest truck the fire had reached, back to where she'd seen the fireball, systematically looking into any structures that remained intact.

Two firefighters, helmets pushed back, faces grimy after completing their inspection of the outermost trailers, got to Thanh's, which was almost completely destroyed. As a result of the main explosion, the sides had buckled and blown out, exposing collapsed cabinets and other fire debris. They examined the back section first, then walked forward, ducking under what was left of one corner of the roof, obscuring them momentarily from Logan's view.

Within minutes things started hopping.

Several firefighters and a man not in uniform gathered around the truck. Logan leaned forward and lifted the window open a few inches, trying to catch what they were saying. She couldn't hear a thing, but everyone's body language said whatever it was the firefighters discovered in Thanh's trailer was important. And from the grim look on their faces, not good news.

37

Joe hadn't slept well. Every rat scratch or bit of trash skittering across the parking lot put him on full alert. Even when he thought he'd identified the sound, and it wasn't the punks or Monster sniffing him out, he couldn't relax. If he'd gotten more than two or three hours rest in the last forty-eight hours, he'd be surprised.

He needed his medicine. He wasn't cut out for the streets anymore. Didn't want to be. He wanted to see his daughter. A few tears fell. "Feeling his feelings" was supposed to be a good thing the counselors in rehab always said, but right now, he'd rather be numb.

He'd finally made it to Blanchet House yesterday morning, but not in time. Ms. Wolfe had left, and he was too ashamed of being late to go inside and ask for help or tell them what had happened. An overwhelming feeling of devastation and loss swept over him, followed by the one thing he knew could take way the pain. A good strong drink.

It was a good thing they'd stolen his money or he'd have walked into the first liquor store he came to. The urge passed, but it left him shaky and scared.

Out of habit, he returned to his old stomping grounds but knew this wasn't for him anymore. Even though he hadn't been off the streets long, he felt, and smelled, the difference. Waiting until it was late enough that most people had gone home, he scouted out a good spot to hunker down for the night. He knew this area. He'd be safe here. Exhausted, he tucked himself under the doughnut truck to grab a few ragged hours of sleep. It had an awning, which was useful in case it decided to rain. Tomorrow he'd go to St. Stephen's, see if the Jesuit could help.

He had to try again. Maybe the Jesuit could give him a ride out to the school, or at least let him use the phone. He'd beg Rita to take him back. He needed that job.

＊＊＊＊＊

4:58 A.M.

Joe felt, as much as heard, the vehicle approaching. Slowly, he raised his head, straining eyes and ears in the fading dark. Tires hummed on the pavement. Getting closer.

Found 'em.

He'd spotted the car. There were two of them. He couldn't see the man in the back, but the driver's face was clear in the moonlight. Young. Scraggly beard. Tall for a gook. What were they doing here? He thought they'd cleared this area.

Just one night, one fucking night's sleep is all I ask.

Joe watched as the man in the back smoothly raised his weapon and fired at one of the vehicles circling the perimeter.

Whomp!

Joe jumped into a crouch, keeping his head down, calling on reflexes he hadn't used in years.

FOREST PARK

A huge fireball whooshed into the air, flames leaping above the vehicle.

The shock wave reverberated through Joe's body. Heart pounding, adrenaline pumping, panic. All senses ramped way beyond normal levels.

Survival in the jungle depended on your ability to assess and react quickly and accurately. That's why he was still here and so many of his buddies were not.

Joe reached for his weapon. It wasn't there.

Using the Jeep he'd been sleeping under for cover, he remained frozen. Was he the only one left? His head hurt. Where was everyone? Maybe they weren't dead. Maybe they got out. Where was his weapon? His helmet?

Squeezing his eyes tightly, hesitating only for a second, he made a decision and took off running, low and in the zigzag pattern he'd been taught, across the open field, hoping the smoke from the fire would shield him.

Base camp. If I can just get to base camp . . .

*****

A frazzled woman, still in her pajamas, was driving her husband to the airport. She'd overslept and he was not happy about it. Going as fast as she dared, she was only a block away from the Cornell entrance to Forest Park, when a crazy man cut in front of her, running like a bat out of hell. She swerved and barely missed him. Or maybe not. It all happened so fast. He had either banged his fist on the hood of her car or she'd hit him. He was still standing there, looking confused. She wanted to go back and make sure he was okay, but her husband started yelling, telling her the guy was fine. They were already late and he had a plane to catch.

*****

After successfully avoiding being run over by an enemy jeep, Joe spotted a narrow path snaking into the jungle. Knowing this path led to base camp, Joe felt a huge sense of relief. He hated being out in the open. Running across the remaining distance, he plunged into the trees.

They moved base camp often, but it was his only hope. As soon as he could, he'd get off the main road. Once he found camp, if they'd bugged out, he'd dig in for the night and reassess.

38

Frustrated she couldn't hear anything, Logan reached for her coffee cup, draining the last bit, and tried Glenda again. Still no luck.

She wanted to let Huey and Thanh know about the fire but didn't have their number. She should probably just stay out of it, anyway, but keeping her nose out of other people's business was not Logan's forte. The trailers were probably registered with the city or something. The police would notify them. She remembered Huey explaining that each vendor rented a parking space in the lot. The trucks were like any other vehicles, only vehicles that were never moved.

She again wondered if Thanh and her mother-in-law had insurance.

None of your business, Logan. Give it a rest. They have everything under control.

Pressing the fingers on her left hand into the small of her back, she stretched to release her stiff muscles. She'd have to find some time to walk or do yoga before Ben got in.

The hotel sent out another robo call, releasing the guests with a reminder to stay well away from the "accident area."

They offered to provide transportation to the airport, gratis, and any other assistance needed, again apologizing, as if they'd blown up the food truck themselves.

Logan saw no reason to check out, and Ben's flight didn't come in for another few hours, so she used the time to write up her notes from last week.

Glancing out the window, Logan saw two new vehicles—an unmarked sedan and a van. The ambulance had left already.

Her cell rang. It was Huey.

Yes! Glenda must have gotten through.

"Logan, thank you for calling and giving me the message. I appreciate it and so does my sister. The police called earlier also and said we can come down soon. They wanted us to wait here, but we are coming down—we want to be there as soon as they will let us in. The fire inspector has to do his job first." He hesitated. "Can you see the truck? How bad is it?"

Logan didn't have the heart to tell him that if anything had survived that fire, she'd be surprised. She did offer to let them wait in the room with her until the cops and firefighters finished what they were doing and released the scene. By the looks of it, they wouldn't be finished for a while. If anything, there seemed to be more action across the street than before.

Huey said they only carried insurance on the truck, not its contents, so he was hoping some of the items inside might be salvageable.

Had Logan seen his mother-in-law? Sundays they weren't scheduled to open until eleven. Mrs. Nguyen usually went in early and prepared for the lunch crowd, allowing Thanh a rare morning off to sleep in. Thanh went in early on Wednesdays to give Mrs. Nguyen a break. Thanh and Huey came at eleven and stayed later.

Mrs. Nguyen must have left early. She usually stopped to

visit with her friend Qui for coffee and breakfast on the way, but she should be there by now. Would Logan mind going down to get her? The sight of the burned truck would definitely upset her. If it wasn't too much of an inconvenience . . . they would be right there . . .

"Of course, Huey." Logan was relieved to hear he and Thanh were okay and Mrs. Nguyen was on her way. She looked up and down the streets as far as she could see.

"I don't see her, but I'll go down to the sidewalk—they're letting us leave our rooms now. She's probably sitting at one of the tables outside of Jake's. I don't think they've cordoned off that area—or maybe she's around the corner at Starbucks. If she's there, I'll bring her up to the room and keep her company until you get here. If not, I'll be downstairs waiting for her."

"Thank you, Logan. I really appreciate your help," Huey said. "We'll be there as soon as we can. What's your room number?"

"Four twenty-three. If I'm not outside when you get here, just ask at the desk for directions. At least you can have a comfortable place to wait until they'll let you back in."

*****

After giving the room a quick once-over, Logan pulled the covers up on the bed, making the room presentable for guests. She grabbed her key card and phone and headed toward the elevator. Planning on going out the back way, she pushed J for Jake's instead of L for lobby, taking it all the way to the ground floor that opened onto the side near the food trucks. She'd keep a lookout for Mrs. Nguyen, and as soon as Huey and Thanh arrived, she'd bring them up to the room. She'd told them they could use that as a temporary base until they knew more from the cops and firefighters and could decide what to do.

A wide corridor, lined with comfortable seating areas, connected the Governor to the restaurant. Admiring the Lewis and Clark mural that took up several large wall panels on her right, Logan was about to take a shortcut through one of the private dining rooms when her cell rang. She swiped her screen to take the call.

"Logan, it's Ben."

"Ben? Wait up . . ." She moved back into the corridor. "Okay, I can hear you now—shoot."

Logan looked at her watch. Shouldn't Ben be somewhere over Sacramento about now?

Silence.

"Are you there?"

"I don't know how to say this, Logan, but I'm going to have to cancel for this weekend."

"Oh."

Her voice couldn't hide her disappointment.

"What happened? Did something happen with the pipe—did the repair job not work?"

More silence, and when he spoke, he struggled to get the words out.

"No, nothing like that. The fountain's fine. I . . . uh . . ."

She could hear his pain—pictured his face.

What? Just spit it out.

Finding her legs didn't want to support her just now, she sank into one of the empty couches, phone glued to her ear. Across from her was the mural of Sacajawea, brave woman of the North.

"It's Julie," Ben finally said.

"Julie? *Julie*, Julie?"

Long, blond Julie. Intelligent, ruthless, seductive Julie. Ben's former fiancé.

"Yes."

He'd told Logan about her on one of their rooftop deck nights, over more than a few beers. Julie was a train wreck.

"She flew in last night from San Francisco."

Ben sounded miserable, but just now, Logan didn't have much sympathy for him. Last night? Where had she stayed? Where had she slept? Had he known this morning when they talked? Had Julie been standing there?

He should have told her to get right back on that plane, not canceled his plans with Logan. On the other hand, she and Ben didn't have enough history together for her to complain. They'd only been seeing each other for six months. He and Julie had lived together for three years and change.

She pressed the phone so close to her ear she accidentally disconnected the call.

"Damn!"

Ben called back.

"Please, Logan. Don't hang up! I'm sorry," he said before she could explain. "I just need to figure things out here."

If you were sure of your feelings for me, there wouldn't be anything to figure out.

"I didn't hang up," she heard herself say, not feeling nearly as reasonable as she was trying to sound. She wouldn't give any man the satisfaction of throwing a jealous fit. "Just do what you need to do."

"Are you okay?"

"I'm fine."

She knew her voice sounded brittle and clipped, but it was the best she could do.

"I need to get off now, Ben—I promised Huey I'd wait for Mrs. Nguyen outside. They're on their way."

He wanted to talk when she got back, but Logan wasn't making any promises.

Sorry, pal. You don't get off that easy.

Let him sweat.

She couldn't get off the phone fast enough. Launching herself off the couch, she stalked toward the exit, surprised at the level of hurt and anger she felt.

How had she gotten herself into this mess?

She wondered how he could even consider taking Julie back, after what she'd pulled!

Did he enjoy being kicked in the teeth? She didn't believe for a second that a woman capable of that level of heartless deception had changed her stripes. There could be no valid reason for her to come waltzing back into Ben's life seven years later. She must want something. If that kind of drama was what Ben wanted, she sure wasn't the woman to give it to him. Logan was faithful as the day was long.

She stalked to the entrance, yanked open Jake's glass door, and plopped herself down at one of the tables.

Merde!

One of the more useful French words her foreign exchange mother shared with her.

Why she expected love to go smoothly, she had no idea. It certainly never had.

Most of the wrought iron café tables were occupied by people craning to see what was happening across the street. After looking up and down both streets again, not seeing Mrs. Nguyen anywhere, Logan sat back to wait.

She could do nothing about the situation with Ben, so she'd do what she always did—focus on what she did have control over, and that wasn't much right now.

Crime scene tape had been strung around the block, making it difficult for Logan to see what was happening. All she could make out were the backs of workers, who seemed to have multiplied during her short trip through the lobby. Two men in blue jumpsuits were taking lots of photographs in and around the burned shell of Thanh's truck.

Everything shifted into slow motion when she spotted the waiting gurney next to a large blue van.

Logan suddenly understood what she was looking at. The gurney, the van—all horrifyingly familiar.

Last summer, when the young glassblower had been murdered, Logan saw her first, and what she hoped was her last, dead body. The young woman's lifeless form had been unceremoniously stuffed into a two-by-three-foot concrete annealing oven.

No matter how hard she wanted it not to be true, Logan realized what must be, who must be, in the burned-out remains of their truck. Mrs. Nguyen wouldn't be coming.

Dreading Huey and Thanh's arrival, Logan sat very still and forced herself to breathe.

39

Sonny took his time getting off the phone. Michael and Teng waited by the door. As was his intention.

When the call was over, he took a drag on his cigarette, pushed his hair out of his eyes, and nodded for them to approach. Leaned back in his new high-tech chair. Top of the line. Laced his fingers across his chest.

"So, how'd it go?" Sonny asked.

Teng threw himself down in one of the chairs opposite Sonny's glass desk, another new addition, all smiles. Michael came in but remained standing. The two visitor chairs were smaller and lower than Sonny's. Even with this transparent power play in place, Teng was a few inches taller, but didn't notice or care.

"Cool chair, Sonny! Gray . . . *nice* . . ."

"Graphite, not gray."

"Oh yeah, graphite," Teng said. "It went great. Just like we planned."

In reality, Teng hadn't planned anything, Michael had done all the planning, but Michael said nothing. He didn't care who got the credit. He just wanted his money. He could barely stand either of them.

Sonny continued, "No one saw you?"

Michael affirmed this with a nod.

Teng said, "Yeah, we were in, over, and back on the bridge by five fifteen, five twenty."

Sonny looked over Teng's shoulder at Michael. He verified this with another nod.

"Good," Sonny said, looking out the window, his thoughts racing ahead.

He swiveled his chair back toward Teng but directed his comments to Michael. "Go back tomorrow. There'll be a lot of people around, cleaning up. No one will notice you. Get her alone and tell the old lady she has to get the money. All of it. No more stalling. She'll find a way. She knows we mean business now. Those old Saigon mamas always have something squirreled away."

Teng grinned, and Michael's face remained impassive.

I really dislike you, Sonny.

"By Tuesday. Bring me whatever's she's got. And the rest of them, you know which ones still haven't paid, right? By Tuesday. Cash or gold or stones only. Wednesday's the deal."

"Will do, Sonny," Teng said, excited about how rich Sonny's big thinking was going to make them. Sonny's uncle had been too timid. Why shouldn't they make some money on all the BC bud coming into Seattle from Vancouver? Sonny was smart. It was easy. Lay down the money, get the bud, sell the bud, make a million. Nobody was hassling anyone over marijuana anymore. It was legal in half the states now, wasn't it? Sonny had explained how the new laws actually improved the drug business, not hurt it. Teng didn't understand it all, but he trusted Sonny. Soon, he could have any girl he wanted.

FOREST PARK

Sonny paid Michael and Teng, then shut the door, went back over to the window, and looked out over the river. He was barely able to contain himself. All those years of doing whatever his stupid uncle told him to do. Boring banking stuff. He couldn't believe his uncle had actually wanted him to go to college like the other losers—major in accounting. Accounting! Said he had to understand the way the banking system, loans, and computers worked in order to skim something from the system for themselves. Make just enough—target only other Vietnamese. They wouldn't complain. They just paid up. Yes, it worked, but it was chump change. He, Sonny, was meant for bigger things.

When his uncle made his ultimatum—finish his degree or get out—he'd had no choice. It wasn't easy. He had to catch him off guard. His uncle knew him, but Uncle didn't know to what lengths his nephew would go to avoid actual work and that he had no intention of curtailing his extracurricular activities. That's when he'd called in Michael.

Just a few weeks ago, he pulled it off. Uncle was gone, the fishes were fed, and he, Sonny, was here.

Finally, things were coming together.

40

Breathing heavily, Joe finally stopped, hands on knees. About five miles in, and off the main road now, he could afford to slow down. Get his bearings.

Right. If he remembered correctly, it was more to the right. He made his way farther up and back into the hills. Almost an hour later, he ducked under a branch, pushed aside a giant fern, and entered a small clearing. A two-foot-wide creek, one of the many tributaries of the Willamette River, burbled around a granite boulder resting between a towering Douglas fir and a lightning-struck cedar snag.

Someone had been here.

Been here and taken everything—or smashed it. Tent, food, his books. Whoever it was was long gone. A solitary can of corn lay rusting in the creek.

Shivering, he suddenly realized how cold he was, and how hungry. He hadn't eaten since . . . when had he eaten last?

Stepping around the boulder and over the stream, careful not to get his shoes wet, Joe selected a reasonably thick stick from the forest floor and began desperately digging into an area of the hillside covered in blackberry brambles. Ignoring the angry scratches on his hands and arms, within a few minutes, he'd retrieved a canvas rucksack, and buckled onto it, a canteen. Inside the pack was a stack of Hershey bars, a gun, and ammunition. All dry.

Thank God.

Last, but not least, he reached back in through the blackberry vines and retrieved two bottles. Big ones. Not exactly Grey Goose, but he'd never been picky.

He could hole up here until tonight. He just needed to warm up, rest a little. Then he could find his unit. He wished he'd put a blanket in that hole. What good was an emergency cache if he froze to death?

Eyes closed, he smiled at the thought of being found stuck to the tree, like a kid's tongue on a flagpole.

Two Hershey bars and more than half a bottle later, Joe sat slumped against the red cedar—feet straight out, loaded gun on the ground beside him. Shadows stretched across the clearing. His mind grasped at floating tendrils of thought that stayed just out of reach.

He was supposed to meet someone, find someone, but where?

41

Two men, dark jackets flapping in the stiff morning breeze, ducked under the crime scene tape, entered the area, and walked back. Logan recognized the black-haired one of the left. Keenan. The shorter, stockier man must be his partner, Romero.

Homicide. Rheanna's boyfriend was a *homicide* detective.

Logan's heart sank.

Keenan squatted down and began talking first with a red-haired man, then a man in a black shirt taking a gazillion pictures.

After much pointing and gesturing at a propane tank lying on its side, rolling it over to expose a big hole on the other side, the red-haired man smoothed his tie, brushed some debris off one of his pant legs, and said his goodbyes. Detectives Keenan and Romero remained, the case now theirs.

*****

Over the next couple of hours as the deputy medical examiner, who preferred the more accurate title of medical legal death investigator, continued his work with the body, the detectives began canvassing the area, interviewing anyone and everyone who may have seen or heard anything, including Starbucks employees, Jake's kitchen workers, and the Governor's guests, night auditor, and porter.

Keenan also sent a couple of uniforms over to Wells Fargo to find one of their night managers. It was a long shot, but their exterior security cameras may have picked something up. They were successful in reaching a woman named Wilma. Said she could be there in twenty minutes.

He went over to the bank, squinted back at the scene.

Could be. Hard to tell. The Korean food truck may have blocked it. You never knew. Guy could have been on foot, but not likely. Unless he had someplace to run to, they were probably looking for a car, not a guy on foot. Still, it would be a tough shot.

Hopefully, someone would show up on the tape. If not, then they needed a witness.

*****

Romero was collecting Logan's statement when Huey and Thanh finally got through. She didn't have much to add to her 911 call. They had that transcript. She still didn't mention GI Joe. If it was GI Joe.

Thanh still wore her work clothes—loose pants, thick-soled shoes, thin blue sweatshirt, warm coat. Huey was in pressed slacks, light sweater, and a leather jacket.

When Thanh identified herself as one of the owners of the food truck that had burned, they had her wait in the back of a patrol car until one of the detectives was free. They got Huey's information at the table. At least he got to sit down.

Detective Romero joined Thanh in the patrol car and apologized for keeping her waiting. After gathering her basic information, he informed her that a death had occurred in conjunction with the fire and asked if she knew of anyone who would have been inside the truck at that time.

"No. None of us come in that early. My mother-in-law was on her way here but hasn't arrived yet. She's probably lost in all this confusion."

She looked around as if by searching the vicinity she could produce the woman.

"When did you last see your mother-in-law?"

"Last night. We saw her last night. She went to bed early, around ten o'clock."

"You didn't see her this morning?"

"No. We never do. She has been going in early on Sundays to let me sleep in. I haven't been feeling well. But she never goes in that early. You said the explosion happened around five this morning? She wouldn't have been here that early."

Thanh looked across the street, then turned back to Romero, who was looking at her carefully.

"Whoever is in there can't be her. She must have decided to stay and visit with her friend Qui a little longer today. Or seen all the commotion and gone back home to let us know."

"Huey and I usually get here by ten, ten thirty. Can't you send someone to look for her?"

Romero obtained the address of Qui's bakery. Said they'd send a car.

"I'm sure this is a mistake. That must be someone else. Someone must have broken in to get warm. We have a space heater in there. Can't they tell anything?"

"It is too early to say anything for sure until the DME completes his work. I'm afraid it is not possible to obtain a positive identification of the deceased occupant in the vehicle at this time."

After completing the initial field interviews, asking a lot more questions about her, Mrs. Nguyen, and Huey. Had there been any recent trouble? Did she, her mother-in-law, or her brother have any enemies? Did they keep a large amount of cash in the truck?

Already tired and upset, Thanh's head started to swim, but finally Romero said she was free to go. He did ask her to keep herself available in case he or Detective Keenan needed any further information. And, of course, to call if she or her brother remembered anything that might be important. If within twenty-four hours Mrs. Nguyen had not returned, they could file a missing person report.

Should their investigation lead them to believe the deceased was her mother-in-law, Mrs. Nguyen, either the detectives or the deputy medical examiner's office would be in touch.

When she rejoined Logan and Huey on the sidewalk, Thanh looked pale, depleted, and was rubbing her side. Huey took her pack, and Logan suggested they get something to eat.

They thanked her, but Thanh wanted to go back to the apartment and wait in case Mrs. Nguyen returned. She looked like she needed to lie down.

As they were leaving, Huey turned back and asked over his shoulder, "Wasn't your friend Ben coming in this weekend? Is he here?"

"Oh, he wasn't able to make it this weekend," Logan said. "Busted water pipe. Had to cancel this trip—I'll see him when I get home," she added, not sure if she would or even wanted to see Ben when she got back.

"But please keep me posted and let me know if there's anything I can do."

Thanh really didn't look well. Huey needed to get her home. Get some food in her.

FOREST PARK

Taking his sister by the elbow, Huey must have thought the same thing. They said their goodbyes and walked across the intersection toward a bus station a block away down the street. Logan offered to call a taxi or Uber or whatever was fastest, but they insisted the bus was fine. Even with the bus having to go around the cordoned-off area, they'd be home soon.

An hour later, back upstairs, Logan looked down from her room. Thankful Thanh wasn't there to see, Logan watched as a black body bag was loaded it into a blue van.

What a day. And it wasn't over yet.

42

Her phone kept beeping. While she was being interviewed, Ben had called at least a dozen times.

More than anything, Logan wanted to hear his voice, talk about what was happening, feel his arms around her, pretend this morning's phone call hadn't happened. Only pride kept her from tapping his name on her phone.

What was the point? If Julie had left, he would have said so. Until Julie was out of Ben's life, there was nothing to talk about. In the meantime, it wasn't Logan's job to make him feel better. This was something Ben had to figure out for himself. She wasn't going to play second fiddle.

She grimaced at the musical metaphor.

*****

Realizing she wasn't going to get any work done in her room, Logan tucked her laptop into her canvas messenger bag with leather straps and went down to the main lobby, bypassing all the action on the other side of the hotel. Surprisingly, Starbucks wasn't crowded, so after ordering, she tucked herself into a corner table, powered up her computer, and got to work.

Work was the reason she was up here in the first place. She owed it to Charles Greuger and Mrs. Houser to do what they paid her to do—her job. She'd fulfilled the first half of her obligations by checking out the New School. Tomorrow and maybe Tuesday, she looked forward to picking some professors' brains, see how their programs went with the brain research happening at UC Irvine back in Southern California.

By five forty-five, Logan finished reviewing the research and bios of the professors she'd be meeting, typed up her questions, printed a campus map in the hotel's business office, tucked everything into her bag, and realized she was hungry. Starbucks didn't do dinner, so she went in search of something quick and easy. A box of Thai takeout later, spicy enough to require another 911 call, she returned to the hotel via the front lobby again and went up to her room.

The fire engines had gone, but the police barricades were still up and workers still milled around inside the yellow crime scene tape. A cleanup crew was working on the sidewalk outside the galleria. Shards of broken glass stuck up out of buckets like deadly bouquets.

She hadn't heard from Huey, and when she glanced at the hotel phone, it was absent any blinking message lights. No news was good news.

Hopefully they'd both gotten some rest. Huey said he already called Rita and was going to take a few days off. Thanh would need help dealing with all the insurance, salvage, and cleanup. He hadn't added that he would also need to be there if Thanh was asked to make a positive identification at the Multnomah County morgue. He knew the person caught in the fire was almost certainly his mother-in-law, but Thanh wasn't ready to accept that yet.

Looking down at the blackened aftermath of the fire, Logan made up her mind. She called the front desk and told them she'd be checking out in the morning after all. Assuming it was due to the fire, which it partially was, they waived the twenty-four-hour cancelation notice requirement. They also offered her an additional free night's credit, redeemable anytime in the next twelve months. She looked around the beautiful room. Maybe if she and Ben worked things out, they'd come back someday.

Next, she got a hold of Rheanna, who knew all about the fire from Keenan and was happy to have her stay the next couple of nights. She didn't challenge the busted pipe story Logan gave her, which was half true anyway, so she didn't know the real reason Ben wasn't coming. Said she didn't go into work until noon on Wednesday and so would help her with which MAX to take to the airport. She recommended Multnomah Falls as a romantic spot next time she came up with Ben. It was in the other direction from the New School, but not far outside Portland, and worth the trip, Rheanna said.

"And you don't even have to hike. You can walk right up to the waterfall. Ten minutes. Spectacular!"

Planning future vacations with a man she wasn't currently speaking to didn't make much sense, so after they hung up, Logan looked around for something else to do.

She packed everything but her toothbrush, then laid a comfortable but polished-looking pair of black North Face yoga pants and long-sleeved T-shirt over one of the high-backed chairs. Bonnie kept trying to get her to buy more color.

"What have you got against pink?" was one of her more tired refrains.

But black went with everything, including other black items of clothing, Logan had patiently pointed out.

The black slip, however, wasn't meant to go with anything. Due to current circumstances, it had been firmly relegated to the bottom of her suitcase.

With nothing left to do until morning, she flipped on the TV and ordered an old movie. Couldn't go wrong with *The Hunt for Red October*. Sean Connery was still hot.

43

The Multnomah County Medical Examiner's Office investigates and determines the cause, circumstances, and manner of sudden, unexpected, violent, or suspicious deaths that occur in Multnomah County.

This one qualified on all four counts.

The medical legal death investigator, Raul Dart, was alone. Due to ever-present budget cuts, he was always alone on the weekends. He had been on duty when the call came in early this morning. He'd driven out, done the initial processing of the body, and returned with his guest. Since there was no one else to help, he wheeled her to the intake area himself.

Although the body was badly burned, he'd been able to do a preliminary identification at the scene. Surprisingly, some of her ID was intact. It had been in her purse, which had gotten lodged under her body during the explosion. It was established that an elderly Vietnamese woman worked there, and she normally worked Sunday mornings, although not usually that early. Still, it never hurt to verify it was Mrs. Nguyen. He'd get some fingerprints for the file.

Heat contractions had caused her fingers to curl in and press firmly onto her palm, thus preserving the pads where the skin touched. To uncurl her fingers and get the prints, he used an old trick. Bending her wrist forward, an automatic reflex reaction caused the fingers to lift, opening the tight fist.

When the fingers popped up, he got a whole lot more than fingerprints.

Tearing off his gloves, he rolled across the hard rubber floor and got the detective's number off the card he had given him earlier in the day. He punched it in and waited.

*****

"Keenan."

"Detective Keenan, this is Raul Dart. I know you're probably halfway home by now, but I started working on your fire victim, and you're going to want to see this."

Keenan couldn't imagine what secrets an elderly woman might have that would require his presence. It had already been a long day.

He and Romero had swung by their apartment and done the next-of-kin notification. The daughter-in-law didn't look good when her brother answered the door, and she looked even worse after they told her. Her grief seemed genuine, so he put off asking them any more questions tonight.

Keenan looked at the clock on his dashboard. Almost four o'clock. Traffic would be a bear. Might as well get this over with. He took the next exit.

"I can be there in thirty minutes."

Twenty-five minutes later, Keenan pulled into the narrow parking lot that formed a wide semicircle in front of the modern glass-and-steel building, parked, and went inside.

No code blues here. These customers were already gone. No doubt about it. The morgue was a creepy place.

He hadn't been to a decomp since July, and he hoped it'd be

another good long while before he had that honor again. Vicks was useless against those.

Turning right, he pushed open one of two doors, saw the medical investigator sitting at his desk. He was hunched over his computer, under an overhead light, looking for all the world like a bookie. All he lacked was the green visor.

Perched on a three-wheeled secretary's chair, upon seeing Keenan, he pushed off the hard rubber floor with a black boot and rolled himself back toward the body, motioning Keenan to follow.

Wanting to get this over with, Keenan's impatience showed.

"Dart, what do you have for me?"

After he regloved, the investigator picked up a long pair of tweezers.

"I waited to finish until you got here."

Keenan wanted him to get on with it, but only nodded patiently.

"As you may or may not know, when the human body is subjected to these kinds of extreme temperatures, the body has a tendency to shrink, to curl up on itself. Whatever they're holding at the time gets captured, clutched in a kind of skeletal claw."

Raul was enjoying himself. The man was not going to be rushed.

Reaching over the body, he pointed toward her right hand, which was indeed curled into a tight fist. He then lifted the corpse's arm so Keenan could see.

Keenan's stomach roiled, but he stayed focused. He just wished the guy would get to the point.

The investigator did his party trick with the wrist and out fell several small, chalky-looking rocks. Delicately grasping one with the tweezers, he triumphantly held it aloft.

Okay . . .

"What am I looking at?"

"Diamonds, Detective Keenan. Diamonds! They've just been frosted a bit by the fire—not harmed at all. Vehicle fires only get up to about four hundred degrees Fahrenheit. That's nothing to a diamond—they form at around two thousand. For some reason, your vic was holding a small fortune in diamonds in her hand before preparing to spend her day selling noodle soup."

✱✱✱✱✱

Not sure yet if the diamonds would be property to be returned to the family or evidence against one of them, Keenan bagged and tagged them before pointing his car back to central. Romero had gone home already. He and his wife just had a baby. He'd fill him in in the morning.

Rheanna was working tonight, so he saw no reason to go to her place. Besides, he liked the precinct better when it was quiet. Gave him a chance to collect his thoughts, get organized, work on the book. What the cops said on TV was true. The first forty-eight hours were the most critical. After that, the chances of any homicide being solved went way down. And this was looking more and more like a homicide.

Keep the momentum going.

Keenan took the elevator up to the thirteenth floor, checked his messages, got a Dr. Pepper and a bag of peanuts from the machine, and parked himself at his desk. He tore off the corner off the peanut bag and shook a few into his mouth. Swallowed them down with a swig of soda.

Leaning back, he folded his hands behind his head. His favorite thinking position.

Follow the money.

44

Ranked in the top 10 percent of American Universities by the Princeton Review, Portland State offered a good selection of degrees, including doctorates in seventeen fields. Two professors, from the music and math departments, respectively, were conducting a joint research project with the neuroscientists Logan had been working with back at UC Irvine. She almost understood what they were talking about. She'd look up the big words when she got back to her office.

She had wanted to bring Huey in and get his take on integrating technology usefully into the mix, but that wasn't going to be possible this trip. Maybe next time. Yesterday, he had given her a login to use, so she could demo MuMu to the Portland U team. She was hoping to interest one of the graduate students in designing an add-on music task.

For the next few hours, Logan immersed herself in scales, intervals, Miles, Beethoven, brain imaging, and chemicals that encouraged not only learning, but the long-term storage and retrieval of memories.

Explosions, fires, and boyfriends and their old girlfriends faded into the back of her mind.

By four thirty, her brain was fried, and as usual, she was starving.

Since Ben wasn't coming, Logan had moved her meetings up a day and checked out of the hotel early. No sense spending money on a romantic corner luxury suite when nothing romantic was happening. Rheanna's was only a few miles away from the university. She got there in less than thirty minutes. She intended to take her out to dinner, as thanks for putting her up, but Rheanna already had something going. The aroma was overpoweringly delicious.

"Hope you like Italian, Logan!" Rheanna said.

"What's not to like? Pasta, butter and"—spotting an open bottle on the counter as she walked into the kitchen—"wine. All my favorite food groups."

Rheanna turned from the stove, lifting a huge pot of boiling water and pasta over to the island sink. She used two huge oven mitts to grip the handles and pour it all into a colander to drain.

"Ever had *pasta a la carbonara?*"

Logan put her suitcase by the couch and took a seat at one of the bar stools along the island and shook her head.

"Don't think so, but it smells wonderful. Is that bacon?"

"Yep," Rheanna demonstrated as she deftly returned the pasta to the now dry pot.

"You just drain it, put it back in the pot, toss it with some bacon—with a little of the hot grease—and crack a couple eggs over it. Stir in a bunch of Parmesan cheese. And"—she ladled a large portion into a waiting pasta bowl—"voilà! Dinner!"

Too hungry to sit, they each polished off a bowl in the kitchen, then took seconds on the wine, and adjourned to the living room, where Rheanna lit the gas fireplace. The view out the floor-to-ceiling windows was still spectacular.

Logan filled Rheanna in, telling here more than she'd intended to about Ben, including Julie's reappearance into his life.

"She really asked him to pack up her stuff, then had the guy she was sleeping with come to their *house* to pick it up? Psycho *bitch*!"

"That'd be my vote," Logan said, taking another drink of wine, savoring its velvet feel in her mouth. Merlot was under-rated. Pretty good.

"What are you going to do?"

"Not much I can do but wait."

That subject closed for now, Rheanna wisely left it alone and asked about the fire. She hadn't taken that 911 call, but Keenan had filled her in Sunday night. He and Romero worked late, canvassing the neighborhood. Everyone heard the explosion, but no one had seen anything except the resulting blaze. One of the kitchen workers at Jake's who was setting the tables, preparing the dining room for breakfast, saw an older car driving away, but didn't get a license number.

"Do they have any idea what caused the fire?"

"Not yet. Keenan said they may have some luck with the bank's surveillance cameras. Wells Fargo is near there—not directly across the street, but within range."

"Do they know what they're looking for?"

"They're pretty sure someone shot one of their propane tanks. The explosion was caused because after the propane tank was damaged, it vented in the direction of a heat source—propane's heavier than gas. Probably the little space heater or pilot light on the stove lit it up. Don't worry, Logan. Keenan's like a dog with a bone. Those guys don't give up. If it's at all possible, he'll find out who set your friends' truck on fire and killed the woman inside. He and Romero are very thorough.

If they don't find something soon, they'll just interview every-body again. It may have been early, but it was right downtown. Someone must have seen something."

Logan thought for a second, then decided to trust Rheanna with a question.

45

Logan tried to sound nonchalant.

"How reliable would a homeless guy's testimony be? I mean, as a witness? If a homeless person was there, would the detectives want to know? Would they believe him?"

Rheanna looked at her like she was nuts. "You saw someone? Why didn't you say anything when they interviewed you?"

Logan filled her in on GI Joe, his participation in the recovery program, and his job at the New School.

"I'm not even sure it was him. I didn't want to incriminate him needlessly. He just started out there, and Rita said he was doing really well. Whoever I saw was probably scared out of his mind and has enough trouble just being homeless, without being hauled into a police station for questioning. Particularly if they couldn't use his eyewitness testimony anyway because he's a street person—maybe an alcoholic or drug addict. Unreliable. I don't know," she added lamely. "It made sense at the time."

Rheanna had little sympathy for and less confidence in GI Joe's reformation.

"You need to call Keenan. If your GI Joe saw anything, they'll want to talk to him."

And if he caused the fire, they'll want to do more than talk to him. He'll be under arrest for the death of the woman in the truck.

Rheanna got Keenan on the phone and Logan gave the detective the general outlines of what she saw. Not happy she hadn't told him sooner, he curtly instructed her to come down in the morning to revise her statement.

As long as she had him on the phone, Logan pushed the envelope and asked him if they had identified the victim in the truck. He declined to answer. Said he understood Thanh and Huey were her friends, but this was an ongoing investigation . . .

Next-of-kin notification was always a priority and would be done as soon as possible.

Blah, blah, blah.

She agreed to be there by 9:00 a.m.

"Central Precinct on Second. Check in at the desk. Rheanna can tell you how to get here."

Frustrated, Logan sat back on the couch, wishing she could alleviate her friends' anxiety but knowing she'd gotten all she could out of Detective Keenan without really pissing him off.

This stress couldn't be helping Thanh, who already looked weak last time Logan saw her. The sooner they notified her it was or was not her mother-in-law's body, the sooner Thanh would be able to accept and deal with it. Logan hoped that would happen shortly.

"They may have already notified them, Logan."

She hadn't thought of that. It was too late tonight, but she would call Huey in the morning.

"Nothing you can do tonight," Rheanna said.

Logan nodded. Patience wasn't her strong suit.

The sun having set completely, fireflies of light now twinkled across the city, and street lamps warmed the winter sidewalks below.

"Okay—enough death and destruction for one night."

Rheanna decisively got off the couch.

"Close your eyes," she instructed.

Curious, Logan obeyed.

"No peeking!"

Rustling in the hall.

"Okay, open!"

Holding a guitar and a battered violin up by their respective necks like two slaughtered chickens, Rheanna grinned. "Take your pick! Joey left these with me for a while. You met him the other night—he was my accompanist at the Hub."

When Logan looked puzzled, she elaborated.

"I'm his sometime pawn broker," she explained. "Give him a better rate than the sharks on Seventh."

Missing Bella, Logan went with the violin, which in spite of its appearance, proved to be not too far out of tune and had a pretty good sound.

Rheanna claimed to be a singer, not a musician, but she held her own with some Keb' Mo' tunes on the big scratchy guitar. The blues didn't require a large repertoire of chords.

After they'd played a few songs they both knew, Rheanna pulled out an original bluegrass/folk piece she'd been working on. Em, A, D, G. She had the music down but was stuck on the final verse—wasn't sure how depressing to make it. Logan reassured her that acoustic songs about unrequited love, written in a minor key, hadn't hurt Alison Krauss's career, so she went with her original draft, leaving the sad parts in.

The two women, happily lost in the creative interplay of emotion, energy, and sound, played and talked into the night. Ancient guardian of women, the moon spilled liquid silver over the smaller woman's blue-black hair, her head bent over a too-large guitar, and sprinkled diamonds on the taller one's shoulder-length auburn waves as she stood tall, serenading the Milky Way.

Life didn't hand you nights like this very often.

Logan was learning to enjoy them.

46

First in as usual, Keenan made a fresh pot of coffee and returned to his desk to organize his thoughts.

Follow the money. That had been their mantra since discovering the diamonds Sunday. Except there wasn't any money. At least not in Thanh Le's bank account or her brother's. They'd checked those.

He'd noted the use of her maiden name on her initial interview. Wondered if that indicated any rift with her mother-in-law. And except for the diamonds Dart found, Mrs. Nguyen wasn't rolling in cash, either. She had a checking account but other than paying a few monthly bills, she rarely used it.

She wouldn't kill herself for her own diamonds, and if the diamonds had been the draw, why would a thief torch the place first? Unless they were dealing with a very stupid thief, of which there was no shortage. No, the three of them were, as far as he could tell so far, what they appeared to be—hardworking people who'd had some tough breaks, Mrs. Nguyen's the toughest of all.

But things were rarely as they seemed. Follow the money.

He needed to know more. The first round with Ms. Le had been gentle. The next round he'd ask a lot tougher questions. Did they get along? Was there a will or life insurance? Was the business insured, or just the truck? He wouldn't mention the diamonds yet. If Mrs. Nguyen was so wealthy, why work in a food truck? What was that about? According to Romero's notes, Thanh and her husband had a nice restaurant in the Pearl District not long ago.

Who benefited from this woman's death?

Once they found motive, they'd narrow it down by opportunity. Thanh and her brother were each other's alibi. Convenient. The truth was, one or both of them could have come and gone in the predawn dark. Just because no one had seen them didn't mean they weren't there.

Last but not least was means. Maybe Hieu was in the military.

Where was that bank tape? Romero said they sent it over.

Two hours later, with the section of tape they had showing nothing but the taillights of an old Subaru, which may or may not have anything to do with the crime, Keenan stood up and stretched. Typical of anything technology related, the previous section of tape was corrupted in the copying process. Or at least, that was the tech's excuse.

Romero stumbled in around eight-thirty. While his partner revived himself with caffeine and looked over the reports, he'd check the homeless-guy-witness box, taking Logan McKenna's revised statement. Probably nothing, but she should have told him everything the first time. Later, they'd take another pass at Thanh and Hieu. Separate them for their interviews. Divide and conquer. Maybe something would shake loose.

Somebody shot that tank and turned that food truck into a firebomb. Like the arson guy said, propane tanks don't blow up by themselves. No weapon or brass recovered at the scene, but a small, clean entry into the propane tank and an exit wound the size of the Grand Canyon pretty much made it arson.

And if they could prove intent to the DA, murder.

47

How Rheanna got by on so few hours of sleep each night was a mystery. They'd stayed up till three playing, and she'd still popped out of bed with a smile and was out the door before the sun came up. Logan kept hitting the snooze alarm and had to hustle to get up and dressed by eight. This morning's attire included a quilted vest. It might be freezing now, but by late morning, if the sun came out, she'd need to shed the jacket but still have something over her henley. She had to be downtown for her appointment with Keenan by nine.

Rheanna gave good directions. Logan only got lost once, arriving at the Second Avenue Central Precinct at 8:57 a.m. If she did nothing else to make Detective Keenan happy, she'd be prompt.

City of Portland Police Bureau was engraved over the glass-and-steel entrance. The arched windows and blue awnings made it look welcoming, even friendly, but remembering Keenan's not-so-friendly tone of voice on the phone, Logan wasn't exactly relaxed. Entering through the revolving door with metal detectors, she went through security and checked in. Keenan was called and came downstairs to fetch her himself.

Back in the squad room, after offering her coffee, which she declined, they sat down. Knowing how bad police station coffee was purported to be, she'd brought her own java.

All the interview rooms were being used by the time she got there, so Keenan took her statement at his desk. He was just as intimidating as she remembered. For the next forty minutes, as accurately as she could, Logan went over the additional facts, telling him what she knew about GI Joe, describing the man she saw running across the parking lot area Sunday morning, away from the burning food truck. Several times throughout the interview, she emphasized that she wasn't sure it was him. Could have been some other homeless guy.

Keenan had a few more clarifying questions, then asked if she had anything else to add. She couldn't think of anything but provided him with Rita Wolfe's number at the New School. Rita and the kitchen staff could attest to Joe's gentle nature.

As she left, she asked if he knew the identity of the victim of the fire yet. He verified that yes, it was Thanh Le's mother-in-law, Mrs. Nguyen. He and his partner had done the next-of-kin notification.

The few times she'd seen Thanh's mother-in-law, she had been scowling and arguing with or screaming at someone. According to Huey, she'd been particularly hard on Thanh, dishing out more criticism than praise, but still—no one deserved to die like that.

PORTLAND PD

10:00 A.M.

Unsolved homicides had doubled since this time last year, and it was only February. Trying to protect 181,160 citizens packed into 821 street miles reported by the Portland Police Bureau's website for Central District, they needed to double the size of the number of officers on the street and detectives working cases, but that wasn't going to happen anytime soon. Like public employees everywhere, the PPB had to work with what they had.

Hitching up his pants, Sergeant Lenton, laid some papers on the podium and began the ten o'clock briefing. It was shift change, so he kept it short. He began with an update on one of homicide's open cases. Reading from the notes Detective Keenan had handed him this morning, he informed his officers to be on the lookout for a Joseph Maynard Watts, a.k.a. GI Joe, age sixty-five, approximately six foot one.

Officers Raitt and Jenson exchanged looks.

The sergeant continued.

Originally of Vallejo, California, currently homeless. Last seen wearing an olive army jacket and jeans, tennis shoes, and a black beanie, behaving erratically in the vicinity of Tenth and Alder, running west-northwest down Washington, away from the scene. For now, he was just a person of interest. Wanted only for questioning in conjunction with the explosion and fire at Tenth and Alder Sunday morning, February 23, but being former military and recently involved in an altercation with one Thomas Abrams of the Road Warriors, who claimed GI Joe initiated the attack, this man should be considered armed and dangerous.

They were also hearing rumors of a big buy going down this week, down by the docks, Wednesday night. Drug enforcement had some undercover guys working that one. Allen and Timmons took notes. That was their area. In the last few months, there had been an increase in hot shots and an influx of drugs from Canada. The BC bud was relatively harmless, but the heroin was another story, and they were practically giving the stuff away, it was so cheap now.

The briefing ended by ten thirty. The sergeant didn't believe in long meetings and liked to get them out on the street as soon as possible so the last patrols could come in, get home to their families, get some sleep. By ten forty, Raitt and Jenson were in their unit, rolling toward Forest Park.

With over five thousand acres of forested and hilly terrain, it was a favorite hideout for a certain component of the hard-core homeless. Most were harmless and just wanted to be left alone. Although there was some violent crime in the park, the unofficial residents mostly stayed off the trails and kept to themselves. The younger guys, Road Warriors and the like, wanted to be near services, so they stayed in town. The crazies could be anywhere.

If GI Joe ran there on Sunday, he'd be getting hungry by now. And if he was injured, as he may have been, considering Monster's reputation, eventually GI Joe would need to come out to seek medical help.

*****

Back on the sidewalk, civic duty done, Logan decided to walk. She needed to work off the stress. She'd been right about the layers and stuffed her jacket into her messenger bag. Much better.

Her thoughts turned to Joe and then, more generally, to people like him. Why were some people able to overcome physical and emotional traumas like war without turning to drugs or alcohol? And for those who succumbed, then tried to pull themselves out, the health care or criminal justice systems made it almost impossible.

Places like Blanchet House were trying to make a dent, Rita said. But the homeless faced endless challenges, where one wrong step would throw you back down. She didn't know Joe's story but remembering how frightened and confused he looked when he was running away, she almost hoped Keenan wouldn't find him.

Lost in thought, she was almost halfway across town before she realized how hungry she was, and she looked for a place to eat. Consulting Yelp, she went a few more blocks to Deschutes Brewery, then spent a couple of hours wandering through Powell's Books again. Her messenger bag now overstuffed with more gifts plus her jacket, she aimed herself toward Rheanna's loft. Remembering the leftover pasta in the fridge, Logan picked up her pace.

48

It wasn't until Logan got back to Rheanna's, kicked off her boots, and zapped some leftovers, that she remembered she'd put her phone in airport mode so it wouldn't ring in the station during her interview with Detective Keenan.

Bowl in one hand, phone in the other, she walked into the living room and plopped down on the couch.

Four messages.

None of them from Ben.

Several were from Huey, she called him first.

"Logan, I'm so glad you called me back."

"I'm sorry, Huey, my phone was off. I just got your messages. You said you're at the hospital. Are you guys okay?"

"Yes, I'm sorry to bother you, Logan, but I didn't know who else to call."

Logan could barely hear him. There was a lot of background noise. She turned up the volume on her phone.

"What happened? What's going on?"

"I'm not even sure where to start. I'll try to make it short. Monday, you know, they—the police, those two detectives—came and gave us the official notification, told us that Mrs. Nguyen was the woman who died in the fire. At least Thanh didn't have to go down to the morgue and identify her, they were able to do that without us, then verified it with fingerprints."

Thanh took it hard. I made her go to bed, but when she didn't get better, I drove her to the hospital."

"Is she okay?"

"She's okay for now, but no, she's not well. She has hepatitis C. She's had it for many years but didn't know she had it or how she got it. She's not a drug user—never has been—and never got a blood transfusion. Probably got it in that awful refugee camp. They told us it's common for people to have the virus for years and not have any symptoms.

"Anyway, since she didn't have any symptoms, she never treated it. It silently worked in the background, destroying her liver. A few months ago, when she first started feeling tired, resting didn't help. When she finally went to a doctor, he had her see a bunch of specialists and they told her she would need a transplant. He put her on the list, but because she was still able to work, she was way down on the list, low priority. Last night, though, she got really bad—her liver was completely shutting down, so her transplant team moved her up to next available."

"I had no idea, Huey. Have they found a donor yet?"

"That's why I'm calling. They found one, but she didn't get it."

"Why?"

Huey's voice took on a bitter, angry tone. "Because earlier today, Detectives Keenan and Romero came back. Said they needed to ask me some follow-up questions. They went over everything I'd already told them, but they sounded like they thought I was hiding something. Like somehow one or both of us was involved with whoever blew up the truck and the attack was our own fault. While I was talking with them, I missed the call."

This last was said through gritted teeth.

"How did they know where to find you? I mean—how did they know you were at the hospital?"

"They didn't come to the hospital. They showed up at the apartment. I went back to the apartment to feed Thanh's cat, Pinot, and get some things for her. After the long night she'd had, they gave her something to make her sleep. Before she went under, she asked me to bring her some things from the apartment. Her rosary and her favorite book, *The Art of Happiness* by the Dalai Lama. She keeps both by her bed. Weird combination, I know. Anyway, while I was there, the police showed up. Said it would just take a few minutes of my time. I shouldn't have let them in, but I thought . . . I don't know what I thought. They didn't make it sound like I had a choice."

"Did you tell them Thanh was sick, that she was in the hospital?"

"Yes, but they didn't seem interested in talking with her, and I didn't think it was any of their business. I just wanted them to finish so I could go. I'm the only contact number the transplant team has. Now that Mrs. Nguyen's gone, I'm all Thanh has. When they find a donor organ, the transplant team has only one hour to reach the family and make a decision. When I finally got their message, it was too late. They told me they were sorry, but they had to give it to another patient."

"Oh my God, Huey, I am so sorry. What happens now?"

Agitated, Logan got up, put her bowl down on the coffee table, and started pacing in front of the picture windows, phone to her ear. The view was still beautiful, but she wasn't looking at it.

"I'm back at the hospital now," Huey said. "I talked with her doctors, and they're going to rush me through some tests and see if I am a good candidate to be a donor for her."

"Can you donate a liver? I mean, I didn't know you could do that."

"You only donate part of it, and then it regenerates—at least most of it. I'm not sure. They explained it to us. I don't know how it works, but they say it can be done."

"I had no idea. Is there anything I can do to help? Anything else you guys need from the apartment? If it would help you guys, I'll be happy to take care of Pinot for you."

Protesting at first, Hieu gratefully accepted her offer. He told her to come by the hospital and he'd give her the keys.

"Thank you again, Logan. Usually it takes weeks to do all the compatibility testing, but because of her advanced condition, they're going to rush them and try to do them all over the next few days. I thought maybe since your brother is a police officer, and you know some of the people up here, you might be able to talk with the police and explain the situation to them. I'll answer whatever questions they want, Logan. But not now. Not until after the surgery."

49

"I'll do what I can, Huey. I can't promise anything, but I can at least let him know what's happening. In the meantime, just focus on what you need to do."

Saying she would come over now to pick up the keys, Logan looked at her watch. Rheanna should be home soon, and would have Keenan's direct number, but this couldn't wait. She looked up the number of the police station.

Before the call got put through, she had to sit through a recorded message advising her that if this was an emergency, to dial 911. *No thanks. Been there, done that.*

It only rang once before a flat-toned voice intoned, "Portland Police Bureau, how may I direct your call?"

"Detective Keenan, please."

After a brief Mozart interlude, she was informed that Detective Keenan was not available at this time. Would she like to leave a message? She left a brief one, simply asking him to return her call. Next, she reassessed her schedule.

She was in no hurry to get back to Jasper and face the Ben situation—this was why you didn't get involved with neighbors, but she could probably fly out tomorrow, Uber in from the airport and sneak into her house under the cover of darkness. She might even be able to take Lola out for a much-deserved spin in the morning.

Public transportation options in Portland were awesome, but she sure missed Lola. Just the thought of cruising down PCH, salty wind whipping her hair around, deeply breathing in the ocean air, made her long for home. She could use a little top-down therapy right about now.

By the time she got back, Ben would have left for work. If she timed it right, she might be able to avoid him for days, or at least until she figured out what she was going to do.

Tabling those thoughts for now, she looked at her calendar and made a decision. She didn't have to be back at work right away. She hoped Rheanna wouldn't mind having a house guest a few more days. Tomorrow she would go see Thanh at the hospital and give Huey moral support. Feed their cat. Check on their apartment. Throw out any perishables in the refrigerator.

Thinking of cats made her wonder how Dimebox was doing. Named after a small town in Texas "no bigger'n a dime box worth of snuff," the tiny kitten had grown into a hefty, mouse-catching hell-raiser. Ben was supposed to feed and water said bruiser until Tyler took over. Hopefully he wasn't too preoccupied with Julie to remember.

Between pet care, visiting with Thanh and Huey and hanging out in the waiting room while tests were being run, she could write up her Portland U notes, catch up on emails, and run interference should Detective Keenan feel the need to harass her friends again. The next few days would be busy. Looking up the number online, she dialed Alaska Air and began listening "to the following options . . . which have recently changed . . ."

FOREST PARK

✶✶✶✶✶

Once she got through to a human being, changing her reservations went pretty smoothly. With that taken care of, she headed over to the hospital to pick up the keys to the apartment from Huey and get Pinot's feeding schedule. She also wanted to stop in and visit with Thanh if she felt up to it.

She found Huey's room without any trouble. He wasn't there when she arrived, but they wheeled him in just as she was about to go ask the nurse how to find him.

"Sorry, Logan," Huey said as he got helped back into bed from the wheelchair.

"Everything okay?" Logan asked.

"I'm fine. They just make you ride in these things everywhere you go." He gave the orderly a thumbs up, adjusted his covers and took a long drink of water from the glass on the shelf next to the bed. "Glad you waited. They've had me coming and going all morning."

Logan nodded and pulled up a chair. She remembered the nurses making her do the same thing when she was in the hospital after the car accident, even when she'd insisted she was fine and could walk on her own.

"The next poking and prodding excursion isn't for another hour, but in case they get here early, the keys are over there," he said, pointing to a small, plastic bowl on the shelf. Logan retrieved them.

"I texted you the address. I really appreciate you stopping by to feed Pinot. He has plenty of fresh water and I changed the litterbox and all that before I left, so he should be good until tomorrow."

They talked a few more minutes and then Logan asked if he thought Thanh was up for a short visit.

"Should be. She's had all her tests," he said. "Should be resting in her room, now. She's probably bored to tears or laying there worried about the operation. Either way, she'd love to see you and the distraction would be good for her. Her room is on the other end of this floor, opposite the nursc's station."

50

When Logan got there, a daytime soap opera was blasting out of the wall-mounted TV. Thanh, lifted up on one elbow, was trying to turn it off with an oversized, plastic-covered remote control.

"Oh, I'm so glad you're here," she said. "I can't get this thing to turn off or do anything. It won't even change channels!"

Logan couldn't get the remote to work, either, so she just reached up and turned the television off manually. A welcome quiet descended on the room.

"Thank you!" Thanh said, sinking back onto her pillow, closing her eyes. "You're a lifesaver!"

Logan found a chair and pulled it up to the side of the bed. It was another one of those hard, plastic, bucket chairs with metal legs, identical to the one in Huey's room. Bright orange. She wondered if all hospital purchasing departments bought the ugliest, most uncomfortable chairs possible in order to discourage long visits.

She asked how she was doing and Thanh filled her in on the upcoming surgery. Thanh wanted to hear about Logan's interviews with the cognitive scientists at Portland U. She shared a few stories but could see her friend was tiring fast. Promising to stop by tomorrow after she went to the apartment to feed Pinot, she got up to leave, but Thanh reached up and touched her arm.

"Wait," she said. "There's something I want to talk with you about."

Logan sat back down, wondering what was on her mind.

"It's . . ." Thanh began, "It's probably nothing to worry about, but I'd like someone to know in case I . . . well, in case I don't make it."

Logan knew better than to interrupt with false assurances. An operation such as the one Thanh was facing was not a sure thing. The best way to show respect was to take her concerns seriously and listen to what she had to say.

"Like I said, it's probably nothing, but I didn't tell the police everything when they interviewed us," she said.

"Does this have anything to do with why they wanted to talk with Huey again?" Logan asked.

"No, at least I don't think so," Thanh said.

Logan sat back down. "Why don't you start from the beginning."

"You need to know Huey has nothing to do with any of this. That's why I haven't called that detective." She picked at the plastic on the useless remote control laying on the blanket. "He already thinks he's involved somehow."

"The beginning . . ." Logan prompted.

"Okay, remember when we were talking about the first wave of Vietnamese refugees, those who left when Saigon fell in 1975?"

"Yes, I remember that conversation," Logan waited to see where this was going.

"Well, some of them were criminals. And they preyed

mostly on other Vietnamese in the area. They all spoke the same language, came from the same culture, and people of my mother-in-law's generation did not understand American banking and had a natural distrust of governments. So, for example, if they needed a loan or got into trouble, they looked to other Vietnamese. These people were happy to hand out loans—at very high interest rates. Even if someone never borrowed from these guys, they still collected monthly 'fees' from each business, just for operating in their area."

Logan wondered what this had to do with Thanh. Had she taken out a loan from one of these guys? Is that why her food truck had been blown up?

"For a long time, a man named Mr. Tran Van Cong ran the operation in our area. He had his people collect from all the food truck vendors and every other small business in the Asian community. Vietnamese, Korean, Thai."

"Did you owe this man money, Thanh?" Logan asked.

"No," she quickly reassured her. "And neither did my mother-in-law that I know of. I never asked her, but I always wondered why we seemed to be exempt. He never sent anyone around to collect any monthly 'fees' from us like they did for everyone else."

"Was your mother-in-law related to him, maybe?" Logan asked.

"No, but her husband and Cong did come from the same village back in Vietnam. But she never associated with him here or there that I know of and people who knew her back in Saigon speak very highly of her late husband. He was a respected officer in the ARVN."

"How did you hear about her husband and this Cong being childhood friends—or at least from the same village? Did Mrs. Nguyen tell you?"

"No, my husband told me. He saw Cong at our restaurant one night, right after we' expanded and moved to the new location in the Pearl District. He pointed him out to me. Told me he was bad news. I'm not sure how he knew of the village connection, must have been something he picked up from conversations he heard at home. He said not to mention Cong being there to his mother."

"So, if neither of you owed this man, Cong, anything, then what . . ." Logan asked. She wanted to reassure Thanh, but this wasn't making much sense.

Thanh scrunched up her face and shook her head. "I don't know, exactly, but recently Mrs. Nguyen was worried. She and I never spoke of it, but I heard through the grapevine about a month ago that Cong died and his nephew, Sonny, took over the business. Since then, he's stepped up collections. No excuses are accepted. Even though we didn't owe them anything, we started getting visits from his two collectors."

"Did you talk about your concerns with your moth-er-in-law?" Logan asked.

"No, they only talked with Mrs. Nguyen," she said. "I guess she thought she was protecting me, because I tried to ask her about it once, but she brushed me off."

The two men she had seen intimidating Mrs. Nguyen at the food truck came immediately to Logan's mind. She asked the obvious question.

"But why would they be hassling someone who didn't owe their boss any money?"

Thanh's eyes filled with tears. "I don't know! I should have insisted she tell me what was going on, but she was so proud. I just couldn't. What if my not going to the police right away got her killed? What if I could have prevented all this?"

Logan didn't know what to say.

"If anything goes wrong tomorrow—if for any reason I don't make it through, I want you to promise you'll talk with that the police and tell them everything I told you. If Cong's nephew, Sonny had anything to do with my mother-in-law's death, he needs to be stopped before he hurts anyone else."

Logan promised. Whether or not the police could prove Sonny was responsible for killing Mrs. Nguyen or having her killed, from what Thanh said, this guy was responsible for a whole lot of human suffering and misery—and he was just getting started.

51

Teresa Slavenka was exactly where she wanted to be.

In the middle of nowhere.

Well, not exactly in the middle of nowhere, but as close as you could get within the city limits of Portland, Oregon.

In January, fresh from a two-year stint with the Colorado Conservation Corps, the athletic twenty-eight-year-old brunette beat out two PhD candidates and a former peace corps director to land the perfect trails manager job with the Forest Park Conservancy. In spite of her slightly over-the-top enthusiasm, the hiring committee loved her. A successful track record and glowing recommendations from her former employer in Colorado sealed the deal. All her references said the same thing: the girl got things done, including completing the final leg of the Pacific Trail last summer.

Few people did much hiking in the park in the winter, which was just fine with her. Her first project, Teresa told her team, was to know their territory. At least that was her excuse for spending this last few days climbing as far up into the hills as she could, ostensibly to check out the condition of trails in this section of the park. With over forty-seven miles of trails, she wouldn't run out of places to explore anytime soon.

Yesterday, she'd hiked up Balch Creek, familiarizing herself with the local flora and fauna. While keeping an expert eye out for any water drainage issues or trail damage as she went, she took notes and pictures with her iPhone. She camped out in the ridge and was planning on hiking back out this morning, across Wildwood, then down one of the fire lanes. She played tourist and took a selfie at the Witch's House, an old, moss-covered stone ruin only partially still standing.

Dousing her small fire with water from the creek, she kicked more dirt on it, making sure it was completely out. She hoisted her pack onto her shoulders, jammed her hat on her head, and looked up to check the sky. A bank of dark clouds were rolling in. *Better get moving.*

Indulging her penchant for wilder places, she'd gone off trail, but if her map was current, she should reconnect with the established trail system at Wildwood in about an hour. She didn't want to go back but knew a pile of paperwork on her desk was waiting for her and would only get higher if she stayed another day.

The prospect of getting wet didn't bother her, but she knew how easy it was to sprain an ankle up here on a slippery rock hiding under a fern. She was adventurous, not stupid. Cell phone coverage was good, but she didn't want to waste anyone's time coming out to rescue her, either. That wouldn't exactly instill confidence in the troops.

Focused as she was on a northern flicker woodpecker drilling into a fallen tree, successfully extracting big, fat grubs, Teresa didn't notice the man's leg sticking out directly ahead, on her path. Dirt and twigs stuck to the dried, encrusted blood on his pants, camouflaging it as effectively as if he'd artfully placed them on purpose. The rest of him lay off the path, hidden under a dense patch of ferns. When her right toe caught on his ankle, she tripped, and the weight of her pack sent her flying.

FOREST PARK

Automatically reaching out her left arm to catch herself, twisting toward him as she fell, she heard a deafening blast she recognized immediately. Someone was shooting at her! Before she hit the ground with a sickening thud, just as her ankle snapped, a wild-haired man jumped up in front of her, looked at the gun he held in his hands in surprise, then plunged into the woods across the path.

Adrenaline coursing through her body, Teresa flinched as the northern flicker, startled off his log, rose in undulating flight.

She reached into her pocket and pulled out her cell. She couldn't give them exact directions, but they would be able to track her phone and get a rescue team up there. No, the attacker was no longer there, but she wasn't sure if he was coming back.

The EMTs took a while to find her but got her to a hospital in record time. She was able to give a fairly good description of the shooter and his weapon to the police. She knew guns. Only fourteen years old when her father died, she'd joined the army right after graduation to avoid her mother's seemingly unending grief. Did a two-year tour in Afghanistan before moving to Colorado.

Once her description of her attacker reached Keenan's desk, they got through to a judge, and GI Joe's BOLO got upgraded to a warrant for his arrest.

52

Back in Rheanna's apartment, Logan forced herself to warm up some dinner before plopping down on the couch. She knew once she sat down she wasn't getting up again. Listening to Thanh's heart-wrenching guilt and concerns about whatever Mrs. Nguyen's unfinished business was had been exhausting for both of them. At least Thanh seemed to be resting easier by the time she finally left.

Logan turned off all the lights and looked out over the city. She made quick work of her bowl of pasta and absent-mindedly licked the spoon. Not her rooftop deck, but close enough. Like a big cat, Logan liked being up high. She found the unobstructed view comforting.

Pulling her gaze back from the stark moon and the faraway lights, she noticed movement just below her, in the building across the street—another loft conversion by the look of it. Different builder, though, she thought. Their windows were average-sized, not panoramic. Of course, they were facing the uphill side of the street, not the city. No view to maximize.

A woman about her age, big screen flickering behind her, twisted shut her louvered blinds against the night. Other windows showed signs of life behind a variety of window coverings. Some were dark, their residents either asleep or the unit empty.

Logan let her mind wander. What lives were being lived out within those rectangles? It brought to mind one of her favorite old movies, Hitchcock's *Rear Window*, a 1950s classic, one of Jimmy Stewart's best, in her opinion. She preferred the black-and-white to the colorized version. In the movie, foreign correspondent Jimmy Stewart breaks his leg on assignment and gets stuck in a cast, and therefore in his apartment. He has only the view out his rear window to keep him entertained. Binoculars at the ready, he soon realizes that all his neighbors have a story, a challenge, a problem, ranging from loneliness to murder.

Looking out across the city, Logan wondered how many of her fellow human beings needed help tonight, and how many would get it. She wished she could do more to help Thanh and Huey.

Who blew up the propane tank and why? Did this have anything to do with Cong or his nephew, Sonny? If not, what other enemies could the two women possibly have had? Logan racked her brain for other options. She thought of the Korean man Mrs. Nguyen had gotten into the argument with. Would he be angry enough to destroy their truck, and if so, had he known she was inside? Or had it just been some random act of vandalism or a gang initiation? Or, going back to her conversation with Keenan this morning, could it be GI Joe having some kind of flashback to Vietnam? But where would he have gotten access to whatever was used to blow up the propane tank?

If someone meant to kill one or both of them, was Mrs. Nguyen the true target, or was it Thanh? Would they come back to finish the job? Was Thanh safe in the hospital?

Logan rubbed her face in exasperation. This wasn't helping. She was letting her imagination get the better of her and she had absolutely no answers to any of her questions. Every avenue of thought was a dead end. She took a deep breath. What facts did she actually know?

Not much. Rheanna said they had a car leaving the scene on tape, but hadn't had any luck tracking it down, yet. Keenan said it was probably long since dismembered at a chop shop or at the very least, driven far away or repainted.

Speaking of Rheanna, Logan wished she'd get home soon. She needed to get through to Keenan and convince him to leave Thanh and Huey alone. It's not like they were going anywhere. They were in the hospital. Hopefully Keenan had other lines of inquiry to follow. There were a lot of other places the cops should be looking besides Huey, Thanh, and GI Joe, a gentle giant of a man who just happened to be a recovering alcoholic with PTSD.

For a moment, the sheer number of messy human problems over which she had no control threatened to overwhelm her. In the last few days, there had been a violent explosion, killing Mrs. Nguyen. Then Thanh, who had already suffered the loss of her husband and her home, was now facing a dangerous organ transplant operation. The police seemed particularly interested in Huey, and if they could find him, the man she saw running from the burning truck. All indications pointed to it being Gentle Joe. As much as she wanted him to be innocent, she had to admit to herself that she didn't know him. He may not be as gentle as he appeared. Maybe GI Joe had done it. But she couldn't come up with a motive or the means.

And then there was the mess with Ben. And Julie. How she wished there wasn't a Julie.

Lost in thought, she was startled by the scraping of Rheanna's key in the door. Keenan was with her.

"Hey, Logan!" Rheanna called out, hanging her keys on the hook just inside.

Keenan remained standing in the entryway, scowling.

Well, she wasn't very fond of him, either. She knew he didn't know he'd caused Thanh to miss a viable transplant organ by delaying Huey, but she was still angry with him, and she definitely wasn't going to let him make her feel like a third wheel tonight. Rheanna had invited her to stay and until Keenan started paying rent here, it wasn't for him to say who Rheanna's house guests were.

Sensing the tension, Rheanna put Keenan to work opening a bottle of wine in the kitchen while she kept up a stream of chatter about her day and warmed up the rest of the pasta. Logan told her she already ate. Following behind her with the stems of two wine glasses woven between sinewed, knobby fingers in one hand, a bottle of Chianti in the other, Keenan set the glasses on the coffee table.

"Ladies?"

After pouring for them, he retrieved a glass for himself from the kitchen. Rheanna, in a show of loyalty, sat with Logan on the couch, while Keenan took the large chair opposite, his back to the view.

While they ate, Logan filled them in. Her goal was not to make Keenan feel lousy, but to make him understand how sick Thanh was and how much she needed Huey right now.

Without making any commitments or apologies, Keenan nodded and thanked her for letting him know. She added the information about the Korean man but left out the rest. It was really Thanh's decision when and if to share that. More nodding.

Obviously, Keenan wasn't going to discuss the case with her. She'd have to encourage Thanh to fill him in after the operation. Until then, she would just have to trust he'd cover all the bases.

Rheanna, always the peacemaker, changed the topic, telling them about some of the calls she'd taken on her shift, ranging from a six-year-old who probably saved his mother's life by dialing 911, then following her instructions until the ambulance got there, and a Forest Park employee who got shot at, falling and breaking her ankle in the process.

"Is she okay?" Logan asked.

"Yeah, they gave her a cast, sent her home."

"Jeez, I hope they find the guy," Logan said.

"Yeah."

Keenan said nothing.

The conversation dwindled.

Not entirely oblivious to the couple's signals, Logan announced she was tired and went to her room. In a few minutes, soft jazz flowed under the door, making her smile.

At least someone was getting laid tonight.

53

Sonny started yelling the minute Michael and Teng walked through the door. Teng wisely took a seat on the new leather couch under the window, out of the line of fire. He'd already heard this. Since Michael had been MIA the last two days, Sonny had been ranting and raving about the botched job—taking it out on Teng. Michael remained standing, facing Sonny.

"Do you see this shit?" Sonny shouted, stabbing his finger at the new, wall-mounted, big screen TV. A local news program was showing the now familiar vivid footage of Than's *pho* engulfed in twenty-foot flames, with bits of smoldering metal from two neighboring food trucks littering the sidewalk.

Shoving yesterday's newspaper across the desk so Michael could see the headline he said, "Explain this to me, Michael. I thought you guys said it was taken care of. You said everything went smoothly. What the hell happened?"

Michael stared straight ahead.

Not only had Michael screwed up, but his going AWOL after the incident allowed Sonny's fury to ramp up to atomic levels. If Michael was repentant, it didn't show. He'd picked up Teng this morning as if nothing had happened.

Finally, Michael spoke. "No one should have been inside. It was early. Way too early for anyone to be there yet."

"Well, someone *was*, wasn't she?" Sonny slowly growled.

After wasting a few more minutes berating him, Sonny moved on. Teng probably expected him to tell Michael his services were no longer needed, but Sonny wasn't ready to get rid of his best enforcer. Not yet. He did, however, need to make his point. Michael needed to know who his boss was. This disappearing shit would not be tolerated.

Sonny wasn't too worried about the old woman's death being tied back to him. No one could identify Michael or Teng and Michael assured him they didn't leave any trace evidence. Neither of them had even gotten out of the car and the Subaru had long since been 'recycled'.

But there was still the matter of the cash and valuables they had been sent to get from Mrs. Nguyen. Sonny had been counting on a few more collections for the Canadian buy tomorrow night. He wasn't done punishing Michael yet, but he decided to give him a chance to redeem himself.

He paused for effect and glanced down at his computer screen, then looked up at Michael.

"Mr. Park. Park liquor store across from the plaza . . ."

Michael nodded. If he had been bothered by Sonny's rant, it didn't show. Teng was kind of impressed.

"Park is paid up, but his brother isn't. He still owes. Pay Mr. Park a visit. They have other family, here, too," Sonny scribbled an amount on a piece of paper. "That's what he owes, plus interest. Don't leave until he pays up."

After Michael left, Sonny turned to Teng and instructed him to search Mrs. Nguyen's apartment.

"What if her daughter-in-law is there?" Teng said. "She lives there, too."

"Then wait 'til she goes out," Sonny said.

"Okay, but what if there's nothing there? What if she was telling the truth and there's nothing to find?" said Teng.

"Those old people always have something hidden away. They don't trust banks. And it's probably small. Something they could smuggle out of Saigon when they left. Gold, silver, jewels. You'll have to really look," Sonny said. "Could be sewn into couch cushions or clothes."

With a nod to Teng's concerns about the apartment being occupied, he added, "And don't go tonight, her daughter-in-law will probably be home. Go in the morning, but don't take too long. We have a lot of work to do before tomorrow night."

Teng shrugged his jacket back on and left.

Sonny sighed and plopped back down into his chair. He was surrounded by incompetent assholes. As soon as this deal was done, he'd have to bring on some new people. People who understood business. The business he wanted to be in, the one he was this close to breaking into, starting by impressing the Canadians.

In their last contact, they said they were coming in on their yacht, "*Quicksilver.*" They were to send an agreed upon signal when they arrived, then wait in a small boat just offshore. Once it was good and dark, a small boat would come out to get them. The meeting would be held onboard the yacht.

Sonny would leave Michael on shore with the cash. Once both parties were satisfied, Sonny would signal him to make the buy. The Canadians would load up the truck and Michael would hand over the suitcase. When the Canadians had their money, he would be ferried back to shore, where Michael waited with the goods. If all went smoothly, this would be the first of many future deals.

Sonny's blood began to race. This was going to launch him into a world he wanted, the one he always felt he belonged in, but could never enter as long as his uncle was alive, holding him back. But now it was within reach.

Nothing could stop him now!

54

Logan felt energized. The early morning air was rain-washed, cold and fresh. Even in winter, Portland was a walking town. Pulling her beanie down to cover her ears, she snugged her scarf around her neck, and tucked it into her jacket. Missing her morning beach run, she decided to get in at least a few miles of city hiking before breakfast. Checking the map the hotel had given her, she headed toward the river.

An hour later, she was ready to eat. Spotting a place called Mother's, she got in the short but growing line out front. She only planned on grabbing a pastry and some coffee, but by the time she was seated everything looked so good she wound up having the Breakfast Double Down: corned beef hash, two eggs over easy, buttermilk pancakes, and a side order of biscuits and gravy. The French Press coffee was excellent, too.

Back on the sidewalk, she loosened her belt a notch and pulled on her gloves. Life was good.

Now that she'd successfully changed her travel arrangements and decided to put the Ben issue on the back burner, she felt better. Living in limbo was not her style. Getting shit done was. One day at a time.

Ben, the police bothering Thanh and Huey, who shot up the food truck and why . . . she had no control over any of that. Those things would have to take care of themselves. Besides, nobody was going to arrest Thanh and Huey while they were preparing for surgery. She needed to focus on what was within her control and mind her own business.

Today's mission: Go to their apartment, feed the cat, clean the litter box, then go to the hospital to visit Huey and Thanh.

*****

Palace Apartments consisted of twenty-four one- and two-bedroom units set in a three-story, utilitarian block building built in the seventies. A far cry from Rheanna's luxury loft in the stylish Pearl District, it boasted no doorman, no topiary out front, no colorful signage, and no awnings or embellishments to soften the façade. The cement was discolored and cracked, and the dirt bare, but both were swept clean and no trash littered the sidewalk or surrounding area.

Logan went inside and took the stairs to apartment 207. She needed the exercise. Besides, there was no elevator.

Jiggling the key in the lock several times—the one Huey gave her must have been a copy, those never worked right—Logan was relieved when the apartment door finally popped opened. Pinot met her at the door, meowing loudly, weaving in and around her ankles, rubbing against her legs.

"Jeez, Pinot, calm down," Logan said. "Huey said he left you plenty of food yesterday and it's not even lunchtime yet."

Logan rinsed out the cat's food dish and made sure his bowl was full of fresh water, then opened a can of Tuna Delight and dumped it in. Huey said one can a day was fine. That with the dry food she could leave out would be plenty. Pinot needed to be on a diet, anyway.

Don't we all.

But Pinot wasn't interested in his breakfast. He seemed agitated and kept pressing against Logan's legs. His meowing intensified and Logan wondered if he was sick or something. Sometimes Dimebox got into things he shouldn't, but Pinot wasn't an outside cat, she didn't think. They were on the second floor.

What could he have gotten into here? Logan didn't see any cat vomit or diarrhea on the floor. Not even a hairball. He seemed okay. It didn't look like there was any garbage spilled on the floor or other obvious things he could have eaten.

She bent down and scooped him up. Holding him firmly in one hand, she gently prodded the protesting cat's abdomen. If it was distended, that might spell trouble. Logan wasn't sure what kind of trouble, but it's what the vet told her to do the time she called about Dimebox. The last thing Thanh needed to worry about was a sick pet.

Pinot seemed to know Logan didn't know what she was doing. With one good twist, he yowled and leaped out of her arms, ran down the hall, and disappeared into one of the bedrooms in the back.

Logan groaned. "You're not going to make this easy, are you?" she said.

She found the number for the vet on the fridge. He was busy so she talked with the tech. She said there was probably nothing to worry about, but if she wanted to, she could bring the cat in and they'd check him out. Logan went into the hallway and started opening closets, looking for a cat carrier. Something was wrong with this cat. If she didn't calm down soon, she'd take him in. Better safe than sorry.

The first closet held nothing but a vacuum cleaner and some coats. She pushed the coats aside, but other than a collection of winter boots lined up in back, she came up empty. The second closet was full of cleaning supplies, some industrial sized. She finally struck gold on her third try. A full-length linen closet with five wooden shelves held neatly folded towels and extra blankets and bedding—probably for Huey to use when he stayed over and slept on the couch.

On the top shelf, she spotted the carrier. Balancing on her toes, she stretched up to get it. Just as she hooked her fingers into the wire edge to lift it down, someone ran past, slamming the door into her back, shoving her into the closet. She heard a loud crack and intense pain shot through her face. As she struggled to remain conscious, she grabbed onto the door jam and lowered herself to one knee, only vaguely aware of blood spurting out of her nose onto the previously clean linen.

The door bounced open on the rebound, so when she turned, she could see straight down the hallway. A tall, young man sprinted out the front door, launched himself over the wrought iron railing and down the first flight of stairs. She could only see him from the back, but when he hit the landing and turned, for a brief instant, they made eye contact and Logan knew instantly who it was.

One of the two thugs she'd seen bothering Mrs. Nguyen. She froze, knowing she had no escape route if the guy decided to come back, but the funny thing was, in the split second she saw his face, he looked as frightened as she was.

Thanh's concerns suddenly seemed a lot more plausible. She tried to remember everything she'd said about the nephew who took over his uncle's criminal enterprises. Sonny. She said he'd been bleeding the local business owners dry. Obviously, Mrs. Nguyen had something Sonny wanted and he'd sent his men to get it. Valuables, or maybe evidence of some kind that connected him to her violent death. That is, if he was responsible for it, which in all likelihood he was.

Speaking of men, Logan hoped the other half of the collection team wasn't waiting inside.

55

Logan wanted nothing more than to dump all this in Keenan's lap. After she got cleaned up, she could stop by the station, look at mug shots until she could put a name to the guy who just mashed her into the closet. She could tell Keenan everything she knew about Sonny preying on small businesses in the local Asian community, a whole underground organization seemingly operating right under the cops' noses, but if she did, that would put the spotlight back on Thanh and Huey and they certainly didn't need that right now.

Right now, she needed to deal with her injury. She struggled to a standing position. Gingerly, she reached up and touched her nose. It crunched and searing pain shot across her face.

Not good.

No one else came running out, so after a quick look around, she shut and locked the front door, then made her way into the bathroom to assess the damage.

Yikes!

It looked like she was going to be taking herself to the doctor, instead of the cat. At least she knew now why Pinot had been so agitated.

She grimaced at the thought, but that brought new waves of pain. Grabbing a pillowcase and towel from the now ruined linen closet, she held the towel up to her nose to staunch the flow of blood and went into the kitchen to make a temporary ice pack out of the pillowcase. She found a bag of frozen peas in the freezer. Those worked better, so she used that. She needed to keep the swelling down as much as possible on her way to the ER.

Cleaning the blood off the closet floor as best she could, she called a cab and grabbed her bag. She'd come back later when she could do a better job and replace whatever towels or sheets couldn't be washed. Pinot seemed to be fine now that the intruder was gone. He was sitting serenely on the back of the couch, eyes closed. She'd check on him tomorrow.

She had planned on stopping by to visit with Huey and Thanh before their surgeries, but decided against it, given the state of her face. She'd leave a message for them that Pinot had been fed and watered and leave it at that. They might be disappointed, but it was better than upsetting them with the bad news some broke into their apartment. And that the man was one of the two thugs she'd seen hassling Mrs. Nguyen before she was killed.

Holding the bag of frozen peas on her face, she took another look into the back bedroom where she assumed the guy had been hiding. Dresser drawers had been pulled out, their contents dumped on the floor, and the bed was all torn up—reaffirming her assessment that the man had been looking for something. None of the other rooms had been touched, so he must not have been there long before she surprised him.

What he was looking for, she had no idea. She couldn't ask Huey or Thanh. At least not until after the surgery. She thought again of calling the police and reporting a break-in? If she did, she'd have to tell them she recognized the guy and that would open the door to another whole slew of questions. Keenan and his partner already suspected the Nguyens of somehow bringing all this on themselves. Well, when they weren't thinking it was GI Joe.

She couldn't think about this now. After locking up, she descended the stairs as carefully as she could, but every change in direction or slight jolt brought a new wave of pain and dizziness. She'd have to tell them to get a dead bolt on that door. No wonder the guy was able to get in. Not that she was an expert but picking a flimsy lock like that would probably take all of 2.5 seconds.

Part of her wanted to hand this off to the police, but she'd promised Thanh. It would just have to wait until she could think clearly. She hoped the guy didn't come back to finish what he started while she was at the hospital.

Outside, trying to avoid the stares of people passing by, Logan waited for the cab. She'd decided against taking the MAX for just that reason. She didn't have to wait long. In just a few minutes her taxi pulled up.

The driver took one look at her and said, "Wow! I don't have to ask where to, right, lady?"

Logan grimaced and lowered herself carefully into the back seat. Yes, the closest ER would do.

On the way to the hospital, she couldn't stop thinking about what her attacker was searching for. Was he just a low-level collector for the organization or had he been the one to blow up the food truck? Had he killed Mrs. Nguyen? If so, why? What could an elderly Vietnamese woman possibly have that these guys would want? Could Thanh and she have borrowed money from loan sharks to keep their little food truck afloat? Was Huey involved? Maybe when they couldn't pay back the loan . . . but, no, that didn't make sense. Why blow up the only source of income the two women had? They couldn't very well pay back a loan if their food truck was destroyed.

Logan squeezed her eyes shut. None of this made any sense. All in all, she just felt crappy. What had started out as a great week, visiting Glenda, touring the New School, meeting the wonderful staff, enjoying great food, talking math and music with Huey and the professors at Portland U, anticipating a romantic weekend with Ben . . . all of that had gone to shit.

Mrs. Nguyen had been killed, Thanh lost her business, her liver was failing, and she was facing a dangerous organ transplant. Huey was risking his life to give his sister part of his. Logan couldn't even go visit them because her nose had been broken by an intruder. A man who now knew she could identify him.

Oh . . . and Julie. With everything else that happened, she almost forgot about her. The return of Ben's old fiancé threw a huge wrench into her relationship with Ben. If they still had a relationship. She couldn't even look forward to going home, which was always her happy place, because now there was the awkwardness—she'd be trying to avoid him. And as if all that weren't bad enough, she *looked* like shit, too.

It was *not* a wonderful life . . . at least not right now.

56

The doctor wanted her to stay overnight for observation, but Logan convinced him she had someone at home who could check on her. He didn't need to know that home was a thousand miles away. All she wanted right now was some time and space to think things through.

Ignoring the alarmed look on the driver's face as she got into the cab, Logan decided at the last minute not to go back to Rheanna's, but instead instructed the driver to return to Thanh's apartment. She wasn't up to answering a bunch of questions, and if Keenan was there, she was sure he'd give her the third degree.

Besides, the more she thought about the whole situation, the madder she got. She was tired of being the powerless victim. Starting right now, she was taking action. And that action started with trying to figure out what Sonny's goon had been searching for. Better than waiting for more bad things to happen while she sat twiddling her thumbs. If there was anything in that apartment that would help Thanh and Huey, Logan needed to find it before Sonny did. Once he got his hands on whatever it was, it would be gone forever.

When the cab let her out, Logan was glad to see most of Thanh's neighbors were home. Lights were on in most units and sounds of people making dinner or watching TV drifted out onto the sidewalk. Hopefully, this afternoon's visitor wouldn't return until tomorrow when most people would be at work. She'd be long gone by then.

Making sure the door was locked behind her, Logan checked on Pinot, who barely woke up from his cat coma on the couch. She went to get a glass of water to wash down one of the pain pills they'd given her at the hospital, then thought better of it. She could manage the pain for now and save the knock-out pill for tonight.

Pinot was a terrible watch cat, so she checked all the rooms just to make sure no one was hiding anywhere in the apartment. She caught a glimpse of her face in the bathroom mirror. No wonder the cab driver had stared at her. Two colorful black eyes were blossoming on each side of her swollen nose. They had her taped up like one of the Mummy's distant relatives. Not a good look. She sighed.

Better get this party started.

She decided to begin with the back bedroom. From her brother Rick's stories from when he was in drug enforcement, she remembered the basics of how to search a room. She began at the door, working around the room clockwise. She had no idea what she was looking for, but hopefully she'd recognize it when she found it. She was going to take her time. The intruder had been in a hurry, but she had all night.

From a framed photo on the dresser of a slightly younger Thanh and a handsome Vietnamese man—all smiles—posing in front of a restaurant, Vietnam Pearl, Logan assumed this must be Thanh's room. That must be the restaurant they'd owned before her husband died. *Happier days.* So sad to have lost her husband, their business, and her home so young.

Logan shook her head and got to work. As she finished with each area of the room, she shook out the clothes the intruder had thrown on the floor and returned them neatly folded to the dresser drawers and closet. She probably had everything in the wrong place, but at least it would be in some semblance of order for Thanh when she came home.

After an hour, all she found were a few dust bunnies under the bed. Nothing of any value or interest to local criminals as far as she could tell. But then again, she had no idea what the man had been searching for, so there was that.

The bathroom yielded even less. The two women were excellent housekeepers. When Logan entered Mrs. Nguyen's room she hesitated at the door. Nothing had been touched in here and it felt disrespectful to go through a dead woman's things, but she couldn't leave anything that might explain what was going on and help Thanh and Huey, so Logan squared her shoulders and stepped in.

She tackled the bed first, undoing Mrs. Nguyen's neat handiwork. Nothing in the sheets or blankets, nothing slipped between the mattress and box springs or hidden inside the solitary pillow. After remaking the bed and checking the nightstand, Logan moved on to the next wall, which had no furniture, just a window that looked onto the street. Thanh's room only had a small window. She'd given her mother-in-law the better room. Pulling a chair over, she checked the tops of the curtains and felt along the window edges, then turned her attention to the closet, opposite the foot of the bed.

Mounted on the wall was another photo similar to the one in Thanh's room. Taken outside the same restaurant, probably on the same day, since Thanh's husband's clothing hadn't changed, this one was of Mrs. Nguyen and her son. His face wreathed in smiles, an arm his mother's shoulders, her expression one of dignified pride and joy.

What was it Thanh said when she had dinner with her and Huey at Jakes? Mrs. Nguyen had given the young couple the money to expand the restaurant. From the look of the neighborhood in the photo and the luxurious design of the building, the new place must have cost some serious money. How could an older woman of modest means give so generous a gift?

Logan looked around the room again. This woman was a mother, and as a mother, she would have found a way. Logan understood. Her own daughter meant everything to her. She would do anything to help Amy.

Maybe Mrs. Nguyen had borrowed money from Cong after all—not for herself, but to help out her son. That would make sense. She wouldn't necessarily have told him or Thanh. In fact, she probably wouldn't. She'd be too proud. And the loan must have been taken out with Cong, not Sonny, because Thanh's husband was still alive when they expanded the restaurant and Cong didn't die until recently.

That's when his nephew, the infamous Sonny, took over.

Logan looked again at the photo on the wall. The restaurant had been successful for a while, Thanh said. Maybe Mrs. Nguyen had already paid Cong back. If so, maybe the thugs were only coming around to hassle her because they were hassling everyone. Maybe they were trying to squeeze protection money from her like they did from every other food truck vendor. But if that was the case, what had Sonny sent one of his collectors to the apartment yesterday? Mrs. Nguyen was already dead. What were they looking for?

Which brought her mind back to the food truck explosion that killed her. Was that connected?

Logan sat down on the foot of the bed and tried to think like a criminal. Thanh said this Sonny was brash and aggressive, unlike his more old-school, patient uncle. For whatever reason, he wanted more and wasn't afraid to use brutal means to get it. If Mrs. Nguyen had taken out a loan with his uncle and had been unable to pay it back, or at least not in full, yet . . . what would Sonny do?

The propane tank had exploded very early that morning—much earlier than anyone would normally have been there. Maybe Sonny intended to send a message, not kill anyone. Mrs. Nguyen couldn't very well pay him back if she was dead. Which brought her right back to square one. She couldn't make any money to pay him back without a way to earn a living, either. No food truck, no money. Of course, maybe the truck was only supposed to be damaged, not destroyed. Rheanna said there had been a small space heater near the door that had probably accelerated the fire.

And what was Mrs. Nguyen doing there at four-thirty in the morning, anyway?

It was like trying to solve a puzzle with missing pieces. Logan doubted she'd find them here, but she had no other leads, so she got back to her search.

In contrast to her daughter-in-law's practical work clothes, the elderly Mrs. Nguyen's wardrobe was decidedly more upscale. Although most did not look new, each item was of high quality. Fine-grained, leather shoes were neatly lined up beneath a small selection of cashmere sweaters, silk blouses, and wool slacks. A single wooden shelf across the top held a couple of boxes, some purses in plastic bags, and an old Samsonite suitcase tucked in the corner.

Starting at the top of the closet, one by one Logan began pulling items down, examining each one. The methodical work was soothing, but she was getting tired. She was glad there were only two bedrooms. She'd finish this one up and then get some sleep. She could do the kitchen and living room in the morning.

When she got to the suitcase—a light blue, hard shell model with a plastic handle vs. roller wheels, a memory of her mother flashed across her mind. Her mother had had one almost just like it out in the garage—a leftover from her college days. One day it was gone. Along with her mother. Logan had only been thirteen years old. Weird how a detail like that sticks in your brain. She thought she'd blocked all that out—she hadn't thought of her mom in years.

Logan pulled the luggage down slowly in case it was heavy, then placed it on the bed and popped open the metal latches. Other than a few sweaters, it was mostly empty. She felt carefully along the seams and both top and bottom inside and out but found nothing out of the ordinary.

Her nose was starting to hurt. After she put the closet back together, she'd call it a night.

Grabbing the suitcase by the handle, Logan pulled it toward her to swing it up onto the top shelf. Something rattled. Sweaters don't rattle. Logan shook it a few times. The sound was coming from the handle.

57

Placing it back on the bed, Logan leaned in to examine it more closely. She hoped she hadn't broken anything. Being nosy was one thing, damaging someone's property, dead or not, wasn't cool. Maybe the handle just needed to be tightened. She took the suitcase over to the nightstand and turned the lamp up to bright to get a better look.

There were two small screws and one was loose. Remembering a small screwdriver she'd seen between two of the purses, she retrieved it and came back to sit on the bed, pulling the suitcase onto her lap. As she tightened the loose screw, a faint line appeared around that end of the handle, quickly widening until it cracked open. Logan watched, stunned, as three clear, brilliant stones, one quite large, tumbled into her lap. *Diamonds!* So *this* is what they were after.

"Nice work."

Logan's head jerked up. A fairly tall Vietnamese man, sharply dressed, arms folded, casually leaned against the open door. Not more than three feet away, blocking any escape.

Sonny.

"Guess I should thank you. My associate's search was

unsuccessful. Although," he added, indicating her nose with a nod, "I can see he made quite an impression on you."

Logan remained silent. She'd gotten over the immediate shock of his sudden appearance, but still didn't know what to do. Listening seemed the best option for now.

One thing she did know. The cavalry wasn't coming. No one knew she was there. Even she didn't know she was coming until the last minute.

Another reality dawned on her. He was making no attempt to hide his face. She could identify him as well as his associate. If this was the infamous Sonny, he had no incentive to let her go. Still, there had to be a way out. She just had to think of one.

Swallowing her fear, Logan began taking slow, even breaths to calm her racing heart.

If she could get him to talk, it would buy her some time. She might even get some useful information for the police if she managed to get out of here alive. Whatever happened, she wasn't going down without a fight.

"I don't normally like to do my own dirty work, but as my associates are otherwise occupied, it looks like I'll have to take out the trash tonight," he said.

Seeing the look this comment elicited in Logan's eyes, Sonny smoothly pulled out a gun and pointed at her before she could react. "I wasn't expecting company, but I'm always prepared for unwanted guests."

Now that his gun was out, he seemed even more relaxed.

"So you thought you'd help yourself to the old lady's stash while your friends are in the hospital. Yes, I heard about that. I knew they'd be gone tonight. I just didn't expect you to be here. Sorry to spoil your little jewel heist, but I've got bigger plans for these and I'm on a tight schedule."

Like most criminals, he assumed she was as greedy as he.

FOREST PARK

In for a penny, in for a pound.

"You're Sonny, right? Did Mrs. Nguyen owe you money, or did you kill her because she refused to give you these?" Logan asked.

If he was surprised she knew his name, Sonny didn't show it. He ignored her question.

"Put those on the nightstand," he said. Then, pointing to a side chair, "Take a seat and do not move when you get there."

Hands shaking, Logan managed to put the diamonds onto the nightstand without dropping any, but as she started to follow the rest of his instructions, she thought of every scary movie she'd ever seen.

He wasn't putting her in the chair to make her comfortable. He was going to tape or tie her up to it, then kill her. And hopefully nothing worse in between. She was not going out that way!

Quickly calculating her odds, several options went through her mind—none of them good. He had a gun. She didn't.

But, if he had any brains, he wouldn't shoot his gun off in an apartment complex. Gunshots were really loud. Someone would call 911 if they heard shots fired. Even if he did follow through with his threat, Rick said even cops didn't always hit their target, even at close range. If she ducked down, making herself as small a target as possible, he might miss. Maybe she'd get lucky.

"The absence of alternatives clears the mind marvelously." Was it Kissinger or Winston Churchill who said that?

Taking the suitcase off her lap, Logan stood and turned to place it on the bed before walking to the chair. An electric silence hung in the air between them.

At the last second, pulling the suitcase up to her chest, she launched herself off the bed like a battering ram and into Sonny's gun arm, knocking him against the door as she jammed past. A very loud bang exploded into the air, temporarily deafening her. If Logan was hit, she didn't know it. Pure adrenaline fueled her out of the apartment and down the stairs. She made it out the front door and hit the sidewalk running.

Somewhere near a CVS, Logan sank down onto a bus stop bench. Normally she could run for miles, but this wasn't normal. Staunching the fresh flow of blood spurting from her nose with one hand, she fished out her phone with the other. At least now she didn't have to worry about when to call the cops. It was time. Her crime-fighting days were over. Keenan could take it from here.

She called Rheanna and asked her to put Keenan on the phone, but Rheanna said he wasn't there. He and Romero caught a case earlier—a homicide near the modern art museum. They'd be gone most of the night.

Logan hated to ask, but she didn't know if she could navigate her way to Rheanna's from here in the shape she was in. All she needed was a ride. To her credit, Rheanna tabled her questions and told her to stay put until she got there. Angel that she was, she brought an ice pack with her, which Logan gratefully accepted. Worried about Pinot, she asked Rheanna to take her back to the apartment just to make sure he was okay, but Rheanna talked her out of it. Cats were independent. He'd be fine for one night. Either he was still in the apartment napping peacefully or had meowed his way into one of the neighbors' apartments and was currently being fed an entire can of tuna. Only when she promised to take her back in the morning did Logan agree to wait. She was too weak to argue anyway.

Logan was actually glad Keenan was unavailable. She wasn't up to answering his 101 questions after what she'd just been through. Rheanna agreed it would be best to wait and give her information directly to Keenan in the morning, after she got some sleep.

Even if she dragged herself down to the station right now and gave her statement and they sent someone to the apartment, Sonny would be long gone. He had what he wanted—the diamonds. And Logan didn't think he'd be coming back for her. She could identify him, but she had no proof of his ever having been there or stolen anything. No one knew the diamonds even existed. Only she and Sonny had seen them, and the way things were going, they'd probably accuse Logan of stealing them. And as for getting them back for Thanh, she doubted that would ever be possible. No, better to let Keenan untangle all this.

Once upstairs, Nurse Rheanna made sure all the locks on the door were secure, then heated up a can of chicken soup and made Logan eat every last spoonful. Surprised at the sudden surge of emotions welling up within her, Logan swallowed the lump in her throat and dabbed at the tears pricking her eyelashes. The hot soup also warded off the shakes she felt coming on as Rheanna sat her down at the kitchen table.

Later, in her room, Logan peeled off her clothes and got into her pajamas. Beyond redemption, her bloody sweater went straight into the trash can by the bed. Too tired to ask Rheanna for a glass of water, she dry-swallowed the pain pill she'd been saving. Lowering herself carefully onto the bed, she pulled the covers up under her chin. Forced to lay on her back because of the bandages on her face, she lay there staring at the ceiling, finding it hard to breathe through her swollen nose. Willing her arm to grow a couple of inches, she finally managed to reach the wall switch and turn out the light.

To sleep, perchance to dream . . .

58

After last night's adventure, Sonny holed up in one of his uncle's properties, making himself scarce in case the police came knocking. But by three o'clock when no one had showed at the office or his home, he relaxed. Thanh's friend, the woman he'd surprised in her apartment last night, was obviously too scared to report anything, and if she did, she couldn't prove he was even there. He'd just call his lawyer. Well, it was his uncle's lawyer, but he was his, now. Good to be king! And kings deserve a nice meal. He'd have plenty of time to enjoy some surf and turf before the meeting. He called Teng to pick him up.

In February, the Colombia river was more than a little choppy. Sonny really wanted to relieve himself of the celebratory lobster he'd had for dinner, let it join its little friends back in the sea, but he wasn't going to give these Canadians the satisfaction. The last thing he wanted them reporting back to their boss was that he tossed his cookies over the side.

Teng had no such concerns. He happily upchucked over the side, then wiped his mouth on the sleeve of his jacket. His undignified actions made Sonny deeply regret having left Michael back at the car. Michael's silent bulk would have made a much better impression, but he was still angry with him for screwing up the last job. He was only supposed to frighten the old lady, not kill her. The police had no way to tie her death back to him, but still, it was a mistake Sonny would not forget. Michael would have to work his way back into his good graces.

Assuming what he hoped was a commander-in-chief stance, Sonny held on to the gunnel and looked straight ahead as they approached the yacht, his eyes glittering with excitement. This was it. The big deal. The Canadians had agreed to a meet but wanted the buy to take place on their territory, their ship. Fine with him. He didn't care where they met, just so long as he got what he wanted. As soon as their deal was made, Michael would take delivery of the shipment container, then send out the rest of the money—they'd insisted on cash for this first deal. Trust was a two-way street, though. They'd soon learn who they were dealing with.

If this first shipment worked out—if all went smoothly— they said there would be more to come. Sonny had big plans. This whole area. And why not? With the white-collar crime organization his uncle created to wash the money, and his own bold leadership, he couldn't lose. Sonny looked ahead at the impressive yacht. *His* yacht would be bigger.

*****

It wasn't until they were back in the small powerboat heading toward the dock that things went wrong.

"This is the US Coast Guard . . . heave to! Prepare to be boarded!"

Sonny heard a splash. To his surprise, Teng dove into the inky black freezing water. The Coast Guard saw it, too, but chose to stick with Sonny. They knew these guys.

FOREST PARK

The bright lights of the two Coast Guard cutters left Sonny nowhere to go but in. Desperately, he searched the shoreline and the dock. If anyone could save him now, it was Michael, but the only driver waiting for him as they disembarked was a federal drug agent. And he wasn't taking him home.

Sonny shut his eyes tight against the view. Bitter gorge rose in his throat. Before he could make it to the side of the boat, the nausea he'd been fighting since he stepped on board won out and he violently emptied his stomach, splattering the toes of his Ferragamos. Teng was nowhere to be seen.

Michael, along with Sonny's new ride and a million dollars in unmarked bills in the trunk, was headed north, driving under the speed limit so as not to attract attention. In the first no-name town he came to with a Ford dealership, Michael ditched Sonny's car and picked up an F-150. Cash, no trail.

One of the guys in his unit back in Afghanistan was from Alaska. Said there was nothing up north but a whole lot of empty, which is exactly what Michael was looking for.

59

"Well, good morning, Sleeping Beauty! Rough night?"

Romero grimaced, stirring two packets of sugar into the strong brew he just poured himself from the communal pot. No one remembered the last time it was cleaned, but it was always in service. Keenan was already working on his second cup.

"Colic. Medical term for screaming baby keeps father and mother up all night."

Not being a parent, Keenan had nothing to add. He hadn't gotten much sleep himself. The case they'd been called out on turned out to be in Vancouver's jurisdiction, but it wasn't until at least two o'clock before he made it home. He hadn't even gone to Rheanna's last night. At least he'd managed a few hours of shuteye. Sounds like Romero was running on fumes.

The landline rang. Keenan grabbed it.

After listening to whoever it was for a couple of minutes, limiting his end of the conversation to nods and grunts as he took notes, he hung up and turned to his partner, a smile on his face.

"Got 'im!"

"Who?"

"GI Joe—they're holding him down at Advent. Turned himself in this morning. Needed treatment for the leg Monster chewed on. Let's go see what our boy knows." Romero put his coat back on. "And by the way, he was in a talkative mood. He admits to shooting his gun at that girl in Forest Park. Says he didn't mean to. Feels bad about it."

Romero pulled on his coat, and they headed for the elevator. "I'm sure that'll make everything all right with the judge. Him feeling bad and all."

*****

They missed the second call, but the duty officer kept the woman on the line—put it through to Keenan's cell just as they got in the car.

"Who is this?" Keenan said.

Tact was not his strong suit.

A young Hispanic woman's voice. "It doesn't matter who this is. But you're gonna want to hear what I have to say. I know where you can find someone you're looking for . . ."

Keenan put her on speaker so Romero could take notes.

"And when you throw that motherfucker in jail," the woman added with malicious glee, "you tell Teng. Make sure he knows it's because that skinny ass of his was in the wrong bed one too many times. It won't be in *mine* again anytime soon."

With that, she disconnected.

Pencil poised above his notebook, Romero mumbled, "Hell hath no fury . . ."

The third call was from Logan McKenna.

This was getting to be a busy morning.

FOREST PARK

✶✶✶✶✶

"You watch television, Teng?"

Teng just glared at them.

It was almost midnight—going on seven hours that they'd had him in here. He'd long since gotten over Vanessa turning him in. He'd deal with her when he got out.

They didn't have anything on him. He hadn't blown up any propane tanks. He hadn't killed anyone. Hell, he didn't even own a gun. He was just a driver. But he knew plenty about Sonny. It was at least warm in here. That dunk in the river almost killed him. His heart almost stopped it was so cold when he dove in.

"You listening, Teng? It's not like it is on TV. We can hold you as long as we have a reason to. And we have lots of reasons."

Teng thought about his options. Michael must have had enough time to get someplace safe by now. No sense holding out. He wasn't going to rat Michael out. Michael scared him, but he'd be happy to sacrifice Sonny. Now was as good a time as any.

✶✶✶✶✶

By morning, the DA's office made the deal. Drug enforcement was only too happy to throw back Teng, the guppy, for Sonny, the bigger fish. And if they were lucky, they'd get enough to land the Canadian whale on the yacht. Interpol had been working that case with the DEA for months.

Teng happily gave them enough information to not only hook Sonny but filet and fry him. He added the firebombing on Tenth and Alder for good measure, reciting in great detail Sonny's personal and business dealings. He only vaguely described Michael and said he had no idea where he'd gone.

277

The connection to their arson/homicide would have taken them by surprise if it hadn't been for Logan McKenna's statement. They'd need more than her or Teng's word, but combined with the bank footage of the car, they had enough to take to thc DA. With Logan's testimony, combined with what she said Thanh would be able to give them, they'd probably be able to get some serious jail time for Teng, too, not just Sonny. Breaking and entering, aggravated assault . . . accessory to murder.

Apparently, GI Joe was just in the wrong place at the wrong time when Teng and Michael blew up the food truck. That meant they'd only be able to get him for the attempted shooting in Forest Park, but all in all, not a bad day at the office.

60

Directed to the seventh floor by the nurse at the admitting desk, Logan exited the elevator and found Huey and Thanh's room. They'd put a rush on Huey's tests and found he was an 85 percent match, which was excellent. The surgery had gone well. Thanh was pale but looked better than she had last time Logan had seen her. The pair had won the hearts of the nursing staff, who'd arranged for them to share a room until they were released. Huey saw her first.

"Oh my God! What happened?" he said.

Logan was hoping to look better by now, but if anything, the bruising around her eyes had become more colorful. She still looked like a raccoon, but at least the scary, large brace and bandages on her face had been reduced to a simple nose splint.

"It's a long story, but I'm fine. Nothing serious," she said. She'd share the harrowing details when they were stronger.

"I promise to fill you in later, but right now, I want to know how *you* two are doing." She put a vase of tulips on the table between them. "Didn't know if flowers were allowed, but they said these were okay."

"Thank you," Thanh said weakly. "They're beautiful. You didn't have to come. You've done so much for us already."

Logan positioned the only chair in the room between their beds and sat down.

"I don't think feeding a cute cat and lolling around here counts as doing too much," Logan said, showing them both some pictures she'd taken of Pinot on her phone at Rheanna's. Since Logan needed to go back to work, Rheanna said she'd cat sit until Huey and Thanh got out of the hospital. In the picture, Pinot was playing with a toy mouse stuffed with catnip Logan had picked up at the grocery store along with fresh kitty litter.

"How long will you need to be in here?" Logan asked.

"They say it varies from patient to patient. As long as no complications arise and it looks like I'm not rejecting the liver, it shouldn't be too long," Thanh said.

Not wanting to tire them out, Logan visited for a few more minutes, then, with a hug for both, said her goodbyes. There wasn't anything more she could do now and Thanh was already nodding off.

Yesterday, Logan had gone back to the apartment and cleaned up the mess. The landlord gave her a spare piece of carpet to replace the blood-soaked one in the closet. She'd washed the towels and would replace those that wouldn't come clean as soon as she could. Two-day free shipping was a godsend. Then she locked up their apartment and went to Rheanna's for her last night in town.

Huey promised to keep her in the loop as they went through the process of healing. He said the New School had generous health insurance for Huey but it didn't cover everything. Between copays and aftercare, it would still be very expensive. Being self-employed, Thanh's health insurance wasn't as good but, after a hefty deductible, it covered the surgery.

FOREST PARK

Logan later learned from Glenda that neither Huey or Thanh would need to worry. Pulling a rich rabbit out of a hat, Rita found a donor to take care of their medications once they were released from the hospital. She also said they could stay in one of the cabins until they were back on their feet. With Nick's cooking, Glenda's nursing, and Carla's oatmeal cookies, Logan knew they'd be in good hands. Huey would be able to return to his job, and from what she had seen of Thanh's resilient spirit, Thanh would figure out a way to rebuild her life, yet again.

*****

Neither Huey or Thanh knew anything about the diamonds in the evidence locker downtown, which Keenan would return to Thanh on Monday. And it would be another few days before the last three diamonds were recovered—the ones Mrs. Nguyen had intended for Thanh and that Logan had almost gotten shot over.

Logan assumed they were lost forever, but miraculously, the police found them laying loose in the top drawer of Sonny's desk. He'd probably assumed he had plenty of time to sell or secure them after his meet with the Canadians. It would take another few months as they worked their way through the tangled bureaucracy of several overlapping agencies, but eventually, even these last three would be returned to Thanh.

After the hospital visit, Logan took another cab back to Rheanna's place. Letting herself in with the spare key, her legs were immediately attacked. Mewing loudly, Pinot wove himself in and around her ankles until she picked him up and fed him. She'd wait for her own dinner until Rheanna got back, which should be any minute now. Since Keenan and Romero would be working late, wrapping up their case,

Rheanna said she'd bring home takeout for the two of them. Logan was grateful. She didn't feel up to making small talk with anyone.

A wave of exhaustion overtook her. She went into the living room and sank onto the couch. Hearing Pinot's claws tap across the polished concrete floor before launching himself into her lap, a longing for home hit her hard. She missed Dimebox, she missed Bella, and she had to admit, she missed Ben.

He'd called earlier but didn't leave a message this time. She hadn't called him back.

Why did things have to get so complicated? Everything had been so beautiful, had flowed so easily between them. Why couldn't things remain the same? She could see his face—wanted to take it in her hands—look into his blue eyes. Lie her head on his chest, one leg crooked up over his, relax against his body. That's how they'd lain on the couch, watching Casablanca, the week before she left.

Unclouded—that's a word that described Ben. Solid and uncomplicated. Open, caring. Until now, anyway. Had it been just a summer romance? Or was there something more worth pursuing? Ben was a one-woman man, of that she was certain. And as long as Julie was in the picture, there was no room for her.

61

John Wayne, as the Orange County, CA airport was called, got mixed reviews. Airline pilots disliked it because of its short runway, but for passengers, it was user-friendly and easy to navigate. Within minutes of disembarking, Logan was in baggage claim, pulling her luggage off the conveyor belt. Rolling her bag behind her, heading toward the wall of glass doors toward the taxi area, her mind filled with ways she was going to avoid Ben until she felt ready to talk to him. Or at least until her bruises faded.

That's when she saw him.

Everyone else continued moving, a river of passengers, flowing around her toward the exit, bags in hand, as if she were an island.

This is why they do that slow-motion thing in the movies, because that's exactly what it feels like.

Crossing the distance in three long strides, Ben engulfed her in his arms, careful to avoid bumping her nose.

"I couldn't wait," he said simply, holding her close, not giving her a chance to pull away.

Then, holding her at arm's length, he took in her face and smiled.

"Glenda called," he said. "She filled me in on how you got those shiners. Can't leave you alone for a minute, can I?"

Ben picked up her bags. Logan came out of her stupor and started to speak, but Ben silenced her.

"Before you say anything, I want you to know Julie's gone. Out of our lives. I put her on a plane."

With his hand on the small of her back, he guided her through the revolving door onto the loading and unloading area outside.

"I wanted to tell you days ago," he added, "but when you didn't answer my calls, I figured you needed more time."

They reached the crosswalk that led to short-term parking and waited at the light. Ben turned to her and smiled.

". . . and I figured you'd have a harder time hanging up on me in person," he added. Doubt flitted across his face.

This was it. This was the big decision. Was she going to trust him or not? Was she even capable of trust anymore?

The light changed and they both ignored it. The moment seemed to go on forever.

Then a feeling of calm washed through Logan's body. She wasn't sure how, but she knew. Without saying a word, she threw her arms around him, lay her head on his chest, and squeezed. Ben let out a deep breath and hung on tighter.

She would hear the long version later, but this is all Logan needed to know. This is what she wanted. This was home.

When the light changed again, Ben picked up both her bags with one hand and put his arm around her shoulders with the other.

FOREST PARK

"How about one of Jean's cinnamon rolls?" he said.

Even if she hadn't skipped breakfast, Logan's mouth would water. Jean's cinnamon rolls were legend. Tava'e's husband, he did all the baking at Tava'e's and was as quiet as she was vocal. Few had even seen him. He stayed in the kitchen, working his baking magic, while his wife held court out front.

✶✶✶✶✶

Twenty minutes later, they found a parking spot on the ocean side of PCH and went inside.

Tava'e spotted them as they came in.

"*Talofa,* skinny one!" she boomed. Gathering Logan in a crushing hug, she kissed both cheeks before releasing her and giving Ben the same treatment. She led them to her booth in the corner, which had been customized to accommodate her generous size. She shifted until she got comfortable. Logan and Ben sat on the opposite side. Tava'e smoothed the fabric of her cool cotton dress. The lush floral pattern of blues and greens flattered her warm, mocha skin.

"Okay, what happened to you?" she asked, pointing to Logan's face.

Logan gave her the fastest version Tava'e would accept, reassuring her multiple times that she was fine, just hungry.

Before they could order, a multiply pierced young woman with short jet-black hair delivered three large cinnamon rolls and coffees to their table, handing Tava'e her own gold-rimmed, steaming espresso cup.

It was from this booth that Tava'e held court every morning, inviting anyone who wanted a game of chess to join her, as many of the old men who lingered outside the café did. Tava'e also made sure that in addition to a game, each man left with at least one of the bakery 'seconds' and a to-go coffee a former customer 'forgot to pick up'. Everyone knew Jean's pastries were all perfect and there couldn't possibly be that many forgotten coffees, but it was a dignified charade everyone was more than happy to continue.

"Thank you, Epiphany. How have you been? How's Danny doing?" Logan asked.

Not being much of a talker, Epiphany took only three sentences to fill them in. She was fine. Danny was fine. Still working with Jean in the kitchen. Doing great. Epiphany and Danny were only two of the young people Tava'e and Jean had taken under their wing.

After polishing off the rolls and promising to stop by on Sunday for her next chess lesson, Logan and Ben said their goodbyes.

As they pulled into her driveway, Logan smiled. There sat Lola, her sapphire self gleaming in the winter sun. Top up, she was getting her beauty sleep. She'd take her out for a spin tomorrow. When they got inside, Dimebox, unhappy with Logan's absence, pointedly ignored her, rubbing against Ben's legs instead.

Par for the course. Dimebox always punished her for being gone. Ignoring her indignant cat, Logan laughed.

Good to be home!

Kicking off her shoes, she did her signature sock slide on the hardwood floor, stopping only when her toes jammed into the thick rug in the living room.

Agreeing on six o'clock for dinner, Ben left to do some errands while Logan showered and threw in a load of laundry. Checking her email, she saw that Amy and Liam (it was Amy and Liam now, not just Amy) had sent a newsy update from Scotland, where they were visiting his family.

Logan loved her daughter's enthusiasm. She would answer her with a long email later. She called the hospital, but they said Thanh and Huey were resting after numerous tests. No complications so far.

Later, she unpacked her suitcase. On the bottom was the black slip. She shook it out and hung it on the doorknob. Straightened up the bed. Made sure she had matches for the candle on her nightstand. Just in case . . .

Ben arrived promptly at 5:55 p.m., fully equipped with his barbecue kit, and fired up the grill. Although Southern California winters didn't justify it, he also lit a fire in the fireplace, leaving the French doors open just enough to keep it cold enough to cuddle. Ben was an excellent cuddler.

Logan hoped his other skills would be called upon later.

Over a bottle of cabernet and two thick medium-rare rib eyes, Logan's favorite, Ben supplied what turned out to be the short version of the Julie saga. Logan knew the basics but had never heard the whole story.

For the first couple of years of their engagement, things had gone well. Julie finished law school and made junior partner. Alan, the man she'd left Ben for, was a full partner. They raked in the money, bought an impressive restored Pacific Heights Victorian, within which they entertained all the right people. But after snorting most of their combined income up his nose, Alan fell from grace within the firm. In truth, Julie had done a little coke herself, although she wouldn't admit it. Losing the impressive, Pacific Heights house was the last straw. Julie dumped Alan and hopped on a plane, assuming Ben would take her back.

Her showing up like that was a shock, to say the least. Ben said he'd closed off that part of himself and moved on with his life, or thought he had. Seeing her standing there on his doorstep ripped his heart open, pouring out a confusing mix of feelings he couldn't handle all at once. That's when he'd called Logan.

But the more Julie talked, the more Ben saw how selfish and manipulative she was. Although still beautiful, in a cold, polished way—long, perfectly straight blond hair and expensive shoes, her Manolo budget hadn't been exhausted—he couldn't help but compare. When he looked at Julie, all he could see was Logan's lithe, athletic body racing him down the beach, her winning, laughing, Purgatory barking at her heels.

Julie was allergic to dogs.

The love Logan had for her daughter, her students, her music, making a difference in the world, and him. He pictured her clear, green eyes, sprays of laugh lines appearing when she smiled at him, the waves of her hair twisting in his fingers as he pulled her close for a kiss.

No contest.

Having already made up her mind to trust Ben, Logan still appreciated hearing the whole story. She needed to know that part of Ben's life was truly and forever behind him. Love without the speed bumps was just lust or infatuation. This was real.

They spent the next two hours talking about anything and everything, catching up and making plans. Around midnight, Ben got to Logan's favorite part of the evening—not talking at all.

62

Generous and welcoming, Forest Park opened itself all summer, welcoming laughing children, families, and nature lovers along its many trails. No fancy gear required. T-shirts and tennis shoes sufficed. Butterflies fluttered, birds sang, and the sun shone, or at least wasn't absent for long. Teresa, whose ankle healed quickly, was back at work and in the thick of tourist season by the end of May. It buckled now and then if she stepped on it wrong, but she upped her physical therapy exercises and even that got better. Summer had been busy. She and her team opened two new trails, cleaned up several more, and expanded a visiting naturalist program to Portland elementary schools.

She checked the numbers on her computer. October. Visitor volume had dropped with the temperature. She and her crew had accomplished a lot. Time to take a much-deserved rest. She knew just who to call.

*****

Early in the morning, their breath escaping in steamy swirls, two hikers struggled up a steep section of a faint, narrow path.

The unlikely pair had been at it for about an hour. It was that hour of the morning when the moon had gone to bed and the sun was approaching the horizon but hadn't yet risen.

"Almost there. Watch your step," the man said.

Six inches and over forty years distant from his companion, he still moved as easily up the rough terrain as she did. Many years of rough living had broken his body down, but three months of rehab and eight months of solid work on the New School's grounds and gardens had worked wonders. More muscled and confident, he looked and felt fifty-five again.

Teresa reveled in the feeling of using her body to reach a goal, which, in this case, was the top of the ridge.

Looking at Joe's back, she marveled at their new relationship. Odd as others may view it, it didn't feel strange to her at all that she and Joe had connected. Both had served in the military, seen combat and all that entailed. It was because of this she'd been able to understand and forgive his actions on the trail that caused her injury.

Beyond that, with her father gone and his daughter rejecting his overtures of reconnection, even though he had been clean and sober for months, they had just naturally gravitated into each other's orbit. She felt bad for him that his daughter couldn't get over the past, but forgiveness wasn't in everyone's DNA. You took family where you could find it.

Joe's family was also expanding to include a warm, wonderful redhead named Carla, who finally had the good sense to kick her worthless husband to the curb. Her shy son, Derek, had taken to following him everywhere, and when he wasn't working with Huey in the computer lab, he could be seen working side by side with Joe in the garden. Teresa visited often. Last week she taught Carla's daughter, Maria, how to braid her hair like Katniss Everdeen. The girl had been thrilled.

FOREST PARK

Joe crested the ridge first, unloading his backpack on a rock, reaching down to offer Teresa a hand up. She accepted his warm, rough hand and stepped up to join him. Pulling out a thermos of hot coffee, some granola, and dried apple slices, they faced east and settled in to wait. No need for conversation.

When the sun arrived in all her silent glory, they simply drank it in with their eyes. It felt as if they were the only ones experiencing this event. Unconsciously, their breathing eased and slowed. All that had brought them to this moment had been worth it. This was enough.

ACKNOWLEDGMENTS

If stories are paintings, writers' paintings would be very dull if we only used one color, our own. But what can we do? Each writer has only one set of experiences to draw from—one perspective on life. Gathering experiences from other people, then—either through interviewing or observation—is our only path to a vibrant story, and the only way to tell the truth, even if we don't discover it for ourselves.

I am grateful to the men and women who allowed me to briefly see the world through their eyes. They've enriched my life as well as my writing.

In every city in America, hundreds of dedicated men and women work at demanding and often thankless jobs, protecting us and keeping us safe. In Portland, Oregon, many of them also took time out of these busy jobs to answer my pesky questions. I'd like to thank Stephanie Solomon, certified dispatcher, and Shawnda McMurray, police officer in the Forensics Department, both of the Portland Police Bureau, for their insights. Arson Investigator, Jason Anderson, of the Portland Fire Bureau, and Lt. Rich Tyler, of Portland Fire and Rescue, provided much-needed technical expertise and a view into how fire and police work together to solve crimes. And without Damon O'Brien, deputy medical examiner, a sticky plot point involving the discovery of some diamonds may not have been solved so elegantly. I hope I represented all your jobs with dignity and respect. Your work is appreciated.

Thanks also go to Rick Stoller, executive director of the Salvation Army Veterans and Family Center, Beaverton, Oregon, who shared valuable perspective on the struggles of homeless veterans. Mary Ann Parker, Interim Director of Veterans Affairs at JGF, gave me a focused primer on PTSD, an affliction all too prevalent among our vets. Kimberly McCallum Vargas, RN, walked me through the finer details of liver disease, its causes, and its treatments.

Whenever you write about another culture, country, or time, you want to get it right. Mr. Hoi Ba Tran, former pilot with the ARVN (Army of the Republic of Vietnam), "generously reviewed the sections regarding Saigon in 1975 for accuracy. The details in Thanh's and Hieu's stories were gleaned from many interviews I conducted with Vietnamese refugees from that period. Those stories stay with you. I wonder if I would have handled being torn from my country with such strength and grace.

Don't know if you can thank a city, but if it's allowed, I'd like to thank Portland, Oregon, for being itself. I fell in love with Portland when I briefly lived there years ago, and I go back as often as I can. Than's *pho* food cart is fictional, but I love the real food cart vendors near Tenth and Alder in downtown Portland. Their delicious food and energetic, entrepreneurial spirit fueled multiple research and writing sessions.

Whenever I am in Portland, I stay at the Governor Hotel and enjoy Jake's Grill downstairs. I was sitting in Jake's looking across at the food carts one morning when the idea for this book began to form. Thanks go to Bethanie Peterson, Sarah

Sanders, and Ryan Smith, of the Governor, who answered endless questions and generously put me in Logan's corner room. Awesome room. Awesome hotel! It's now called the Sentinel, but to me, it will always be the Governor.

When I first started writing, I did not always have the luxury of top-notch, professional editing, so I can tell you what a difference it makes to work with someone like Laura Petrella. Delightful, insightful, and professional.

I'd also like to thank Kimberly Peticolas for her creativity, skill, and dedication in giving all the books in this new edition of the Logan series powerful, new covers, and fresh, clean interior design.

Family often gets mentioned last, but comes first in my life. Special thanks go to my husband, John Davisson, my sister, Michelle Montclaire, my father-in-law, Maurice Davisson, and my father, Darrell Fleming, for their unflagging support and spot-on critiques. All are valued.

Thanks to all these people for helping me produce and polish Forest Park. All remaining errors are mine.

ABOUT THE AUTHOR

A self-admitted book addict, Valerie Davisson was the kid with the flashlight under her pillow, reading long after lights out. After a life of travel, she now lives on the Oregon coast with her husband, John, and their new puppy, Finn. When not working on her latest book, she's probably in the kitchen, cooking up a storm for family and friends.

Enjoyed the Book?

If you enjoyed *Forest Park*, please consider leaving a review on Amazon or Goodreads. And be sure to check out the rest of the Logan McKenna series.

Shattered (Book 1)

Devil's Claw (Book 3)

Vanishing Day (Book 4)

Safe Harbor (Book 5)

Lies That Bind (Book 6)

Whisper Creek (Book 7)

Want to know more about Valerie Davisson or her next book? Make sure to visit www.valeriedavisson.com and sign up for her newsletter.